Santa Fe

Love Is a Legal Affair

Maxine Neely Davenport

To Kayte—
Merry Christmas!
Maxine Neely Davenport

LANCE
PUBLISHING

Santa Fe, NM

Love Is a Legal Affair
A Novel

By Maxine Neely Davenport

First Edition

Printed in the United States

Published by: Lance Publishing
Send all inquiries to: lancepublishing@davenportstories.com

Copyright © 2016 by Maxine Neely Davenport

Love Is a Legal Affair is a work of fiction. Names, characters, and incidents are products of the author's imagination and are not to be construed as real. Any resemblance to actual events, organizations, or persons, living or dead, is entirely coincidental. Legal citations, descriptions of court, jury, or criminal actions should not be cited as real.

ISBN: 978-0-9972088-0-1 (paperback)
ISBN: 978-0-9972088-1-8 (epub)
ISBN: 978-0-9972088-2-5 (mobi)
ISBN: 978-0-9972088-3-2 (pdf)

1. Fiction. 2. Pedophilia. 3. Religious ethics. 4. Cub Scouts.

Cover design and interior layout by www.MediaNeighbours.com

In memory of William Jarrett Neely and Maud Mae Lance Neely,

who had so little and gave so much

Chapter One

Despite the fact that Yolanda sat in the outside office within speaking distance, Judge Salazar yelled into the intercom. "Yolanda! Make sure Jared's in court tomorrow. I want her on this pedophile case."

The clerk quickly closed the file drawer where she stood sorting documents from last week's trials and returned to her desk. The judge's order surprised her. She understood that Carmela Jared remained on contract to serve as an attorney for the public defender's office when it was overloaded—but appointing her to defend a possible pedophile? She rarely handled criminal cases. Yolanda wondered what the judge was thinking.

She picked up the telephone, pleased to be working with the Jared law office. Chatting with Rosemary, the friendly, outgoing secretary at that office, always brightened her day. Plus, Yolanda's successful efforts to smooth the sometimes-prickly relationship between the judge and attorney had allowed her to develop a close connection to the firm. From the first day Carmela appeared in Judge Salazar's courtroom, usurping the space he believed would be better held by a male attorney, the two had engaged in a subtle battle to define territories. On the surface, their encounters appeared neutral, but Yolanda suspected the judge consistently appointed Carmela to obviously unwinnable cases. However, she knew the elderly judge grudgingly admired the fact that Carmela bent—rather than broke—under the pressure he exerted. In spite of everything, he had come to depend on this woman, not long out of law school, to guide him through the intricate changes in the law without embarrassing him in front of other attorneys. He needed her to prop up his waning years on the bench, but he'd be damned if he would admit it.

"Carmela Jared's office. This is Rosemary. How may I help you?"

"Hello, Rosemary. This is Yolanda. Judge Salazar asked me to notify your boss of a new appointment from the public defender's office. The client's in jail. Carmela will have to attend the first hearing in front of Judge Casey in municipal court tomorrow afternoon. It will be transferred over to our court after the arraignment." She paused. "I'll email you the order."

"Wow! That's all she needs right now, Yolanda. She doesn't know how to say no when someone needs help, so we're always overloaded with pro bono cases. Appointments from the public defender's office come close to being pro bono."

"I'm sorry, but the judge was adamant about this one."

"May I tell her what it's about?"

Yolanda hesitated. "Why don't I just send you the order?"

"Okay. I'll put the hearing on her calendar. Tuesday afternoon in municipal court with Judge Casey?"

"That's right. Also, Judge Salazar has a meeting in the morning and wants to do civil cases first. Criminal cases won't be heard until afternoon. The order's on its way." She replaced the telephone quickly, before she gave away information that might cause Carmela to think twice about accepting the appointment.

Rosemary frowned. Carmela had a civil case in district court before Judge Salazar. Yolanda should have noticed that. She shrugged. The clerk was used to handling those kinds of problems, so she'd leave it in her hands.

As soon as the order arrived, Rosemary placed it on Carmela's desk, expecting she'd have time to read it before she left the office. As luck would have it, though, Carmela went straight home from the courthouse.

Chapter Two

Carmela woke the next morning with the warning that a migraine headache was brewing, but she had to rush. She grabbed a pill bottle and tossed it in her briefcase. At the office, she noted that Rosemary had not arrived and assumed she had detoured to pick up her favorite muffins. While she emptied her briefcase, she leaned over her desk and stared at an order her secretary had placed for her immediate attention. She read it and lowered her body into the leather chair as if eggshells covered the seat's padding. Settled in, she shook the order, as though the blurred wording would come into focus, and then laid it aside, daring to hope it was a figment of her imagination. Judge Salazar had appointed her as legal counsel for the Reverend Paul Morrison, who had been arrested last Saturday.

She shook her head in disbelief and winced from the pain. This can't be the man who had flirted with her in spin class, or perhaps she had misread his intentions when he began arriving early to set up his bicycle next to hers, all smiles and light chitchat. Weeks had passed before she discovered that he was the minister of a conservative church on the south side of town. Soon after, as their relationship seemed to be warming, he stopped coming to class, and it had mystified her. Could this case shed some light on that mystery?

She moved to her computer and checked the county's latest filings. There was his name, Paul Robert Morrison, with the following charges: *On or about the 6th day of September, 2014, the above named defendant was in a position of authority, and he used his influence to touch the genitals of a child who was younger than eight years old.*

Carmela sighed. He'd seemed like a really nice man, but now he stood charged as a sexual predator. It must be a mistake. But, true or false, there was no way she wanted to get involved in his problems. She had to inform Judge Salazar as soon as possible that she couldn't take this appointment. Besides, the judge surely knew that her inclination would be to represent the victim in such a case. She didn't look forward to a confrontation with the judge and hoped her withdrawal could be settled with his clerk.

Nauseated, with her headache spinning out of control, she dug inside her briefcase and discovered the pill bottle was empty; she'd forgotten to refill her prescription. Since Rosemary had not checked in, a text message would have to do. She typed, "Headache. Cancel morning appointments. Back after lunch, in time for court." Thinking only of relief, she failed to notice the modified schedule for her civil case.

Needles of pain jabbed at the edges of her eyesight as she drove on narrow streets along the San Carlos River. She pulled into the drive-in lane at the CVS drugstore, thankful that her call-in prescription had been filled. She swallowed a pill immediately and headed home.

The sun shining through the yellowing leaves of cottonwood and elm trees along the narrow riverbank smeared rainbow streaks across her vision. The traffic was light, and her cop—as she called Detective Travis Hawk—was either on call or, more likely, picking up a sack of breakfast burritos as an excuse to stop by the office to share her company. His early morning drop-ins, which began after his wife deserted him last month, no longer surprised her. Since childhood, he had been a people person, and eating alone did not suit him.

Carmela's five-foot-eleven-inch frame fit comfortably into the old Cadillac she'd inherited from her grandparents. She wasn't sure which ancestor passed on the tension headaches, but her muscular arms and broad shoulders were products of her parents, both six-foot-plus California hippies. Proud of her appearance, she honed her physique at the gym and rode her horse on weekends. Her long, black hair, shining with highlights, framed light freckles sprinkled across her nose and cheeks, skin damage she'd earned as a child while racing with Travis under the burning New Mexico sun.

As she neared home, she glanced at the chamisa bushes lining the acequia—an ancient water trench branching from the river, formerly used to irrigate the farms and gardens of early settlers. Today, the dirty water that flowed in the river never reached the dry trench, which served instead as a cops-and-robbers' playground for the neighborhood children. Carmela remembered the morning she'd hidden behind those bushes as her parents began packing their crafts equipment—including Savanna's fortune-telling apparatus—into their old VW van, headed for a hippy commune in the northern mountains outside of Taos.

Unknown to Carmela, they'd stopped over at Grandma's and Grandpa's with plans to leave her there so that she could be enrolled in public school. When they told her of their plans, she bolted. Torn between wanting to join the children playing in a schoolyard just four blocks from her grandparents' home and terrified that she'd never see her parents again, she ran away, hiding behind the bushes in the acequia. Their promise to visit her on weekends and take her to live with them in the summers she could understand. The unknown was what frightened her. What if the town kids made fun of the way she talked or dressed? And what if the teacher she'd seen on the playground yelled like her father did when she made a mistake?

Hiding among the bushes, Carmela almost wet herself when she saw a patrol car turn the corner and come to a stop behind the van. Fate, or good fortune, had sent a nice, young policeman to find her hiding place behind the bush. He took her hand and led her to the worried relatives.

She clung to her mother and cried when Buck ordered Savanna to "Get in," cursing the delay the search had caused them. He yanked Carmela from her mother's arms, and the memory of her long, wet eyelashes, heavy with tears, would haunt Carmela forever.

While Carmela sobbed, the policeman called to his son, who was playing soccer with friends in the vacant lot across the street, and told him it would be neighborly to invite Carmela to join the game. Travis kicked the ball toward her, and she vented her anger by returning it straight into his chest, dumping him into the dirt. The policeman laughed and headed for his patrol car. From that day, Carmela became the first choice as a member of Travis's teams, and most days the pair dashed around tall backyard fences, through utility easements, jumped over clumps of chamisa, crossed lawns and rocky driveways, never slowed by gawking neighbors who stopped their gardening to admire the speed with which the two traveled.

All that racing couldn't make up for the fact that Carmela's parents rarely returned to visit. Before long, she was told their old van had broken down, and the visits stopped altogether. She kept letters from her mother in a wooden box in her dresser drawer.

Carmela slowed the Cadillac as she entered the neighborhood where she had grown up. Children, playing in the street near the bus stop, waved when they saw her car. She returned their greetings as the school bus pulled to a stop at the corner of Ash and Rosita. The street emptied as the children crowded to be first aboard. Carmela eased her car into the driveway, glad the noisy children were leaving and she could rest in peace.

The heat from New Mexico's sun fell over Carmela's shoulders like a Native blanket as she exited the garage and headed toward the back door. She grimaced at the sight of her trashcan. She should have placed the container on the curb for pickup this morning, but now it was too late, which was just as well, because her headache would not withstand a meeting with neighbors inquiring about her health, who really were more interested in the pickup truck frequently parked in her backyard. Carmela wondered whether the ladies raised their eyebrows and clicked their tongues while waiting to solve the new mystery in the neighborhood. More likely, they hoped she would marry the nice policeman who, from outward appearances, seemed to be courting her. She felt sure they weren't aware that Travis was married, although separated—a complicating factor in their present relationship.

It had seemed natural when his wife, Carolyn, left him that Travis would turn to Carmela for consolation. They had been close buddies since that day her parents left. What Carmela hadn't expected was the difficulty of maintaining their childhood relationship now that they were consenting adults. Following her return to San Carlos after law school, she had been careful to avoid solitary meetings with her former buddy, now married.

Inside the house, she brushed aside a guilty feeling of relief that Travis was not around. Sharing his problems was reason enough to give one a headache, especially when he seemed reluctant to resolve them legally. Still, there were many things about Travis she admired. His uniform covered a body with muscles crafted in the weight room. He wore his thick black hair—compliments of his father's Navajo heritage—trimmed in a neat, military-style crew cut. When he smiled, his clean-shaven face revealed a swath of beautiful white teeth and deeply dimpled cheeks. Dark eyes teased with laughter or sparked with anger when he was crossed. Best of all, he loved to tinker with house repairs and took pride in keeping her old car running. He carried a key to her house, and she was never surprised to find him working away on some improvement when she came home. On weekends, they played tennis, and occasionally she won. Professionally, he loved his job, which allowed him to spend much of his time out of the office, overseeing criminal investigations. The officers in his division respected his leadership and worked hard to gain his approval.

Also, to his credit, he understood her headaches and had learned not to call Carmela during one of these debilitating occurrences. Instead, after her medication knocked her into Neverland, she often woke to find a single rose or a cup of tea on the warmer beside her bed.

"Ohhh!" Pain stopped Carmela's rambling thoughts as she dropped her briefcase inside the door. She set the clock alarm for twelve p.m. and crumpled on the bed, shirt and pants thrown across a chair.

She woke before the alarm and paused to see if the headache had disappeared. She smelled coffee and opened one eye. Nothing happened. She opened both eyes and heaved a sigh of relief, pushing aside the covers, noting that the dream she'd had of being tucked into bed had, in fact, been a reality. Travis had no doubt been a silent but busy visitor. She threw aside the blanket, sat up, and sniffed again to make sure the coffee smell wasn't a dream. She grabbed the robe, folded with military precision, at the foot of her bed and padded to the kitchen.

"Bless you," she said to the air around her, sure that somewhere in his cop car or at the office, Travis was smiling and saying, "You owe me one." It was getting harder and harder for Carmela to hold him at arm's length.

The coffee hit her empty stomach with a stabilizing jolt. As she relaxed under the shower's jets of hot water, her mind wandered to the afternoon hearing concerning a six-year-old who had been removed from the family home. The girl had told a teacher that bruises on her legs were caused by her father's spanking. Carmela had reviewed the doctor's report and had inspected the family's mobile home—which the police had reported as filthy, with mice feces scattered around the cabinets. However, in San Carlos, mice feces were a given, even in the most expensive homes. At her inspection, she'd found the floors clean, dishes washed, and beds neatly made. She'd talked to neighbors who were noncommittal and suspicious of the police, not willing to be described as snitches. One next-door neighbor had agreed to testify on behalf of the mother if the matter went to trial.

Finally, Carmela and the parents met with Aviva Romero, the social worker from Child Protection Services, and all came to an agreement to return the child to the home, provided the parents attend parenting classes and cooperate with frequent follow-up visits from social services. Today, Carmela would be presenting that agreement to the court for approval and implementation.

She arrived in Judge Salazar's courtroom expecting to meet the child's family, hoping she had time for another cup of coffee before the civil docket was called. She headed for the hall, just as her name boomed from the judge's dais.

"Attorney Jared!" Judge Salazar's voice was unnecessarily loud in the crowded room.

"Yes, Your Honor?" She walked toward the attorneys' podium.

"You failed to appear this morning when your case was called, first on the docket. In your absence, a representative from Child Protection Services reported that she had met with you and the parents and that you had reached an agreement to recommend that the parents be ordered into parenting classes and the child returned to her home, with scheduled oversight. Was that your client's agreement?"

"Yes, sir." Carmela spoke firmly to assure the lawyers snickering behind her back that she could take whatever the judge meted out. She understood their delight in watching a colleague, whom they considered too pretty and too smart, brought down a notch or two. Tomorrow it would be their turn.

"Next time, Counselor, check with the court in the morning for schedule changes. And don't charge this morning's non-appearance to the state." The snickers became guffaws. Carmela didn't bother to answer. She turned to leave, angry at herself for flubbing the timing and with the judge for not passing on her case until she arrived—which was standard practice when an attorney was late.

"Miss Jared!"

"Yes, sir?"

"I believe you've been notified of your appointment to represent Paul Morrison on a contract basis with the public defender's office. If you haven't done so already, pick up the file at municipal court and attend the initial hearing at four o'clock." He looked at the courtroom clock. "You have time to meet with your client before the hearing." He dismissed her and called the next case.

Carmela's ears rang. She shuddered to think of the criminal charges against Paul. Even if he weren't an acquaintance, she would have hesitated to take his case. She had opened her office as a general practitioner four years ago, and the majority of her criminal cases involved teenagers on drug or theft charges. She didn't advertise services as a criminal defense attorney.

Why had the judge placed in her hands a case that could become a hot political issue? The child in the case would be represented by District Attorney Roman Sedbury, who would use the notoriety that springs from a sexual-abuse story to boost his re-election campaign. There was little chance that representing a client accused of sexually abusing a child would enhance Carmela's reputation.

Hurrying down the hall, she made her way to the judge's chambers behind the courtroom. Yolanda issued her usual cheery greeting. She was the only court clerk who smiled no matter how grumpy the judge or how impolite the lawyers were that day.

Carmela forced herself to match the cheerfulness. "Hi, Yolanda. Rosemary did let me know of the court's appointment on the pedophile case, and you know how much I appreciate appointments, but please tell the judge it will be impossible for me to take this one." She paused when Yolanda failed to respond. "I have a conflict of interest."

"Oh, that's too bad. The judge has his mind set on your carrying this case for him."

"Me? Why me?"

"The judge is afraid it will go viral if it's linked to the recent stories about the child abuse charges against New Mexico's Catholic priests. You may have seen the latest story in yesterday's paper. He doesn't want some headline-seeking law firm involved."

"But I wouldn't be representing the child. The appointment is to represent the pastor."

"Well, the pastor's innocent until he's proven guilty." Yolanda leaned forward and looked toward the door to make sure no one could overhear their conversation. "The judge says you do the best job on messy cases, and he's very concerned about this one in particular. The pastor is a highly respected minister in town. He's the secretary of the Chamber of

Commerce and belongs to the Kiwanis Club. The judge hopes this can be settled out of court. When he learned an Albuquerque law firm had filed seven new lawsuits on behalf of adults who claim they were childhood victims of sexual abuse by priests, he just about flipped. Those cases are bound to stir up enough controversy to put our case on the front pages."

"Perhaps that out-of-town law firm could carry this case also."

"No. This one's different. The judge doesn't want them tied together. The abuse happened this week, right here in San Carlos in one of our little south-side churches, where there's never been any such scandal."

Carmela blinked and stared at the ceiling, wondering where the difference lay, but she had no time to bother with semantics. "I'm so sorry, but I do have a conflict of interest."

"Can I tell him what your conflict is?"

"Well, I . . .," Carmela gulped. How could she make her weak excuse stick? She was sure her casual friendship with Paul Morrison didn't rank as a conflict of interest, so she'd have to think of something else to get herself out of this mess. Their meeting in spinning class had become a friendly but limited relationship. It was impossible to ignore his beautiful smile, misty blue eyes, and melodious voice. Must be some movie star in town, she'd thought. Only later, seeing him at the vegetable bin in Whole Foods, had she discovered he was the opposite of what she had imagined. She'd tapped his shoulder to say hello while he sorted through a just-sprinkled pile of Swiss chard. Surprised, he flipped the leaves upward, sending drops of water raining over Carmela's head and face. He laughed as he grabbed a paper towel and dabbed her face, apologizing for administering what he called a "Presbyterian baptism."

"While my church allows for sprinkling, I prefer taking penitents to the lake for immersion, the way Jesus and John the Baptist did." His voice was strong but pleasant, as if that statement represented normal, everyday conversation.

Carmela's mouth had fallen open, but she could think of no reply as he waited for her response. Her first thought was that he was pulling her leg. What church could he mean?

"You do baptisms—at the lake?" She couldn't imagine a modern church not having a baptismal font.

He smiled. "Southern Pentecostal Holiness Church. We're on the south end of town. Our baptisms are held at Bonita Lake. We make it a day of celebration with a potluck lunch, singing, games. Actually, we eat all day! You should join us sometime." He ducked his chin and raised his eyebrows as if questioning her.

Carmela searched his animated face, looking for a clue to the man's story. She'd never attended that church, but she would have guessed its minister to be shouting hellfire and brimstone sermons, like those in the movies. He wouldn't be caught attending spinning classes or shopping at Whole Foods. On the other hand, she recalled that the Lujans, her next-door neighbors, did attend that church. She would never have imagined that Maria—who wore ankle-length dresses, sleeves covering the elbow, opaque cotton stockings, and flat shoes and who combed her hair into a bun fastened low on her neck or braided, encircling her head—belonged to the church where this charismatic man led services every Sunday. She envisioned such conservative ministers as much older, possibly wearing long, white beards and preaching before a congregation shouting "amen" and waving their hands as the sermons progressed.

In retrospect, she recalled being invited to join the Lujans at their church one Easter morning and now regretted that she hadn't accepted the invitation. How was she to know? She suspected there was more to this reverend than showed up in his Sunday sermons.

Yolanda frowned, concerned by Carmela's difficulty in describing her conflict of interest with the Reverend Morrison.

"Well," Carmela finally said, "I'm not sure it's a conflict, but he . . . he baptized me."

That was the best spur-of-the moment excuse she could think of. She knew she was stretching the truth—some might call it lying—but it sounded as if it might work to get her off the case. She knew there was a legal privacy privilege between a pastor and his flock, the same as that between a lawyer and her client, or a doctor and her patient. If she could sneak in the idea that she was somehow connected to the minister's church, she could use that privilege to avoid this appointment.

"Ohhh," Yolanda cooed. "I didn't know you belonged to that church. I'll tell the judge. I'm sure he'll want to discuss it with you."

Carmela cringed. Lying to Yolanda was one thing. Convincing Judge Salazar would be like trying to tell God he'd made a mistake dropping a snake in the Garden of Eden. But how else could she get out of representing a pastor accused of groping a Cub Scout?

She waited as Yolanda's elbows moved to her desktop and her chin rested on her entwined fingers, while she contemplated Carmela's problem. "Maybe he can call to discuss this with you between his cases this afternoon, but you'd better show up for the arraignment if he doesn't reach you. It's at four o'clock today over at municipal court."

Carmela nodded. "You heard the judge tell me to go meet with my client before that hearing. I guess that can't be put off?"

Yolanda shook her head as Carmela left, her voice trailing behind: "I'll ask the Reverend Morrison to tell the judge he doesn't want me to represent him. That should resolve the problem."

Chapter Three

Having picked up the new case file, Carmela dragged herself out of the municipal courthouse and walked toward her office. An undercover police car slowed down and Detective Hawk pulled over to the curb. Carmela looked around to see how many of her colleagues were observing this encounter, glad that it wasn't a patrol car he was driving.

"What are you doing here?" she whispered as she bent through the passenger-side window to glare at him.

"I was thinking of arresting you for jaywalking. You know how crazy the drivers are here. You could get yourself killed wandering around in a fog. Jump in. I'm going your way."

"Travis, you know my office is only three blocks away, and besides, you shouldn't be seen picking me up in front of all the legal buzzards in town. They'll think you're arresting me. Worse, you know our being seen together could compromise any testimony you may give in my trial next week."

"Hey, I'm just killing time waiting around for PT. I have to pick her up after a doctor's appointment. She has a sick kid. And I'm sure the chief would prefer I pick up an attorney, as much as he hates them, rather than that sexy wench on the corner." He raised his eyebrows and tipped his head toward a busker strumming a guitar and singing on First Street, probably without a license.

"Thanks for the comparison, you jerk. Fact is, I just got out of court and half the people coming out of the courthouse heard Judge Salazar slap me around for being late."

"Didn't you tell him you'd been sick?"

"Lawyers don't get sick. Especially women lawyers."

"Poor baby. Get in. I'll take you home and give you a massage."

"Travis, it's two o'clock in the afternoon. Don't you have better things to do than harass the public?"

"Nope. You probably read about the new sexual-abuse case we got today, and my job is to harass every witness I can find before they all get together and start remembering the same exact thing."

Oh, my God, Carmela thought. Travis is in charge of investigating the pedophile case? Now I have a real conflict of interest. But how does a respected attorney tell the judge that her conflict of interest lies in the fact that she and the chief investigator are having—or verging on having—an affair? San Carlos was a small town and most locals had gone to school together. Classmates often married, as Travis and Carolyn had done, or became lovers. That problem was exactly what worried Carmela: attorney and police relationships often caused ethical conflicts. She grimaced, realizing that Travis's assignment also presented another problem. She could imagine the jealous reaction he would have if he interviewed the people at the gym and someone described the friendship she and the preacher had nurtured during spinning class. She had always shared news and feelings with Travis, and he would be suspicious that she had never mentioned this man to him.

She breathed deeply. "Why don't you give this case to one of the other investigators, or maybe PT can do it? A woman would be perfect for the job."

"I thought of that, but her husband's due back from Afghanistan next month, and I'm trying to lighten her load so she can take some time off when he gets home. Everyone else is tying up loose ends on that gang murder case. Get in. I'll drop you off at the office and we'll talk about it."

"No thanks." Carmela sighed. What other complications should she expect?

"See you after my shift?" Travis called as she crossed the street in front of him. She ignored him and he cruised past her, smiling.

Inside, Rosemary looked up from her desk, her mouth poised to clamp on a glazed donut. "You're back early," she mumbled. "Did you get the child returned home?" She delicately wiped glaze from the corner of her mouth with a long, purple fingernail.

"No and yes. I missed the hearing, but Aviva was there to present our agreement. Otherwise, my whole day would have been wasted." She tossed a file on Rosemary's desk. "Here's the paperwork. Please get Aviva on the phone, and set up a meeting as soon as possible. Her department is supposed to be checking on the family frequently, and I need to keep up with what they find."

Carmela moved into her office and dropped her briefcase atop the console. As soon as she slumped out of her jacket and sat down, Rosemary appeared with a cup of coffee.

"I have to get over to the jail by three o'clock to meet with the Reverend Morrison before his initial hearing, which is set for four."

"Oh, on that subject, you just got a call from Yolanda, and she says Judge Salazar wants to see you immediately, if not sooner. It's about that appointment. She hinted that the judge doesn't believe you have a legitimate conflict of interest." Eyebrows raised, Rosemary turned at the door. "Frankly, we don't need another low-paying government case that will take up all your time. I talked to Lucille over at the utilities department, and she says we should make a small, good faith contribution to our overdue electric bill, before the lights go out." She shrugged and allowed her head to lean in a questioning tilt. "If we pay that bill, though, there won't be enough in the bank account to pay my salary at the end of the week. My car payment is already late. I'd hate to have them repossess it. I keep expecting to get that check from the state for your work last month. It's way late."

"It always comes, Rosemary. Please stop worrying."

"If you say so. First you have to see Ms. Peña. Her cat is up the tree again, mewing her head off. Post traumatic stress syndrome, the vet says."

Carmela stared at Rosemary, positive the story was one of her secretary's jokes. They burst out laughing, and Carmela banged her forehead on her desk. "This can't be," she said. "I may go crazy."

"Hey, be careful how you treat that noggin. It's our bread and butter," Rosemary hurried out to comfort Ms. Peña.

Carmela bit her upper lip as she stared at the closed door of her office. She could hear Rosemary's sympathetic conversation with their client. Man or woman, they all seemed to think she could wave a magic wand and their problems would disappear. Today, she wasn't sure how she would get Prissy out of the tree if the fire department refused to cooperate. She reached for the telephone. Travis answered on the first ring of his cell phone. "Have you changed your mind about that massage?"

"No, I have other problems. How's your research going?"

"I'm just getting started, but the first lady I talked to doesn't believe their pastor would grope the kids he works with. She says his reputation is super clean."

"That's great. Salazar appointed me to represent him, and if we can get the case dismissed before it starts, I'll be obliged."

"You're looking for my help on a criminal case? That's pushing boundaries, you know. We agreed when you became a lawyer that I wouldn't hand out any police goodies just because we're friends."

"The initial appearance is this afternoon. But I didn't call you about that. I have another problem I'm hoping you can solve. It doesn't interfere with your job. It's personal."

"Well, that's different. I'll come over after work."

"Can you get away now? This is an emergency."

He heaved a sigh. "Hold on a minute." She assumed he was talking to his secretary.

"Okay. I'm clear. What's the problem?"

"Have you ever climbed a tree to rescue a cat?" Carmela held the phone away from her ear to lessen the roar of laughter hitting her sensitive eardrum.

"I just thought I'd ask. You don't have to make fun of me."

"You don't own a cat. I was the only animal around the last time I visited."

It is Carmela's turn to laugh. "Okay. Forget I asked."

"No, no. Where's the tree and whose cat is it?"

"Do you remember last week when Ms. Peña's cat had to be rescued by the fire department?"

"Uh huh."

"It's up the tree again, and the fire department refuses to help because the parties didn't pay for the first rescue. I'm broke or I'd pay it."

"Why don't you call the mayor? This sounds like a great public relations case, and he's coming up for election next spring. He could get a reporter to take a picture of him climbing the tree."

"Travis, be serious. It may come to that, but first, I thought you might do me the favor. You always have such great fix-it ideas. You could do it after work."

"You're buttering me up. You should know by now that I come already basted."

"Ummm."

"What's it worth to you?"

"I'll fix you meatballs and spaghetti for supper." There was silence on the phone. "Starting with guacamole and cheap wine." Still no response. "Chocolate pie for dessert?"

"That all sounds good, but as Coach Wingard would say, it's short of a bases-loaded homerun."

"Travis, you're pushing your luck."

"Eating your cooking is where I push my luck, honey. As I recall, I'm the cook when I get something decent to eat at your place." Carmela grimaced.

"Where's the cat?"

She relaxed and smiled. One problem solved.

Chapter Four

In the judge's reception area, Carmela was greeted by a stern Yolanda, who asked her to have a seat while she notified the judge of her presence. That bad? Carmela was well aware of punishment meted out to a lawyer who lied to a judge.

The door opened and Judge Salazar greeted her with a hardy handshake, as if the morning confrontation had never happened.

"Come in. Come in," he said. "How are you, Carmela?"

"Thank you, Judge. I'm fine."

"Now, what's this conflict of interest all about?" he asked as he wandered near the windows, his back to her.

Carmela slipped into the chair facing his desk and laid aside her briefcase. His pacing didn't bode well. "I'm sorry to be bothering you with this, Your Honor. I know how busy you are, but Reverend Morrison and I are closely acquainted through his church and . . . and so forth, and I'm afraid I'm too close to his case to do it justice. Wouldn't it be better to put it in the hands of a law firm from Albuquerque, or the lawyers in Roswell who are pursuing similar cases against the Catholic Church?"

The Judge made no response, and she felt compelled to add, "You know I don't take criminal cases full time."

The Judge continued to stare out the window for a long moment before turning his gaze to Carmela and settling behind his desk. "Thank you for your suggestions, Carmela. However, I believe the question at hand is whether you have a legitimate conflict of interest. Yolanda said you were a baptized member of this man's church. Did she misunderstand you?"

"I . . . I'm afraid I may have misled her. I'm not a *member* of his church." She paused while he continued to stare at her, then mumbled,

"He sprinkled me with water from wet chard at the grocery store. He said it was a Presbyterian baptism."

"Hmmm. So you're friends, not church associates. I don't think that counts."

"Yes, we're friends."

"That settles that," he said as if to dismiss her. "Just being acquainted with the minister is not a reason to withdraw your representation, and despite your well-taken advice as to who should represent him, I trust my first decision. It was not hastily made. You have shown a remarkable ability to win cases that everyone believed were unwinnable. If the minister is satisfied with your representation, then so am I." He rose to dismiss her. "The arraignment will be videotaped at the jail, so if you hurry, you can get over to meet your client just in time."

Carmela's breath quickened. This case would most likely be precedent setting, and Judge Salazar was tossing it into her hands for better or worse. If she won, he could bask in having done the proper thing. If she lost, he could put another notch on his "gotcha" pistol.

Carmela realized the argument was over. She thanked the judge for his confidence in her and hurried out, too upset to wave goodbye to Yolanda. Her only hope for getting off this case was to have the minister request a substitute. The jail sat only ten minutes from the courthouse, and she herded her Cadillac to Clarke Road, heading south.

Inside the jail, she was greeted with smiles by the guards, neat in their uniforms, guns snug on their hips. After a light patting search for weapons, she was told to wait for an escort to her interview. Down the hall, a guard ushered her into a small soundproof room with a long table and four chairs. A wide, one-way window covered the upper half of one wall. Police officers or attorneys could stand behind the window and view a prisoner's reaction to questions. Carmela pulled the shade over the window to ensure their privacy. She clicked off the open mike so that her interview didn't carry outside.

Guided by two officers, Paul entered the room with his head lowered, his eyes averted. Seated, he turned his profile to Carmela. The officers left, closing the door quietly.

"Good afternoon, Paul," Carmela said. "How are you doing?" She was immediately embarrassed by her stupid question. How would anyone be doing under the circumstances?

"I'm okay."

Up to this moment, when reading of the numerous pedophile cases in New Mexico, she had felt confusion, anger, betrayal, frustration, disbelief—but mostly outrage at a system that allowed children to be abused and, worse, made it easy for pedophiles to operate in a religious ministry. That's the last place child abuse should flourish, and while she had to admit she fought a prejudicial leaning toward *guilty* every time she read of a priest charged with sexual abuse, she couldn't believe this man had committed such a crime.

"The judge says you agreed to my appointment as your counsel. Why? You hardly know me."

He turned, and those misty blue eyes pierced the short distance between them. "I didn't know you were an attorney at the time we were in spinning class, and I didn't know your last name, so when you were appointed, I didn't connect the two. My cellmate later described you. He'd seen you represent someone when he was in jail before."

"It isn't too late to tell the judge you would like to change counsel, Paul, and I recommend it. Furthermore, I'm wondering why you're being represented by a state-appointed attorney? Can't your family and church members come up with money to pay an attorney who specializes in this field?"

"No. I have no savings. My father is dead. He was the minister of this church for thirty years and died while still in service. There were no retirement funds, so my mother lives on a small Social Security check with a little help from me. My salary is a percentage of the weekly donations. We're not a rich church."

So he was at the mercy of the court, Carmela realized. However, that didn't mean that he had to settle for the first appointment the court made for him.

"As I said before, you have the right to ask for different representation."

"I have no reason to." His voice was flat, but after a time, he looked at her and smiled. "A Presbyterian sprinkle is better than no baptism at all."

"Paul, I'm sure your occupation may prejudice you in that direction, but there are better standards for choosing an attorney than whether she's baptized."

"You're right, of course, but my God does not reside in a specific church or sect, and he doesn't judge non-churchgoers. Neither do I. I suspect a jury will trust you. The question is whether you believe I'm innocent and will fight to win my case."

Carmela was flummoxed. Her job as his attorney would be to fight for his freedom whether he was innocent or guilty. She could not be influenced by what he claimed, and while she couldn't believe he was guilty, she'd have to fight for his freedom despite the truth of the matter.

"Tell me what happened."

Paul aged in front of her. Wrinkles appeared down the side of his cheeks and above his eyes. The corners of his lips sagged, and his voice cracked as he began to talk.

"Some of the Cub Scouts were helping me clean out a space in the church basement where we were creating a crafts room—a place where they could build their race cars and have our annual race. We could also work on other projects. Cody arrived late, and I could see he'd been crying. Following his father's death, he'd gotten into the habit of hanging around after the meetings, just to talk. I counseled him through the crisis of his father's death and also helped him adjust to his mother's remarriage. He trusted me, and when he arrived that day, I assumed he'd tell me what was wrong after the others left." There was a long pause. "He did. When we were alone, he clung to me, sobbing. I put my arms around him and lifted him onto my lap. He kept saying he'd sinned. At one point, he jumped down, leaned over, and clutched his privates, as if he were in great pain. I was so shocked, I couldn't speak. When I regained my voice, I asked if he'd hurt himself, and he nodded. I asked how it happened, and he said, 'He hurt me.' I asked who did it, but he wouldn't answer. I told him I needed to call his parents, and he became hysterical. I did call his home and told the mother that they needed to come pick Cody up, that he had reported to me that someone had abused him, and I had to call the police. She was upset, of course, but said they'd be there.

"When the parents arrived, Cody was so frightened he couldn't speak or look at me. He asked to go to the bathroom, and Marvin took him. It dawned on me that I had been lax in following the rule that two adults should be present at all times when we worked with Cub Scouts. But I'd worked so long with Cody and his mother during their bad times that they almost seemed like family.

"When the police arrived, I told them what had happened, but I'm not sure they believed me. They listened closely to what the stepfather said. My relationship with Lucille and Cody changed when Marvin Stokes entered the family. He didn't seem to like me from the start, and I assumed it was because Lucille had depended so heavily on my counseling before he entered the picture. That day, as I finished explaining what happened, the stepfather interrupted and said that's not what Cody told him in the bathroom—that I had put Cody on my lap and squeezed him. The police asked Cody if that was true, and he nodded yes every time he was asked. Marvin later told the police that Cody was mad at me. I never knew why."

"Was this questioning done in front of you and the parents?"

"Yes."

"That's improper procedure. He must be a new cop. The CPS representative should have intervened. They're there to protect the child."

Paul wiped tears from his eyes. "It became obvious to me that I hadn't handled the matter properly. It isn't as if I haven't been trained to handle these offenses, but I've never had to. My mind went blank when Cody first told me what had happened, blaming himself. I was so horrified, I didn't stop to think it through. It seemed so cut and dried. I never dreamed he would change his story."

"You have no prior criminal record?"

"Of course not."

"Think back to your school experiences—Boy Scouts, sports, things like that. Were you ever propositioned as a boy?"

Paul's eyes narrowed. "Is this necessary?"

"I'm sorry, Paul. We haven't even touched on what will be necessary to talk about in a case like this. You asked if I believed you, and while my duty to represent you doesn't rest on whether I believe you, it's important for you to be honest with me. I have to know all I can about you. Please answer my question."

He stood and walked over to the wall, his back to Carmela. "There's no reason to go on," he said. "You're wasting your time." He leaned his arm against the wall and dropped his head.

"I'm the lawyer, Paul. You'll have to let me decide that."

He turned, facing her. "No. This one is decided for you. No jury is going to believe a gay man is innocent of touching a little boy. Especially with all the priests in this state who've been charged with child abuse."

The chill bumps on Carmela's arm now turned icy. She should have suspected he was gay. She'd had friends in college who lived in the shadows of homosexuality, because it was not safe to reveal it. She could see the chances of winning his case diminishing.

"I've known I was gay since high school, but I was already called to the ministry by the time I acknowledged it for what it was, and I thought the ministry would be the perfect place to hide the fact. I suppose all gay ministers think that, even the Catholics. When I took the job at Southern, I pledged to God and myself that I would live a celibate life." He glared at her. "And I have."

She suspected that the gays in San Carlos did their socializing in Santa Fe, where they were openly accepted in many cases. It was certainly possible that Paul had remained celibate in this small town, but would a jury believe it? And being celibate did not rule out pedophilia.

Suddenly, this case had taken an unexpected turn that challenged her. She had always been intrigued by civil rights cases, but had never dreamed she'd be involved in one.

"Sit down," she said, and waited while he fortified himself against the truth he knew he had to face. He sat straight in the chair with crossed arms, a firm jaw, and narrowed eyes, waiting to hear bad news.

"It's true members of the gay community don't get a fair hearing in our courts in most cases. However, San Carlos is moving into the modern world. Not everyone supports those colleges and churches that teach that homosexuality is immoral, or an illness. Your own church is guilty of that, I suspect, but this community has an increasing number of people who settled here because of the scientific jobs in Los Alamos. They come from San Francisco, L.A., New York, Washington, and Europe. The gay world is not new and frightening to them. I've lived in San Carlos nearly my whole life, and I believe it's possible to seat an open-minded jury in our courts." She paused. "However, we have the option of asking to move the case to Santa Fe or elsewhere, where a more liberal jury could be seated. We'll talk about it."

Paul shook his head. "I've lived here nearly all my life, too, and I see ignorance and prejudice against anyone who's different more frequently than I see acceptance. When I answered the calling to my church, I thought I could make a difference. But I doubt that I've made progress in that direction." He shifted in his chair, looked away, and then lowered his eyes. "You may not understand why, under the circumstances, I'm preaching in such a conservative church. It's where I grew up and where

I'm accepted as one of them. As I said, my father was the minister here for years. My status has never been questioned." He looked again at Carmela and spoke with resolution. "God found me here, and he hasn't told me to leave. Maybe he's telling me now that I'm needed in prison."

Carmela leaned toward him. "Don't try to impress me with that 'poor victim' reaction. No God would wish prison on any person, certainly not a gay man or lesbian."

"I guess that's supposed to make me feel better, but it makes me wonder if you live in some fantasy world. I suspect you're much too optimistic in thinking you can find a jury pool in this community that wouldn't vote to hang us both." He paused when she didn't respond. "However, I'm willing to try it if you are."

"If you're sure you want me to represent you, you need to convey that to the judge at the hearing coming up shortly." She looked at her watch. "This first hearing is set before a municipal judge for the purpose of reading you your rights. The judge will no doubt find probable cause and transfer it over to the district court for prosecution." Carmela stood.

She handed him a business card. "I'll have a bondsman contact you. In the meantime, I have a long list of questions I need you to answer so that I can interview you adequately and come up with a list of potential witnesses as to your character, your association with children, and with the gay community. Do you have a partner now?"

The pastor hesitated. "No. I told you I've been celibate since I became a minister."

"Paul, you also said you trusted me. There's a law that protects the conversations and written information between a lawyer and her client, so that I'll never be required to reveal to the court or the opposing counsel the information we exchange, unless it involves a crime you confess to me. Even with these protections in place, many clients find it difficult or impossible to be open with their attorneys. You may find it especially difficult to talk to a woman. It will require that you reveal very personal, no doubt painful, life experiences. Can you do that?"

"Do I have a choice?"

"No." She checked her watch again and opened her file. "We have just enough time to go over the charges, the punishment you could get, and the procedures ahead of us. Here are the charges: *'On or about the 6th day of September, 2014, the above-named defendant was in a position of authority, and he used his influence to touch the genitals of a child who was younger than eight-years-old. Whoever commits criminal sexual contact with a minor in the second degree is guilty of a second-degree felony for a sexual offence against a child and shall be sentenced to a minimum term of imprisonment of three years, which shall not be suspended or deferred.'"*

Carmela looked up and added, "You *could* be sentenced for up to six years in prison and fined five thousand dollars. The judge will ask if you understand the charges. She will ask how you plead, and you'll say 'not guilty.' I'll stand beside you and confirm that decision to the court. It's important that you look involved—but never smile. She wants to know that you take this matter seriously. The DA will ask for a high bail, which will assure you stay in jail. I'll argue that the bail should be minimal because of your stature in the community, but don't count on a favorable ruling.

"In a few minutes, you will be taken down to the holding cell, and when your case is called, you will be brought to stand by me at the podium in front of the TV cameras, where the judge will address us. I will be responding to the judge, except when she asks you direct questions, such as whether you accept me as your attorney. If you have any questions, we'll turn off the speaker and talk privately. Do you understand?"

Paul nodded.

"I hope you don't mind being manipulated by a female. As your attorney, it will be necessary for me to order you around quite a bit. My first order is: don't talk to a person other than me about this case! Not your mother, your best friend, relatives, especially the district attorney's office, anyone from Child Protection Services, my secretary—all conversations are off limits when discussing this case, unless I am present with you. Do you understand?"

"That sounds pretty clear." He smiled. "Shall we move in together?"

Carmela laughed. "Well, it would stifle the rumors that you're gay! I'm sorry. I know these rules are burdensome, but there are good reasons for them. Anything you say can be twisted around to mean something else, and the district attorney is a master at getting defendants to admit their guilt. You need to understand that nothing you say will convince the accusers that you are innocent. They are not interested in a fair and thorough investigation. They are only interested in finding you guilty as charged.

"I have a private detective who will search for the real culprit in this case. Finding him will be our best hope. Think of names that might help us with that investigation." She looked at her watch again. "We need to get downstairs. They have the cameras set up so that we'll appear in front of the judge via video from here at the jail."

Finished, she pushed a button near the door, and the jailer escorted Paul away. Carmela followed the uniformed attendant downstairs to wait for the hearing.

The municipal courtroom was packed for what should have been a routine hearing. There was standing room only, with a crowd of angry, frightened parents, shocked members of the Southern Pentecostal Holiness Church, and curious bystanders intermingled with bottom-feeders looking for a sexual rush. Though six prisoners were on call, it was Paul who drew the mob. His arrest had turned the day's hearing into a high-profile community gathering, with the religious and non-religious both disappointed that the pastor and his attorney weren't present in the courtroom. Many felt cheated by the fact that San Carlos courts allowed the prisoners to appear before the judge via TV. Their anger lost its power to punish the accused, since he or she couldn't see or hear their grumbling.

The court clerk called for order and announced the arrival of Judge Casey, who asked everyone to be seated. The clerk called the roll of prisoners, who were led to the podium, and the judge explained their constitutional right to plead guilty or not guilty to the charges filed against them, setting the stage for release from jail or a speedy trial.

At Paul's turn, Carmela argued that he should be released on his own recognizance because of his good reputation and permanent connection to the community, knowing the judge would be more concerned with the fear and anger of the community than whether the defendant would return to court. She was thankful for the video appearance, glad her client would not be exposed to the vitriol in the courtroom. In cases of sexual abuse of a child, some citizens still harbored the belief that the case should be settled with a rope thrown over the lower limb of the historic hanging tree down by the river, where cattle thieves had met their fate.

As expected, Judge Casey set Paul's bail so high—a cool million—that he would not be able to pay it.

Unsurprised at the negative rulings, Carmela argued that the judge had not taken into account her client's impeccable reputation, his good standing in the community, his family's longtime residence in the community, his employment in the church, and his history of serving the poor and homeless. As she made her argument, Judge Casey peered over her glasses at the camera, impatient to get on with the crowded docket. "The bail stands. Motion denied," she said and looked at the DA. "If you plan to take this to the grand jury, get it set immediately." She banged her gavel and picked up another file.

Guards led Paul back to his cell, and Carmela headed to the office, wondering where she would find the time to prepare for the preliminary hearing that came next in a criminal procedure. At this point, she suspected the district attorney had insufficient evidence to support the finding of probable cause to bind the case over to the district court for trial. The judge was giving him the benefit of the doubt. It was Carmela's duty to prove her wrong. If the case did go to trial, she'd have to consider a change of venue. Santa Fe would be an improvement. Citizens there were more open to different lifestyles.

Chapter Five

The next morning, Carmela entered her office through a back door that allowed her to avoid the crowded reception room. She hoped some of the clients would pay their outstanding bills. Rosemary slipped into her office, closed the door, and waved a number of checks. She grinned. "Let there be light, for another month at least."

"Did you ever doubt it?"

"No, someone up there looks out for us. How did the interview with the pastor go?"

"Just fine. It's an interesting story, and I'll need a lot of help from you. Let's talk about it later. Did you hear anything about the rescue of Ms. Peña's cat?"

Rosemary giggled. "It's a good thing you know people in high places—pun intended. Captain Hawk called and said 'mission accomplished.' Seems he sweet-talked Prissy down with some tuna and a sprig of catnip he found in somebody's yard. He said to tell you he'd collect the reward promised, plus interest, as soon as your schedules mesh." Rosemary sat in the chair in front of Carmela's desk, crossed her beautiful runner's legs, and whispered, "What did you promise him?"

"Not as much as he'd have you think. Let's get on with our work. Who's first?"

The hours flew by, and late in the afternoon Carmela received a message from Travis, saying he had to run over to Santa Fe for a conference and would be back late—but to hold dinner for him. She closed her file and silently thanked him for reminding her of her promise to feed him.

By the time he arrived, Carmela had the house smelling of home-made meatballs in spaghetti sauce from a jar, chocolate pie made with a store-bought crust, and boxed pudding. It's a step up from takeout, she thought.

He kissed the cheek she offered him before sniffing toward the kitchen. "I love a woman of her words," he said. "I told Ms. Peña not to worry about the bill for rescuing her cat. You were paying it."

"You're great at getting me into trouble, Travis."

He pulled her into his arms and rubbed his rough stubble on her cheek. "I've been trying to get you into trouble for months, and it hasn't worked. What am I doing wrong?"

She circled out of his arms and reached for the spaghetti bowl. "Nothing wrong with your efforts, but your timing is bad. Dinner is ready. Get yourself some wine and cheese while I toast the garlic bread."

"This is great. I'm starving. And I get to sleep late tomorrow, thanks to the hours I spent out of town today. Maybe I can bed down here?"

Carmela smiled at the fact that he never stopped asking. She removed the salad bowl from the refrigerator, pretending not to hear him. "So you won't be interviewing parishioners in the morning?"

"No. Tomorrow I meet with your friend Aviva or some other chick from Child Protection Services. They never trust the police to do a proper job of investigating these cases."

"Make sure you call her 'chick' when you meet with her. That'll fry any testimony you might have against my client."

"Your client?"

"Didn't I tell you Judge Salazar appointed me to represent the minister in the sexual-abuse case?"

"No."

"Yes, I did. And I tried to talk the judge out of the appointment, but his mind was made up."

"You know you can't do that, Carmela. I told you yesterday that I'm doing the investigation for the prosecution!"

"Travis, wash up while I put the food on the table, and we'll discuss it later."

"I don't want to discuss it later. I want it settled right now."

"Okay, okay. Have your say . . . for what it's worth." Carmela turned off the burners, picked up her wine glass, and headed for a chair across the living room, where she could stare him down. Despite his childish temper-fit, she knew the matter could not be settled between them, but she'd let him release some steam.

Chagrined, Travis faced her cool glance from across the room. "I'm sorry," he said. "It's been a long day. I shouldn't dump my frustrations on you, but I hate sexual-abuse cases." He set aside his drink and leaned forward, his forehead resting on his fists. His voice cracked. "I should have put this investigation into someone else's hands. PT's good at it, but I wanted her to have some free time when her husband gets home. Everyone else is tied up." He sat up. "Sex offences drive me crazy."

"I'm so sorry. What makes them worse than murder? You deal with that all the time."

There was no answer, and Carmela sipped her wine, wondering why they'd never discussed this problem.

Travis folded his arms across his chest as if to shield himself. He stared at Carmela. "It's not something I talk about. All I know is, a kid never gets over that kind of experience, and it's also hard for me to believe that you will be spending your time protecting the guy who did it."

Carmela set her wine glass on the side table and stared at Travis. What was he saying? She moved over and bent to her knees in front of him. His distress seeped into her own body as she pulled his face toward her. "You've never mentioned this before, Travis. What happened?"

He pushed her away and began pacing. "I feel stupid. It doesn't make sense to worry about something that took place so long ago. And it wasn't even my problem. I've tried to forget it, but it keeps coming up when I get assigned to one these cases."

Carmela, sitting on the floor, waited for him to continue.

"When we were seniors, Coach Wingard allowed some college boys to come over during their school break to help with our training. They got college credit for it. Problem was, they started taking showers with us. One day the coach kept me and Billy Joe after the game to go over some plays, and Billy Joe left the field before I did. When I got to the showers, he and this guy were . . . kissing and fooling around with each other, and I just went bonkers. I broke the guy's nose, and to tell you the truth, I wanted to kill him." He turned to Carmela. "I've never been so upset."

"I remember when you and Billy Joe quit hanging out together. And you wouldn't talk about it, but I had no idea it was so serious."

"Billy Joe was so mad at me, he wouldn't talk to me. To make it worse, I learned later that he was the one who started it, so I wasn't about to be friends with him anymore. I knew I should tell the coach, but I didn't tell anybody anything. I took my anger out on the football teams we played, which may be why I was a star player."

"It's not too late to get some help, Travis. Counseling helps. But you're right—you shouldn't take any more of these cases until you have a better understanding of what you and Billy Joe went through."

"Us? I blame the college guy. He was old enough to know better." He picked up his drink. "That's why I don't like you working with this creep."

"I'm sorry for what happened to your friendship, Travis, but Paul Morrison isn't a creep. And why do you put blame on the college kid, when you said Billy Joe wanted it?" She stood, with her hands on her hips. "My client is innocent until you or somebody else comes up with hard facts to prove he isn't. You just described how people can be so wrong at times, how mistaken first impressions can be."

"Why do you think he's innocent? I understand the kid in this case was very specific about who did it. What's your guy's story?"

"First of all, the kid was not specific about who did it. The parents were specific. There's a big difference. Adults put words into children's mouths, and the kids are too afraid to disagree. Anyway, I can't discuss Paul's story until the pleadings come out, and you shouldn't judge him until you've heard the evidence. In the meantime, you should ask Aviva to recommend a therapist for your problems."

"No. This is not something I want to get around town. Everybody knows I was one of Billy Joe's friends. What does that say about me? If I decide to get therapy, I'll go out of town."

"It isn't something to be ashamed of, Travis. Besides, therapists don't talk about their cases to other people."

"Maybe not, but it always gets out somehow, and it will affect my career if it becomes known that I'm going to a head doctor. It goes on my personnel records." He disappeared into the kitchen and came back with cheese and crackers. "I talked to your spinning teacher today."

Carmela stopped breathing. Now we're getting to what started this outburst.

"She says you and this minister were chummy, and sometimes left the class together. Why didn't you tell me that? How the hell can you represent somebody you've been involved with?"

Carmela laughed out loud. "You sound jealous, Travis. I've done nothing but chat with the man. I certainly haven't 'been involved' with him. He came to our class for a few weeks, plus I met him once in Whole Foods. We had coffee and ate a snack there. He quit the class, and I never saw him again until I interviewed him yesterday in jail."

"Your teacher said he quit the class. Was that because of you?"

"Don't be silly. Why would I have anything to do with it?"

Travis smiled. "He couldn't resist you, and his religion doesn't allow him to play around with beautiful women."

Carmela sat shaking her head.

"Swear on a stack of Bibles?"

"I will not. And don't think you can get away with loose accusations. I'm not one of your scumbags." She held up her bare left hand. "In fact, I don't belong to you or anyone else. Last time I looked, I was free as a bird." She rose and headed for the kitchen. "You shouldn't judge people based on your prejudices, Travis."

"I know, but Dad expected me to look out for you when we were kids, and it's still in my blood. The idea of some guy taking advantage of you burns me up."

Carmela smiled. How would he feel when he learned that the man from whom he was protecting her was gay?

"It's nice of you to be concerned about me, Travis, but your worries are misplaced. Come on. Let's eat. I'm starving."

Travis relaxed, took off his uniform jacket, and rolled up his sleeves. "I'm coming, but this conversation isn't over."

Carmela nodded. She was sure it wasn't.

After the dishes were washed, they sat on the couch, and Travis repeated his frequent suggestion that he spend the night. "We have to get our relationship settled, Carmela. This stalemate is driving me crazy."

"Travis, our having an affair while you're still married puts your reputation at stake as well as mine. You work under department rules against married officers having affairs. The public judges me, and I've never thought of myself as 'the other woman' in your life, or anyone else's. If that makes me a prude, so be it."

"Okay. Okay. How about I get a divorce? I've just been putting it off, thinking Carolyn would file. Would that change your mind?"

"I have no rules against marrying a divorced man. Of course he'd have to propose."

"I can do that right now. I love you more than anything. Will you marry me?"

Carmela patted his cheek. "Show me the decree. I'm sure we can work something out."

Travis kissed the palm of her hand while his hand moved to cover her breast; he nuzzled beneath her ear. She was somewhat surprised at her body's eager response to this unexpected approach.

"Travis . . ."

"Umm?" He covered her lips with the first long kiss they'd ever shared, and she was reluctant to push him away. She was being a prude, she thought, but one of them had to be sensible. What they both wanted so badly could wait a little longer.

Before she could say it, Travis brushed his lips across her closed eyes and rose from the couch. "I know. I know. It's what my dad would say. And he was right most of the time. I'm sure he'd have no qualms about sharing meatballs and chocolate pie, though. Let's eat."

Chapter Six

The next morning, on her way to the judge's chambers to set a preliminary hearing date, Carmela met Aviva.

"We need to talk," Aviva said. "Got time for coffee?"

Carmela glanced at her watch. She hated to be late for her appointments, but Rosemary was great at making excuses for her. "Why not?" she said. "I've had nothing but junk this morning."

Carmela maneuvered to the far corner of the room, where their conversation could be private. After stacking their files on empty chairs, they went to the bar for lattes and muffins. "This will be lunch," Carmela promised.

Aviva's beautiful, dark eyebrows rose. "Speak for yourself. Tony is coming in to pick up some medicine for one of the horses, and he promised to meet me for lunch. He's paying, so I plan to order big."

Carmela laughed. "What do we need to talk about?"

"Your new case. The minister—Paul Morrison."

"Are you working that case?"

"Yes. We had a new worker go out on the first call, and I'm embarrassed to say she made some mistakes. I'm trying to clean it up. I've put the child in foster care until we get some answers to what happened. I'm worried about him. He was like . . . in shock. Very quiet. I talked to the guardian *ad litem* this morning—John Palmer. He tells me the child was practically hysterical when he talked to him, more from being taken out of the home than from the abuse, he thought."

"I hope you've gotten a therapist appointed for him."

"He'll see Sandra today."

"I am curious about one thing, Aviva. Paul said the social worker who came out when he called the police didn't take the child aside to question him. Nor did the policeman. It was all done in front of the parents. That's way out of line."

"That's what I'm trying to overcome. I was called in when the order to put him in foster care arrived. Apologies don't mean a lot, but I'm sorry. We're so understaffed." She sipped her latte. "What I don't understand are the charges against your client. We've heard such great things about him."

"It is hard to believe. He just doesn't fit the pattern."

"I don't suppose any of those priests who've been charged with dozens of cases up in Roswell fit a pattern either."

"Yes, they do. We just haven't been given the facts."

"It makes one sick to see what's happening to this child. He'll never get over it, and while you may think your client is innocent, the public is up in arms."

"What are you hearing?"

"For one thing, my mother-in-law's in a book club with the preacher's mother. The group meets in individual homes, and when they're at the Morrison's, your client sometimes joins them for the discussion."

"You're kidding."

"No kidding, and the women love him. Mom thinks he's sexy, but wonders if he isn't gay, since he isn't married and doesn't date."

Carmela gulped her hot coffee and frowned. "How does she know that? I hope she's not spreading that rumor."

"I told her to be careful who she said it to. But if she's suspicious, others must be curious, too, don't you think?"

Carmela pushed her muffin away. "It doesn't seem to be an issue with his church members. And besides, being gay doesn't prove he's a child molester. Does your mother-in-law understand that?"

"We talked about it. I'm still concerned about rumors and what this attitude might do to your case if it becomes general gossip."

Carmela frowned. "Thanks for letting me know what the public is saying. That assumption makes my job more difficult, but not impossible. Maybe you can do a little educating about pedophiles if it comes up." She stared at Aviva. This was not an issue the two had ever discussed. "You do support me on this, don't you?"

Aviva laid her hand over Carmela's. "Of course. Tony and I hope you win this case. We're just worried."

Carmela collected her briefcase and rose. "Thanks, Aviva. I appreciate your support. Enjoy your lunch and tell Tony hello for me."

In the judge's chambers, Carmela looked over the choice of three dates that the DA and Yolanda had agreed upon, picked the earliest, and headed for her office.

With the telephone to her ear, Rosemary handed her a stack of messages. "Ms. Peña called to thank you for sending that lovely officer over to rescue Prissy. I think she fell in love with him and may let her cat out again on purpose."

"She wouldn't dare."

The lovely officer left a message saying her spaghetti and meatballs were the best, but most of all he enjoyed the dessert. Remembering his proposal, she doubted that he meant the chocolate pie.

"So what happened last night?" Rosemary asked. "Did Travis get his reward for rescuing the cat?"

"Yep. Meatballs and spaghetti."

"What did you fix for dessert?"

"Chocolate meringue pie."

"Ooooh, that's what's in the refrigerator. Looks yummy."

"That's your piece."

"Thank goodness. I ate half of it, hoping you wouldn't miss it."

Carmela laughed. She knew Rosemary well.

"You didn't tell me how the preacher's hearing went."

"About the way I expected. I understand there was a large crowd in the courtroom, which doesn't surprise me. Most of them no doubt believe he's guilty."

"Is he?"

Carmela grinned at her secretary. "Of course not. I don't represent guilty clients."

Rosemary shook her head. "I hope the jury agrees with you."

"It's my job to make sure they do. Let's get started on the file. Call Harry Rodriquez and see if he'll start an investigation with a small down payment. Last time I talked to him, business was slow. Prepare a subpoena to get church records and membership names, and I'll get the judge to sign it. Tell Harry to go over that list and talk to the men who coach tee-ball. Oh, and Paul says he was born on a farm outside of Pecos, so there should be people around who knew his family then. He went to San Carlos High, so ask Paul which of his teachers might be good reputation witnesses. And tell Harry to do a thorough check on the stepfather, Marvin Stokes. See if he or any of Cody's contacts has a criminal record, particularly child or sexual abuse, and whether they are gay or lesbian."

"Why are we getting into that subject?"

Carmela shuffled her notes from the interview. "Paul is gay and we need to know who his contacts are. This isn't for public consumption right now, so be careful when you discuss this case with other offices."

Rosemary's shoulders fell. "Woman, you're crazy. You know there's no way you can win a sexual-abuse case if your client is gay, no matter how innocent he is. Why doesn't he just admit he's guilty and throw himself on the mercy of the court, instead of taking it to a jury?" She paused, perplexed. "It's too bad we only get the set fee the state pays for this case. It sounds like it would be a money-maker."

"This may be my last case for the department. When I hung my shingle, I needed clients from anywhere, but now we're getting overwhelmed. I just don't have time for these kinds of cases."

"I keep telling you to raise your fees."

"I know. I know. I suppose the day will come, but right now I feel obligated to help the kind of people I grew up with."

"Gays and lesbians?"

"Ms. Peña. Poor people. We didn't discuss sexual orientation when I was young." She laid aside her pen and stared at Rosemary. "Tell me how you feel about gays and lesbians."

"You know I'm not prejudiced. Remember how I became friends with Lisa and Jackie when we worked on their co-habitation agreement? They praised my work highly."

"I know, but you've stated a fact that ninety-eight percent of the people in the courtroom will agree with. Sexual orientation wasn't talked about in families or *polite* company. That's why I see this case as a challenge. The whole country will be surprised when we win."

"The whole country? What are you getting us into?"

"I'm not sure, but I would guess that this is not just a local-interest story. It will no doubt be tied into the Catholic Church's problems with sexually perverted priests. Be sure you don't answer reporters' questions. Tell them they'll have to talk to me."

"Reporters? Sounds to me like this is out of our league."

"Rosemary, I can do this blindfolded, and you'll be headed for paralegal school by the time it's over. Especially if we win."

"Well, if anyone can win it, I suppose you can." She walked to the door. "My inbox is full this morning. I'll open this file after lunch.

Chapter Seven

The next day, Harry Rodriquez dug a handful of bedraggled chocolate Kisses out of the pocket of his long, well-worn cotton sweater and laid them on Rosemary's desk. Pulling a dog-eared Grisham paperback from his briefcase, he settled into the corner of the couch, his smudged glasses hanging low on his blimp of a nose.

"Is this the best you can do?" Rosemary asked, one hand on her hip as the other pointed toward the candy.

"Is there anything better than chocolate Kisses—other than the real thing? I gave up trying to get that from you a long time ago. A fellow can take rejection just so long."

"We both know you don't want any kisses from me. What would Silvie think if she knew you went into every office in town and flirted with the secretaries?"

"She knows I don't mean anything by it."

"She deserves a golden crown in heaven for living with you."

"I tell her that, too. When's your boss coming in?"

"She should be here soon. The judge asked for a report on the child he sent home this week. The police reported the home was the next best thing to a pigsty. Tell me, how do people live like that?"

"It's nothing new. I'll bet there was trailer trash in the Garden of Eden, don't you? They'll always be with us."

"I never thought of it like that." She circled her desk and dropped into her chair, smiling. "At least Adam and Eve didn't have to worry about going to the Laundromat."

Harry chuckled and turned the page in his book. He liked Rosemary's smart mouth. Before he could finish the page, the door opened and Carmela entered with an armload of files.

"How long have you been here?" she asked and waved him to follow her.

"Oh, an hour or two."

"That's a lie," Rosemary called. "Don't let him charge you for more than ten minutes."

Carmela laughed with Harry and fell exhausted into her leather chair.

"I need you to get started on the latest child abuse case—the Reverend Paul Morrison of the Southern Pentecostal Holiness Church. Have you read about it?"

"Oh God, yes. What are you doing on that case?"

"The court appointed me to represent the preacher."

"You're going to defend him?"

"That's what defense attorneys do."

"You'll need some luck, Counselor. Child abusers don't get the time of day in this county. You know that."

"This one's different. I know the man. So does half the county. He's innocent."

"Well, you wouldn't want to be caught dead defending a pedophile who's guilty!"

"Who said he was a pedophile? He's gay. The words are not synonymous."

Harry stared at Carmela with a pained look. "I'll be damned. Are you sure? I'm afraid that's what the public believes."

"Which is why this will be a difficult case, and it means you will have many hours of lucrative work ahead." She laid aside her pen. "Needless to say, let's not be discussing this subject in public."

"Yeah. Knowing he's gay paints a different picture for the trial, I'd say."

"You're showing your ignorance, Harry. Facts show that the majority of sexual-abuse cases involving children are perpetrated by adults whom the children know and trust—a family member or people in positions of authority—who are usually heterosexual, not homosexual. In fact, heterosexuals can be attracted to both boys and girls, while homosexuals are attracted primarily to the same sex. But you're right. It is harder to prove the truth when a gay man is involved. I can't argue with that."

"You sure the man is innocent?"

"I am. You have to believe that too, Harry, or your heart won't lead your search for the guilty person."

"I have to tell you, my experience with homosexuals has been limited."

"Most people would be surprised how many of their contacts every day are gay men or lesbians—very likeable people until they're known to be gay. I'm sure you've had several such clients and didn't even know it."

Harry slapped his hat on his knee and thought a while. "I suspect I could have figured it out but didn't want to."

"Well, spend some time thinking about the preacher. Do your investigating with church members first, and then you'll need to meet with him. Like I say, I want you behind me one hundred percent or not at all."

"What if I find out he's guilty?"

"I'm not worried that you'll find he's guilty. I'm worried that you won't find out who did do it. Without finding the perpetrator, it may be impossible to convince the jury that Paul's innocent. The state won't be looking for someone else, because they don't want doubts about his guilt."

"You sure know how to make a job impossible. I'm almost sorry I came by." He stood. "I don't suppose, since it's the end of the month, you have a down payment for me?"

"Talk to Rosemary. We're expecting a state check any day. I'll tell her to make it a priority."

He nodded. "See you tomorrow." He left the office, his shoulders drooping. Carmela was a good lawyer and a tough cookie. He hated to see her take on a fight that would leave her bruised and, perhaps, defeated. Rosemary was on the telephone, so he waved a weak goodbye and left.

Chapter Eight

A quarter of a mile from Carmela's home, where pastures had been turned into a new, low-income housing development, Lucille and Marvin Stokes sat on their portal with Coke and beer, respectively. Neighborhood children filled the streets on the way home from school, and Cody was not among them. Tears formed in Lucille's eyes as she mourned recent happenings. Cody had been placed in foster care following the fiasco at the church. It could be weeks or months before his return. The minister was denying the child's accusations, and trials took forever.

"I just don't believe Pastor Morrison did what Cody accused him of." Lucille's tears turned to sobs.

"Then why would he say that?"

"I didn't hear him say anything. He just nodded his head every time someone asked him something. What did you ask him, and what exactly did he say?"

"I asked him when did it start hurting, and he said 'on the preacher's lap.' That's what he said."

Lucille quietly wept into her Kleenex. "This could scar him for life."

"God, I hope not. But you know state workers are neurotics when it comes to sex. That sort of thing happens to lots of kids, and no one ever knows about it. Happened to me when I was a kid, and I lived through it. My dad told me to forget what happened and not talk about it. That's what I did."

Lucille sat staring across the undeveloped land stretching behind their backyard, unable to speak.

"I sure hate this happened right now," Marvin said. "The boss told me this morning that one of the girls who rides up at the stable may have been raped, and the police are nosing around asking questions about everyone who works there."

Neither of them spoke as Cody's dog wandered around the porch, stopping in front of Lucille and then Marvin, tipping his head as if questioning what was going on in his household. Marvin patted his head and walked over to the porch railing, not looking at Lucille. "I'm thinking it would be better if I left town for a while, till this blows over. The boss even said I might be laid off if people started pulling their kids out of the riding program."

"Why would they stop the riding program? Was she raped in the barns?"

"He didn't say. Just that the police were nosing around."

The telephone rang and Lucille went into the house. It was a wrong number. She returned and began collecting empty glasses. "How can we be sure it was the preacher? What if Cody says something different when they start questioning him and we're not around?"

Marvin choked on his drink and sputtered. "We can't be certain." He coughed again. "That's why I told you at first that we ought to drop it."

Lucille paused and mulled her husband's opinion.

She didn't understand why Cody refused to talk. They usually couldn't keep him quiet. She carried the dishes to the sink and rejoined her husband on the portal. "What worries me is that I'm not sure Cody's telling the truth. Pastor seems so nice, and Cody has been so happy in church. He loved Cub Scouts. Maybe someone else hurt him, and Cody is all mixed up." She sniffed and wiped away tears.

"Aw now, honey, I told you this thing is being overblown. We know Cody liked that preacher, but that just makes it more believable."

Lucille shook her head. "Maybe he'll tell the therapist the truth."

Marvin squirmed in his chair. "I'm not so sure about therapy. How we gonna pay for it? I told you I may lose my job."

"She said it was free."

"Well, I guess. While we're on the subject, that lazy brother of yours should find a job, too. He has to start paying rent if he stays on here much longer. "

"I told Rusty he should start looking for a place of his own."

They sat quietly for some time before Lucille stood. "He doesn't have to be in a hurry to leave now. Who knows when they'll let Cody come home?

Harry drove to the parking lot of the Southside church. He frowned at the patrol car parked near the door. He might be too late to sweet-talk the church secretary into confiding congregational gossip. The police no doubt were telling her not to cooperate with the lawyers or their investigators. Inside, he found Captain Travis Hawk leaning over the secretary's desk, setting down a cappuccino and a blueberry muffin. Harry cursed to himself and let his eyes slide over the secretary's nameplate. "Howdy, Ms. Winifred." He smiled and nodded to Travis. "Captain?"

Travis frowned. "What brings you out to this God-fearing, born-again neighborhood, Harry? Kind of off your beat, aren't you?"

"That question fits you better than it does me, Captain. I'm not limited to a beat like some policemen I know. I thought yours was downtown, closer to where the lawyers have their offices." He turned to the secretary, ignoring Travis's grimace. "Does this officer deliver coffee and muffins regularly, or is this something special?"

Winifred giggled and hid her protruding teeth behind a hand wrinkled with freckles and sunburn. She felt uncomfortable being the center of attention. "I guess it's something special. What can I do for you gentlemen?" She smoothed loose strands of gray hair behind her ears.

"You go first," Travis said to Harry.

"No, you go ahead. I have a long list of wishes and you got here first."

"Suits me fine. Especially since one of my orders is that the church not open its records to any ol' private investigator who comes around poking into places he shouldn't be."

"That won't do you a lot of good, Travis. I come armed with a subpoena. Ms. Winifred knows what to do with a demand from the court, I'm sure."

"Getting a subpoena on this case was pretty fast work, Harry. You getting paid by the defense or the prosecution?"

"I believe you're intimately acquainted with the lady who hired me, Travis. She's defending the reverend."

Travis looked back at the secretary. "As you know, the police department did a thorough search of the basement where the incident allegedly happened. The door is locked and is off limits to the public, which includes Harry, here, even if he has an ill-gotten subpoena. There should have been a hearing on that where the DA could have asked the judge to protect the site from the public. My order stands. If this man gives you any trouble, let me know."

Harry grinned as they watched Travis retreat and slam the door.

Winifred sipped her coffee. "You're not going to give me any trouble, are you?"

"Why would I do that? You and me are on the same side. Carmela thinks the reverend is being accused of something he didn't do. We need to find out who did abuse that boy, and to do that, I'll have to talk to a lot of your church members. Here's what I need." He handed the subpoena, properly signed by the judge, to Winifred, who glanced over it and laid it on her desk.

"It will take me a while to run off a list of our members. With the preacher being gone, I'm having to do everything around here, and the phone hasn't stopped ringing since I opened the door this morning. We're 'spose to have a lay preacher any day now. That will help."

"There's no order from the court saying you can't talk to me, so let me ask you some questions before everybody else starts bothering you." Harry settled into a chair in front of her desk, pen and paper in hand. "Are you surprised by this boy's charge against the pastor?"

Winifred threw up her hands. "Land sakes, yes. Pastor is a wonderful man. He'd never do anything like that. He's a big brother to the kids, girls and boys alike. They love him." She blushed. "That doesn't sound so good, does it?"

"I understand what you mean. The preacher isn't married, is he?"

"No."

"Ever been?"

"No. He came back here straight out of college, and he didn't bring a family with him. He was born over in Pecos, and his parents moved here when he was about five years old. He's always lived with them. An only child, you know."

"What does he do for fun?"

"Oh, he goes camping up in the mountains sometimes, on his days off. His father left him a cabin up on Mirror Lake."

"Does he take friends with him?"

"I don't know. He's sort of a loner. He likes to fish, and he rides his bicycle every day, sometimes with the Wheels Club. I'm sure he has friends there. His weekends are busy with church duties."

"Has he ever asked you for a date?"

"I'm married, Mr. Rodriquez."

"Oops, sorry. Well, no I'm not sorry you're married. I mean . . ."

"It's okay. Most people assume I'm an old maid, since I don't wear a ring. The church frowns on an unseemly display of worldliness."

"Well, the church is right. And besides, you don't need any sparkles to improve your looks. What about the little boy's family? You know his mother and father well?"

Winifred took a sip of coffee as her eyes wandered around the room. When she spoke, it was with a sense of authority. "Marvin is a stepfather to Cody. Lucille has been a church member here since she was a girl. She married her high-school sweetheart, Tim Vernon, but he was killed in the war when Cody was just a baby. She's one of the women who found a lot of comfort in Pastor Morrison's counseling. In fact, they seemed so close, some of us hoped they might get married after her husband died. She'd make a good pastor's wife, but it never happened. She finally gave up on him and married Marvin Stokes last spring. He grew up around here, too, but he went to the army, and he'd been gone for years. Then he came back and got a job up at the Las Haciendas stables. He looks like a movie-star cowboy, and Lucille fell head over heels for him. Marvin started coming to church, and right after he got saved, he and Lucille were married."

"Anything else I should know about him?"

"He's sort of a backslider, I guess you'd say. Doesn't come to church regularly anymore. I hear he goes to bars by himself. Lucille brings Cody to church by herself most of the time now. She says Marvin is working at the stables on weekends."

"You say he goes to bars. Does that cause talk among the congregation?"

"Mr. Rodriquez, you got a way of making me say things I oughtn't to. I don't gossip, and what you're asking borders on gossiping."

"I'm sorry, I won't repeat what you say. It's just between you and me. But it's important to get as much information as I can to help your pastor. You want to help him, don't you?"

"Oh yes. We need our minister back."

"I understand. It's my job to prove he's innocent, and I appreciate your help. Can you tell me what sort of mother Lucille is?"

"Oh, she's the best. She takes good care of Cody, and he's attached to her more than his stepfather, of course."

"What's their relationship—Cody and his stepfather?"

"It's okay. I've never seen them fighting, but I've never seen them act close to each other, either. Cody's not into cowboy stuff."

"And how about the teenage uncle who's living with them now? Does he come to church?"

"Oh yes, but I don't know how long he'll be here. He hasn't had any luck finding a job."

"I hear he's working at McDonald's. He may stay. One final request, Winifred: is there a back door to the basement where the Cub Scouts meet?"

The secretary froze, distressed at having to discuss the area the police detective had warned her was not open to anyone other than the police.

"Yes, there's an outside door. We keep it locked these days, since the police said not to let anyone in."

"I suspect they meant not to have church meetings down there where there would be a crowd, don't you?" Harry said. "Just one person can't do much harm."

Winifred laid the keys on her desk and moved them around with her fingers, absentmindedly, while she considered his argument.

"I promise not to bother a thing. I'll drop back in when I'm finished looking around." He reached for the keys, brushed his fingers gently across her hand, and hurried outside to find the door. The hinges squeaked, but he regularly carried a small can of WD-40 for such emergencies. He pulled it out of his pocket and sprayed the bolt—just in case he decided to come back on the QT.

Downstairs he found a hall that led to different rooms, which he scanned quickly and then hurried to the roped-off area where the Scouts had met. The room was crowded with tables made from unfinished doors laid across sawhorses. An eight-by-twelve-foot rug lay in front of a couch, circled by eight folding chairs. This must be where the pastor comforted Cody Vernon, after the other Scouts departed. The garden-level windows had no curtains and were too dirty to allow one to see out, or in, for that matter.

Harry looked over the yellow plastic ribbons that the police had tied around the Scout meeting area and wondered if the room had been vacuumed since the alleged abuse. He was sure the police had searched for semen and bloodstains, information Carmela could get through the court.

What Harry really needed was a good search of Paul's office, to look at his computer and files of correspondence. Carmela might have asked the minister for them, but she hadn't mentioned it. And he was willing to bet that the police, even if they had confiscated evidence, probably overlooked some useful nuggets, like daily calendar entries that would give Harry a clue as to meetings the pastor may have had outside the office.

The question was how to approach Winifred for permission to enter the office. It was now five minutes till five o'clock. She should be preparing to leave. He went to the garden-level window, struggled to open the latch, and then lifted the frame a quarter inch. He breathed deeply, made up his mind to lie if he had to, and went back outside and through the front door of the church. The secretary rose, picked up her purse, and prepared to leave with him.

"Winifred, you've been very helpful. If you'll call me when you get those records together, I'll bring you a cup of coffee and a blueberry muffin when I pick them up."

Winifred shook her head. "You don't need to do that. It's my job."

"And you do it really swell. By the way, is there a meeting here tonight?"

"Not tonight. Tomorrow will be busy till late, though."

He pulled the door closed and called out to her as she ran down the steps toward the parking lot, past the window he'd left unlocked. "Winifred, if that Detective Hawk—if he comes back, you be nice to him. He's a good ol' boy." Harry chuckled all the way to his car.

Chapter Nine

On Monday morning, Harry arrived at Carmela's office early, hoping to have a word with her before her scheduled clients arrived. She pulled in beside his beat-up, top-down Karmann Ghia and waved. "What's up?" she asked.

"I ran into that boyfriend of yours Friday. He wasn't all that warm and cuddly towards me."

Carmela unlocked the office and he followed her inside.

"I can understand that. If you're going around telling people he's my boyfriend, I'm not sure I'm going to be so nice to you, either. You've been told what I do outside the office is not for public consumption."

"I don't chew on it in public, Carmela, but I couldn't resist teasing him a little."

"Maybe you'd better tell me about it."

"Well, we both showed up at the reverend's church at the same time, and he got the better of me by bringing the secretary some Starbucks and a muffin. Seemed plumb unfair to me—so I poked him where he has a weakness. He asked who I was working for and I told him he knew you intimately."

"Harry, Harry. You should have learned by now not to make policemen angry. They have ways of getting back at us."

Harry sat up and glared at Carmela. "Are you telling me that so-and-so is mean to you when you challenge him? You just say the word, and I'll meet him in an alley some night."

Carmela chuckled. "You know darned well I wouldn't put up with abuse from anyone, and besides, Travis is a pussy cat when he's around me. You quit prodding him, hear me? And quit talking about my private life in public. What will the church secretary think? She'll tell the whole world."

"I think it went right over her head."

"If it didn't, and it gets back to me, I may send my cop out to meet you in an alley some night. Now, tell me what you learned."

"The pastor leads an interesting life."

"He does?"

"He does."

"How so?" Carmela's jaws locked, and she spoke through tight lips.

"I went out to the church. The secretary told me I could get down to the basement from the outside door in back."

"And?"

"Didn't find a thing. I decided I needed to get into his office, check out the computer, his daily calendar, and so forth, if the police hadn't raided it first."

"And she let you do that?"

"Nope. I went back after dark."

"Wasn't the church locked?"

"Yep. A little thing like that never deters me. I'd never learn anything interesting if it did."

"Breaking and entering is a felony."

"Only if you get caught. I don't get caught."

"Never?"

"Never. Do you want to know what I learned, or is there a law against listening to a potential felon who never gets caught, because it makes you an accomplice?"

Carmela sat back in her chair. "Right on all counts. Shoot."

"Well, for some reason they hadn't taken his desktop computer, so I opened it. It seems your client spends a good deal of time visiting pornography websites—or, I guess I should say, porno addicts spend time visiting him."

"And?"

"He tells them they should shun pornography, not pass it on. And he'll pray for them."

Carmela relaxed. "That sounds like what any good pastor might do."

"There is one interesting contact, though. A Dr. Barkley, here in town. I ran their correspondence off so you could digest it." He handed sheets of paper across her desk. She glanced through them and laid them aside.

"What else did you get?"

Harry grunted. He'd dug up a potential bombshell in her case, and she brushed it off like so much dust. Did she know more about this guy than she was telling him?

"His calendar. Look at that carefully."

Carmela scrunched in her chair and chewed on a pencil. Harry handed her more papers. "He's had several meetings with a 'DR.' and a 'JB.' Could be doctor's appointments, but they meet in different places, for dinner, parks, et cetera." Harry kept a cool, indifferent manner, refusing to act as if this were important information, although he knew it was. Carmela glanced at the calendar copies and laid them on top of the other computer printout without reading them.

"Anything else?"

Harry handed over a zippered journal. "You'll like this. I found it in the drawer of his desk. The guy writes poetry."

"A journal?" Carmela was almost speechless. Did she dare impose on his privacy? How could she not? She would ask his permission.

"You'll find almost daily contact with the preacher and Cody's mother for a couple months. That happened after her first husband got killed in Afghanistan. Secretary said everyone hoped they might get married."

"'They' meaning Paul and Lucille?"

Harry nodded.

"Seems strange." It must be true, then, that church members didn't suspect he was gay.

"Well, everyone was rooting for her, according to the secretary," Harry said, and then he spent the next quarter hour going over the Vernon-Stokes family history, as the church secretary had revealed it to him.

"Have you had time to look into the stepfather's history? I think that was on your to-do list."

"Not yet, but I'll dig there next. Sounds a little suspicious that he went to the trouble of getting saved at the altar shortly before they married, and then he returned to his heathen ways shortly thereafter. Interesting story, anyways."

Rosemary buzzed her office to let her know a client was waiting, and Carmela looked at her watch. "Thanks a lot, Harry. You've done a good job."

Harry left, scratching his head. He had expected greater enthusiasm for his revelations.

Carmela reached for the pile of documents, her hand pausing, unwilling to pick them up. She wondered how she would get them back to her client without showing she'd gone behind his back, without his permission, to get them. She wished she had time to read them without interruption, but her day was filled with appointments. She decided to take them home. They'd have to wait until after supper, since Travis, no doubt, would be by after work. Remembering she had frozen the remainder of last week's spaghetti, she wondered idly what else might be thawing out.

Chapter Ten

Carmela twirled her fork in warmed-over pasta and glanced at the clock. She was eating late, having waited for Travis to turn up. Surely he didn't need an invitation; he had been dropping by her home or at the office daily, without pre-arrangement. Carmela scolded herself for worrying, but looked at the clock again. If he didn't come, she'd have time to read the documents Harry had given her, a task she wished to complete in privacy.

She sopped the slightly tough garlic bread in the spaghetti sauce, wondering if his absence was connected to his tirade about her connection to Paul. His jealousy signaled a distinct change in their relationship. Since the night he wound up on her doorstep, weeping because Carolyn had deserted their home to live with the local high-school music teacher, Carmela had assumed her role was comforter, the same as she had been when his team lost a big game in high school.

However, she wasn't surprised that the green-eyed monster had hatched between them. A new intimacy was soaking into their relationship, deepening with each contact they made. Travis was no longer a best friend or a handyman she could call at the drop of a hat and expect him to come, as if it were strictly business. They were no longer children or high-school friends.

She knew they'd always been in love, from junior high on, and wondered what had kept them from exploring sex in high school. Could it have been his experience with Billy Joe? She recalled how he had withdrawn in their senior year from handholding and how his goodnight kisses became a peck on the cheek. She sighed. What a waste.

She had to admit she was partly to blame when he married someone else. His jaw had set angrily when she told him about winning a college scholarship, begging him to go with her to Washington University. However, his dream was to follow in his father's footsteps and become a policeman in San Carlos. All he needed was a college degree from NMU, with a follow-up at the police academy in Santa Fe. He wanted her to stay with him.

She'd left on a bus, fully expecting him to be waiting for her when she returned. He had always been there for her, since the day she toppled him with a soccer ball. She remembered the day she learned from third parties back home that he had eloped with Carolyn Mayfield, the high-school football queen. Crushed by the news, she wondered why he hadn't shared those plans with her. How could he have married without even telling her he was dating?

With a light knuckle rap on the door, Travis walked in. This time, as he wrapped his arms around her and moved his lips to hers, she allowed it to happen.

"Ummm, garlic," he said. "I hope you saved some for me." She tried to pull away, but his arms tightened, his chin resting on her hair. She relaxed in his arms.

"Sorry I'm late. There was a God-awful wreck on I-25. Some drunk hit a car full of kids on the way home from a band concert in Albuquerque."

"Dear God," Carmela said. "Anyone in it we know?"

Travis pulled off his jacket and washed his hands at the kitchen sink. "Can we talk about it later? I lost my lunch by the roadside hours ago, and I'm starving."

Carmela filled his plate and poured wine. She sipped her own, recognizing, as he did with her headaches, that sometimes one needs to be surrounded with a healing silence. His appetite was voracious, and she emptied the wine bottle into his glass.

Finished with the meal, he asked, "How about massaging my headache?"

Minutes later, his head heavy on a pillow in her lap, Travis began deep breathing—just a decibel short of a snore. Good, she thought, he'll be able to deal with dead teenagers once he gets a good night's sleep. She slipped her hips from under the pillow and bent down to kiss his lips before heading to the bedroom.

She carried the documents Harry had left with her to the bedroom, shaking her head. She had forgotten to get Paul's permission to read his journal, but her guilt seemed small compared to the problems arising among the policeman, the lawyer, and the accused pedophile. Carefully reading the notes Harry had made, she thoroughly reviewed the documents he had copied. She'd have to discuss them with her client.

The headline in the morning paper shocked Carmela: MUSIC TEACHER, TWO STUDENTS DIE IN CRASH. Smaller type declared: SUSPECTED DRUNK DRIVER, TWO TEENS SURVIVE. Pictures of the teacher and students who died in the crash surrounded a three-column photograph showing the twisted wreckage of a vintage Chevy. They told the story Travis had not been able to. The music teacher was driving four of his students home from a district music festival when a drunk driver crossed the median and hit the driver's side of the Impala, crushing the teacher and two teenagers to death.

Carmela returned to her bedroom and stared down at Travis, lying on top of the covers. His eyes opened and he smiled, lifting his arms toward her. "I didn't wake you when I came to bed, did I?"

"No." She bent into his arms and kissed his cheek. The newspaper crumpled between them.

Travis pulled it aside and glanced from the headlines to Carmela's face. "Hell of a mess, huh?"

She nodded. She wanted to ask if this was the music teacher his wife had moved in with, but it was Travis's place to bring up that subject, and he was ignoring it.

"I have to get to the office. I'm sorry I woke you." Carmela picked up her briefcase, worried about what effect Paul's counseling to gays and pedophiles would have on her case. It was not something she could discuss with Travis. She left him on the bed, reading the newspaper.

At the office, she urged Rosemary to hold her calls until lunchtime, while she sat at her computer researching cases. The question she had to answer was, "What are the best defense arguments for a gay client accused of pedophilia?" There must be one or more cases where the defense had won.

Two blocks away, on the roof of the city jail, twenty inmates dressed in orange jumpsuits and flip-flops circled the exercise area, walking alone or in pairs. Two stories above the street, a twenty-foot metal fence topped with knife-like blades enclosed the area. Inmates were forbidden to congregate or move near enough to the fence to view the cars or pedestrians on the street below. Paul glanced sideways as Troy Leader moved in beside him. They had been arrested the same day but had not spoken since Paul was moved to a private cell at the request of his attorney.

"Nice to be out in the sunshine," Troy said.

Paul nodded.

Troy's brown skin and coal-black hair, brushed behind his ears, spoke of an Indian heritage. His square jaw and broad forehead were a giveaway. He was taller than Paul, a muscled athlete. His curiosity was interrupted when Troy asked, "So how is your new attorney working out?"

"Good, I guess."

"You guess? Was she the chick I described?"

Paul nodded again.

"She cut out your tongue?"

Paul smiled and shook his head. "I'm sorry. I can't even talk to myself about this case. She says I'll have to, but I'm not there yet."

"I read about the kid's charges in the paper. You've got some strikes against you in this state, what with the Catholic debacle and all."

Paul sucked in hot air and stared at Troy. Was that comment what he could expect from every person he met for the rest of his life? Would the next question be, "Are you gay?"

Troy looked at the heat waves rising from the concrete roof and wiped sweat from his forehead. "Not much else to say about the weather except maybe 'we could use some rain.'"

Paul smiled. "Sorry, buddy. I appreciate your kindness. Let's talk about you. Where were you stationed?"

"All over. Enlisted in California, where I was going to college. Was sent to Fort Bliss in Texas for basic. On to Arkansas for officer's training. None of them were vacation spots of the world. Did my time in Iraq. Talk about heat. This place is cool, compared."

"What are you doing in San Carlos?"

"Just passing through. I was born in New Mexico, at a religious commune up in the Sangre de Cristo Mountains." He shook his head. "It wasn't all that religious—just a bunch of flower children who wanted to live without rules."

"I wasn't aware Indians joined the communes."

"It wasn't an Indian commune, although there were some pueblos that came close to communal living. I was told while I was growing up that my mom showed up at this place, all beat up, saying she'd been raped and asking to stay. A married couple took her into their home, and she became a second wife to the man. Everybody believed in free love in those days, so no one asked questions."

"You say that was the story you were told, as if you question it."

"Yeah. My mom had Indian blood for sure. That's pretty obvious, but I wonder what really brought her to the commune. Why did she run away from the pueblo? Who beat and raped her?"

"Did you find out?"

"No. I was told she died when I was born, and they buried her in a Taos cemetery. The couple who took her in raised me as their own child. Sent me out to California to live with my dad's sister, so I could go to college. Then I joined the army. When I came back after the war, the commune was deserted. I couldn't find them and someone told me they'd changed their names on official papers when I was little, to avoid the police. Lots of Indian babies were kidnapped and sold to white people in those days. That's part of why I'm here—to see if I can trace my ancestry. I'd like to know who my real father was."

They walked another half circle until Troy stopped and faced his new friend. "Pardon me for being curious, but I've been reading the papers, and I'm guessing your story is more interesting than mine."

Paul stared ahead, wondering what Troy might have read. "You can't believe everything you read in the paper."

"I know. I'm a photographer. I sell my work to newspapers and magazines. It's hard to argue with what the camera says. Too bad you didn't have me around to record what happened that day at the Cub Scout meeting."

They continued walking in silence.

"Did Indians suffer a lot of discrimination in the army?"

Troy laughed and flexed his triceps. "I didn't, but I'm pretty easy going. I don't look for trouble." He stared at Paul. "So you never went to Iraq?"

"No. Didn't think I was cut out for it."

"Most of us weren't. Circumstances make men killers."

"You think so? What circumstance pushed you in that direction?"

"The military offered the best career in photography I could find. It was that or wash dishes in a greasy spoon. Construction jobs, maybe, if I could find them."

"How'd you get into jail here?"

"I made the mistake of going to Cowboys for a drink and was picked up by the police with some hash in my pocket. Bad timing. I got the habit overseas, where it's part of life. Same here, but your police department thinks a certain number of people have to be arrested to prove they're working hard, and that burden falls on Mexicans and Indians."

A bell rang to signal the end of exercise time, and Paul breathed a sigh of relief. Troy deserved some answers, but Paul hadn't come to a firm conclusion about how he got himself incarcerated. Probably he had allowed himself to believe he was invincible, that God would protect His shepherds. Yet he knew as well as anyone the history of saints who had died in prison.

The door to the stairs leading from the exercise yard down to the cells opened. The prisoners were herded toward the door except for Troy and Paul, who were pushed aside until the others had descended and were locked in their cells.

"What's keeping you?" a guard abruptly yelled at Paul, and as he moved toward the door, a second guard stuck out his boot and smiled as the first guard pushed Paul forward. He fell headfirst and rolled to the bottom of the steel stairs.

"Why the hell did you do that?" a guard asked Troy. "You probably killed the fuckin' pervert."

Troy's fist slammed into the guard's mouth and bloody teeth fell inward, leaving black holes. A third guard slammed a billy club against Troy's head, knocking him unconscious.

Two hours later, at the hospital, Carmela watched as three women and a man knelt in the hallway near their pastor's room, praying, their lips moving, with hands lifted to God, begging for His mercy. The women wore long dresses with sleeves that covered their arms, thick cotton stockings, and flat shoes. Long braids neatly encircled their heads. The man, dressed in black, carried a straw hat. Each of them clutched a small, well-worn Bible. Carmela resisted an urge to join them, to find out what God was saying about her client. She showed her credentials to a deadpan staff member, who led her into Paul's room, past a policeman standing outside the door.

Gauze covered Paul's head, leaving little room to breathe. His strong, suntanned hands, well-suited to support the penitents who gathered at the lake to be baptized, lay inert on the covers, one wrist in a heavy cast.

The story being told by the guards was that all the inmates, except for the pervert and the Indian, had returned to their cells. These two were dawdling in the far corner of the yard. The stories differed on whether they were arguing. When they reached the stairway, Troy pushed Paul, and he tumbled to the bottom of the stairs. They called the police, who escorted both men to the hospital and notified the courts to charge Troy with attempted murder.

Carmela knew the story had to be a lie. Troy had been Paul's cellmate, the one who described her as an attorney to Paul. It made no sense that he would push Paul down the stairs. That left the guards as suspects in the crime, but what if Paul died or was brain-damaged and could not testify against them? Troy Leader would be charged with murder and found guilty. Paul would die under the presumption that he was guilty of sexual abuse of a minor.

The door to the hospital room opened, and Travis entered with a short, dark man wearing horn-rimmed glasses. He held his hand out to Carmela and introduced himself as Dr. Barkley. Travis pointed to Carmela. "This is his attorney, Carmela Jared." To Carmela he added, "Dr. Barkley was on duty when your client was admitted."

Carmela was too shocked to respond. This must be the man Harry described as Paul's friend, whose initials were printed on the calendar. About the same age as Paul, maybe five years older, a narrow mustache unlike the locals wore. A smaller build. Must spend more time in the library than in the gym, she thought.

"I was on duty when your client was admitted," he said, with a quick dip of his head. He thumbed through the patient file at the foot of the bed. "Lots of damage. He suffered a concussion, but we won't know how bad until all the tests come back. Cracked forehead, possible spine fractures, and a broken wrist. He will need plates in his skull."

"Any guess as to how the damage was caused?" Travis asked.

The doctor looked at Carmela. "I understand there's an investigation underway."

Travis's jaw tightened. "Can you guess whether he was beaten up with fists or whether he fell down some stairs?"

"You couldn't cause this much damage with fists."

Travis turned and left the room, closing the door behind him.

Carmela stood beside the bed with her eyes closed. Why had she allowed Rosemary to pursue the bail instead of doing it herself? She should have tried harder to get Paul out of jail at the arraignment, to hell with Ms. Peña's cat in the tree or returning a child to a home where she might be abused again. When she opened her eyes, the doctor was gazing at her as if to read her mind. He glanced toward the closed door.

"Ma'am, this isn't the first time a prisoner has landed in the hospital because of an *accidental* fall down jail stairs. The detective tells me you will pursue charges against the staff if evidence can be found that he was pushed. Please don't let the police cover it up." He handed her his card. "The other victim is in the room next door, but he will be released and sent back to jail tonight, after everyone's gone home. I fear both their lives are in danger. Please do what you can to protect them." The doctor turned and walked out of the room.

Carmela's anger stiffened her muscles, and she fought an urge to slam her fists into something solid. She touched her client's hand. It was icy, and she rearranged the light covers to protect it from the air conditioning. "I'll be back," she said and hurried from the room.

At the office, she pulled out copies of Paul's calendar and examined the five notations of meetings with DR and JB. There was little doubt that these were appointments with Dr. Jason Barkley. However, there was no indication of where they had met or what they may have done. She picked up copies of three notes and two business letters bearing their initials or signatures. "Enjoyed the ball game. When's the next one!" She threw the documents aside. Lunch? Dinner? A tryst? There were late evening meetings on Mondays and Tuesdays, the days when Paul took time away from his church duties. It appeared Paul had lied to her about not having a male partner. Her anger increased.

Travis must know something about this doctor or he wouldn't have brought him in to meet her. She punched his direct number into the telephone and his answering machine clicked on. Careful not to leave a message that could become a public record, she hung up, sure he would recognize her number.

Fifteen minutes later, he knocked and entered her office from the back door.

"You got my call?"

"Yep. What's up?"

"Who was the doctor? I'd never seen him before."

"J. P. Barkley. He's new in town. Moved here from the Mayo Clinic in Arizona. Doesn't have a lot of patients yet, so the county uses him to fill in when they get overloaded. He testified in the last child abuse case we had and wiped out the defense. He's bright and up on the latest research. I was very impressed."

Unwilling to tell Travis about the connection to Paul, she agreed. "He should be very helpful in a suit against the city for what happened at the jail. He seems very interested in helping with charges against the staff. I'll contact Tom Garrison in Albuquerque to see if he will pursue a class action. It's right up his alley."

"I'm glad you're not taking it on." Travis slumped into a chair in front of her desk and propped his hat on a knee. "That suit will put me in a precarious position, you know, since the police department runs the jail, and the government pays my salary."

"I know. Even my case may cause you trouble. You should have thought twice before bringing the doctor by while I was there. Will you get into trouble for that?"

"I didn't know you were there, but that's beside the point. I was interested in his analysis of the jail debacle. It's obvious we have some housecleaning to do, and we need advice from experts who aren't influenced by insiders."

"Sounds like he's your man."

"Those damned jail guards have too much time on their hands. This isn't the first time they've pushed someone down the stairs, but it is the first time there's been a witness with enough guts to challenge them. Have you met the Indian who's being accused?"

"No. Paul mentioned that they were cellmates when he was first arrested."

"That guy will be lucky if he doesn't wind up on the end of a rope in his cell." Travis shifted in his chair. "There's a problem with where you and I stand in all this. Every move I make will be watched and recorded. I can't keep sharing evidence with you."

"I understand. We've always known the day would come when our careers would come between us. I agree that it doesn't make sense for us to keep seeing each other, at least until Paul's trial is over." She suddenly felt sharp pains shoot from one side of her head to the other, and she knew a dreaded migraine was building up behind her eyes.

Travis cleared his throat. "That's not my only problem." He looked away. "Carolyn's having a breakdown. She blames herself for Brian's death—for no good reason I can think of. Her brother, Chuck, took her to the psychiatric ward last night. The doctors say that my involvement in her therapy is important." He looked at Carmela. "With Brian gone, she wants to move back into our house. The doctor says she has to stay in the hospital another week. I'd like to tell her she'll have to find some other place to go, but if I don't take her in, Chuck will have to, and he and his wife have four kids. Besides, the doctor thinks she needs the stability of her own home. She and Brian were just camping out in a garage apartment at his brother's. Bottom line is, Chuck and Barbara can't take care of her." He reached for a Kleenex on Carmela's desk.

"Travis—" the buzzer on her desk interrupted her. "Yes?"

"Yolanda's on the line. Judge Salazar wants to see you and the DA in his office at four-thirty, about the pedophile case. "

"Tell her I'll be there." She looked at Travis. "You do what you have to do, Travis. Don't worry about me."

"I can't help but worry. I don't feel good about allowing her to move in, with me thinking things can never be the way they used to be. Maybe when she first left, it would have been possible." He stood, his voice harsh. "It's not what I want, Carmela, but I just don't see that I have a choice."

"I understand that. And I can't expect you to compromise your investigation into the pedophile case while I'm defending the suspect. We just have to stop seeing each other until this case is over." She couldn't believe how calm her voice was; inside, she felt as if her body was rebelling against the shocks she'd had to face today.

Without responding, Travis left by the back door. Nauseated, she rushed to the bathroom. She heard his tires screeching as he pulled away.

Chapter Eleven

Carmela and the DA didn't speak while they sat in the judge's waiting room. When Yolanda told them to go on into the judge's chambers, Sedbury made an elaborate gesture, inviting Carmela to enter first, and then preempted her greeting by calling over her shoulder, "How are you, Judge?"

Salazar nodded. "Fine. Be seated. Sorry to keep you waiting, but I've been reading this report from your office"—he looked at Sedbury—"concerning the accident at the jail this morning." He turned to Carmela. "The victim of this fall is your client in the pedophile case, isn't he? Reverend Morrison? How's he doing?"

Carmela blinked rapidly, hoping to wipe away the aura that accompanied the migraine that began while Travis was in her office. It circled the judge's head like a frame around a portrait. She struggled to concentrate on the conversation. "I saw him in the hospital shortly after the accident, Your Honor. He was under sedation."

"The report says he and another inmate"—he glanced at the report—"Troy Leader, were fighting in the exercise yard, and then Leader pushed the pastor down the stairwell. Is that your understanding?"

"That's what the report says. It's not what happened, according to Mr. Leader."

The DA snorted, and the judge glared. "I don't recall asking for your opinion, Roman, and when I do, I'd like for it to be delivered in the English language!"

Sedbury flushed and shuffled papers to cover his embarrassment.

The judge sighed and looked at Carmela. "What's his story?"

"They had been exercising, walking around the yard. When the bell rang, they got into line to return to their cells. Guards took them out of line and held them in the yard until all the other prisoners were dismissed. Then one of the guards pushed Reverend Morrison toward the door, where another guard tripped him as he started down the stairs. Mr. Leader says one of the guards then asked him why he pushed the pastor and said he probably killed—and I quote—'the pervert.' Mr. Leader hit the officer in the face with his fist."

The DA closed his folder. "Your Honor, I trust the court will take into consideration the fact that counsel is somewhat prejudiced about the facts in this case. She has no proof whatever of the truth of Mr. Leader's statements. It poisons the court's reading of the report."

Judge Salazar smiled. "You're right, Mr. Sedbury. However, I will instruct myself to forget I ever heard it, and I will not let it sway my opinion in the present case. As you know, I won't be hearing the civil case." His smile gone, he looked at Carmela. "I assume the city will get sued over this."

"I'm sure. I'm told it isn't the first such accident at the jail, so I anticipate a class action."

"Again, I object to this discussion."

The judge shook his head at the DA. "Roman, your locution has improved, but we are not in court. This is a discussion between the court and both attorneys. We're not making a record. You can object all you want to, but as long as Counselor Jared is responding to my questions, I'll appreciate it if you keep your objections to yourself. Do we understand each other?"

Sedbury neither answered nor nodded.

"Now. Let's get back to the sexual-abuse case. Can the two of you find a time soon for a preliminary hearing on the sexual assault charges?" He looked at the DA.

"We've already set the date, Judge."

Carmela nodded. "However," she said, "under the circumstance of Reverend Morrison's hospitalization, I must ask for a delay. And I'm also seeking a reduced bail, since there is little possibility that he can leave the jurisdiction. It won't be safe for him to go back to jail."

The judge looked at Sedbury, who understood he would lose this one. "We won't object to lowering the bail, Sir, but we have deadlines to meet for the preliminary hearing. I assume Carmela wants to protect her client's right to a speedy trial."

"I will agree to extend all deadlines, but preserve Reverend Morrison's right to a speedy trial."

"Good," the judge said. "Talk to your client. We're making progress."

"Your Honor, one more thing," Carmela said. "We need access to the child to get his side of the story. The DA is objecting to it."

The judge looked at Sedbury, with his eyebrows lifted.

"We all understand that interrogating children is not a given," the DA said. "I'm objecting to it in this case because the child is severely trauma-tized. His father was killed in Afganistan; he's been sexually abused; and he has been taken from his mother and put in foster care. What more can we do to this child? He should be protected from further interrogation."

"Has there been an interrogation already?"

"The police and a social worker from Child Protection Services asked him questions at the time he made the accusations. That session was videotaped."

"Both those agencies are trained to protect the child, Roman. Get me a copy of those records, and I'll make a decision on whether the child should undergo further questioning, but I must remind you that inter-rogating a child is an accepted defense right, and I will not object unless there is something egregious in the way the first questioning was done, or evidence that the child has some disability that would be aggravated by it." He looked at Carmela.

"There is no evidence of that, Your Honor."

"It's always my position that videotape of the interrogations of child victims should be used in court so the child has to appear only if his absence prejudices one side or the other. If there are special circumstances in this case that require his presence, then that's what I'll order. He looked at Carmela. "You can file an objection if you wish, of course."

"I'm afraid I must, Your Honor. The child did not say who abused him at the time, and there is no evidence to prove that my client did it. If the cur-rent videotape is all the evidence the state has, I'm requesting that the court preview the video of that interrogation and dismiss the case on the basis of lack of evidence. It's as plain as day that the child has not accused my client of abusing him. Only the district attorney's office has done that."

The judge turned his attention to Sedbury.

"We concede that the child so far has not said who abused him. But he has never faced the man we believe did do it. He has a right to testify in person, where he will have the opportunity to face the pastor and point to him as the man who abused him. He didn't do it at the time the video was made because he was too stressed. Time has passed, and we believe he will point to the pastor when he sees him in court. Therefore, we're asking that he be allowed to testify in person." The judge frowned and turned to Carmela.

"Your Honor, I have already filed a Motion in Limine asking the court to dismiss this case for lack of evidence. My position is that it should be dismissed before we go to trial. If the court chooses to let the child testify in order to allow him the opportunity to point to his abuser, he will indeed be further traumatized. If the court has not already had the opportunity to review my motion, I will ask the court to address it as soon as that video is played."

The judge tossed the file aside. "The state is correct. The law says an abused person has a right to appear and identify his abuser if he is present in the courtroom. The child shall testify, and we'll go from there."

Carmela was not finished. "Your Honor, I also need an order continuing the police guard at the hospital until my client is released."

"Prepare the order. I'll sign it. Anything else?" Both attorneys shook their heads. The judge spoke to Carmela. "Keep me informed about the civil case, will you?"

Carmela left the courthouse feeling a little lighter. The pill she had taken after Travis left her office was taking effect. She refused to dwell on the thought that he was disappearing from her life. It was a good thing that she had plenty of homework to keep her from going crazy at night.

However, her expectation that he was out of her life proved false. Travis's pickup was parked in the alley behind her garage, and she found him in the dining room, reaching into the cabinet for glasses.

"I charge rent for that parking space, Captain Hawk."

"Name your price." Travis grinned and poured Jim Beam from a fresh bottle he'd opened. He handed her a glass and bent over to kiss her lightly on the lips.

Carmela felt the beating of her heart as she swirled the ice in her drink with a forefinger and sucked it clean. She lifted the glass. "This will make a nice down payment." She didn't smile. "I thought we came to an understanding in the office today that we would stop seeing each other until this case is over. Did I miss something?"

"You should have put that in writing, Counselor."

"Travis, quit joking. Your job is at stake if you get caught sharing police investigation reports . . . or for having an affair while you are married. Put the two events together and you could be in big trouble. Plus, Carolyn's illness makes anything between us untenable. We agreed to stop seeing each other. What don't you understand about that?"

Travis picked up his glass and walked to the window, his back to her. "I've been thinking about it, and that's not a solution I can live with." He turned. "I talked to the chief this morning, and he's agreed to transfer me to a different department."

"Travis, you have your dream job. You've always wanted to head investigations. You're good at it. You can't give it up."

"That's not how I see it. I've been at this job so long I'm getting stale. I need a new challenge, and the chief said he'd find one for me. He hinted that he could use some help in his office, maybe an assistant chief." He took a sip of his drink and lifted the glass toward Carmela. "And I went by to see Raymond Ortiz this afternoon. He's filing my divorce papers next week. Any other roadblocks you can think of?"

"You haven't addressed the biggest one. Carolyn's health. That's what derailed us in the first place."

"I've decided to move out of the house and give it to her. Her brother said he'd find her a live-in caretaker. She'll get better once she's over the shock of Brian's death."

"You're sure?"

"Nothing is totally certain in this world, Carmela. Except for the fact that I love you, and that I screwed up badly by marrying Carolyn. I have a chance to correct that mistake now, and I don't plan to screw up twice. Tell me this is what you want, too."

"You know I love you, Travis. We've been on each other's team from the day Mom and Dad left me here. I thought we both understood we belonged to each other. I can't tell you how hurt and shocked I was when you married Carolyn. No one had ever come between us before."

"I know. I shouldn't have let you go off to college by yourself. I'll never stop regretting that decision, but I don't accept that it's too late to make things right: to be together, to have some children. We can raise our own football team . . . with maybe a girl or two."

Carmela moved into his arms and placed her fingers over his lips. "You are shameless," she said, surrendering her mouth to his. Her eyes closed and she felt transported to Eden, where only the two of them lived, free of entanglements, nothing but love to bind them together, a place where children could run free, as the two of them had done in their youth. It was a sweet thought.

Her head dropped to his shoulder and she wondered: was there room in Eden for a football family? She could see that, in his mind, their story was ending with a last-minute, winning touchdown and an extra point. But in reality, she was afraid the team was vulnerable. The football could be dropped, intercepted, or maybe it would miss the uprights by a good two feet.

He lifted her face to his. She'd worry about the dangers in Eden tomorrow.

Chapter Twelve

The next day, Harry entered the rectory office to pick up the documents he'd requested in the subpoena. Winifred frowned while she considered whether she should accept the gift of a Starbucks package, which he placed on her desk. She glanced toward the pastor's office on her left.

"New boss move in?"

She nodded.

"Can I talk to him?"

Winifred shook her head. "He's counseling with Ms. Stokes."

"Cody's mother?"

Winifred nodded. "She's having problems since her son was abused. She no longer has Reverend Morrison to counsel with."

"Poor woman. I can't imagine. How often does she come in?"

"Almost every day."

Harry pushed the Starbucks gift a little further on the desk. This must be a difficult problem for the new pastor. He couldn't be happy with what transpired before he replaced Paul or with the problems dumped in his lap because of it.

Winifred accepted the coffee and handed him a manila envelope. He nodded his understanding and left.

Across town, Carmela walked into the hospital carrying a large bouquet of lilies and a box of milk chocolate bars that would melt in a mouth sealed almost shut. She was hoping Paul would feel well enough to answer some of the questions she had concerning evidence Harry had accumulated. Today's prayer group outside the Reverend's door consisted of two older women who had been given chairs to ease their vigil. She was glad some of the congregation still supported Paul. Harry reported that other church members were angry at the man they suspected had hidden his sexuality, fooled them, and made them look like ignorant backcountry folk taken in by a smooth talker.

Carmela smiled and nodded to the police guard standing between her and the door and then entered Paul's room. Much of the gauze and tape had been removed from his face, revealing bruises, black eyes, and cuts on his lips. His head remained bandaged. He was sitting up in bed, reading the morning paper. The smile he offered was crooked.

"Hey, you're still alive!"

"As of today." He looked at the flowers and mumbled, "You've been to Whole Foods without me."

"Mmm. Returned to the scene of the—baptism."

"They're very beautiful. Thank you. They'll help me remember happier times. You look very beautiful today, too, if I may say so."

Carmela felt her face warming and turned to fumble with arranging the flowers on a table near the window.

"I'm sorry," he said. "Did I embarrass you? What I said was out of line between a pastor and—and almost everybody. My sentimental side sometimes conquers my better judgment. Please forgive me. For some reason, I feel free to say what I'm feeling when I'm with you. There aren't many people with whom I can do that. Maybe because you're a lawyer and I trust you to respond logically."

"I'm of the opinion that people shouldn't have to apologize for expressing their deepest thoughts," Carmela said. "Aren't Christian ministers allowed to admit to normal feelings?" She was beginning to understand why he had sometimes avoided talking to her at the spin classes, and why he quit coming to class after their meeting at Whole Foods. *Put thee behind me, Satan*, she remembered from her own Sunday-school class. Was his sudden openness a sign that his religious constraints were loosening? She couldn't resist challenging him on the subject of following his church's mandates, especially when he didn't agree with them.

"Is that why you preach in a church filled with little brown hens who wear clothes that cover up any sign that they're feminine? Not to mention a church that doesn't approve of a gay minister living with his partner?" Carmela teased, knowing she was being unfair.

Paul's face hardened, his eyes narrowed. He didn't fall for the bait. "Not all the women in my church are 'little brown hens,' as you describe them. Perhaps we should stick to the facts of my case."

Carmela opened her briefcase. She had touched on a sensitive subject, which he didn't wish to pursue. She turned to a review of the meetings she'd had with the judge and DA, and informed Paul that he would be released on a lowered bail when he was dismissed from the hospital.

He closed his eyes and sank back on his pillow. "Thank God. Have you talked to Troy? I worry about him in that jail."

"He's been moved to the county jail, and I doubt that they will allow him to be attacked in their facility. The case is too hot in the papers, and his attorney is on top of the situation. He called and suggested that we get a law firm he's associated with in Albuquerque to carry the civil case, and he and I can join them and do whatever work is necessary in San Carlos. The advantage to you is that this arrangement will put the case in the hands of experienced tort attorneys, and I can concentrate on your criminal case."

"But what makes Troy any safer in the county jail?"

"The city knows it will be sued for causing your accident, and its only defense will be to convince the jury that you and Troy had been arguing, and that he pushed you down the stairs. The best way for them to do that is to vilify Troy as an Indian who has been arrested for drug possession and who knocked out the teeth of one of the guards, and therefore he will be guarded carefully. I'm not sure his attorney can get him out on bail, but I'll keep you informed. Has the doctor said when you'll be released from the hospital?"

"Next week. The MRI and other tests take several days. But my back is okay. That's the biggest relief. Will I be put back in jail?"

"I don't think so. I'm asking the judge to release you on your own recognizance."

"That's great news."

"Do you feel up to more work on the case? I have Harry interviewing people from your church, and I want to review their input with you as soon as I get it. I also need the list of questions I asked you to answer. Did you get them completed?"

"They were almost finished when this all happened. The papers should be with my things at the jail."

Carmela cringed. The information should have remained private; now there was a real possibility that the jail personnel could have shared his answers with the city attorney or even the DA.

"I'll go out and get them," she said and rose to leave.

"Carmela, do you think it's possible for us to be friends—like real friends—instead of professionals?"

She returned to his bed, lifted one of the lilies from its vase, dipped it into his drinking glass, and sprinkled water over his head. "I baptize thee 'friend.'"

He grinned, wiping water away with his one good hand. "We'd better keep this a secret. I suspect it's anti-religious, and the church would frown upon a Southern Pentecostal minister accepting a sacrament from a sacrilegious female."

"It's okay. You tell them you're trying to save my soul."

Following her visit with Paul, Carmela pulled into the parking lot at the city jail and hurried to the front desk, ignoring a cell phone call from Travis. They needed to talk, but it would have to wait. She had made an embarrassing beginner's mistake in taking the list of questions to her client in the jail. They might refuse to release Paul's personal items to her, or the questions and answers could have disappeared—either "lost" by the staff or sent to the DA's office. When a pleasant secretary handed her the large envelope containing the material, she chastised herself for thinking the worst of the jail staff.

On an impulse, she decided to visit Troy Leader and drove the short distance to the county jail. In her last discussion with his attorney, she had asked for permission to visit his client, and true to the attorney's promise, the jail personnel found her name on the visitors list. She was taken to a glassed-in interrogation room and seated at the table. Minutes passed before Troy entered, dressed in a sleeveless sweat suit, perspiring as if he has come from the gym. He carried a towel, which he wiped over his face and arms before reaching out to shake hands. Carmela was struck by his eyes, which reflected a pale green sea. Where had she seen such eyes before?

"Gosh, I'm sorry, ma'am," he said, drawing back his damp hand. "We get an hour to exercise, and I've been running the whole time. It helps to keep me sane. It's nice of you to come. How's Paul doing?"

"He's doing very well. He'll get out of the hospital next week. He's worried and asked me to check on you. Are they treating you okay?"

Troy looked around to see if they were being observed. The guards outside the door tried to look disinterested.

"Truth is," he whispered, "I'm being treated with special care. I think they're scared out of their jockey shorts." He blushed at the language he'd used and laughed as if the whole thing were a joke. He sobered, and his eyes revealed deep concern.

"The attorney from Albuquerque came by and said he was working on a class action against the city. Sounds complicated, but he hopes to get me released before long, if I can find some local resident who will take me in and give me a job. I contacted an army buddy, and she's working on her boyfriend, who owns a restaurant." He grinned. "The problem is, it's in Albuquerque, plus I joined the army to avoid working in a greasy spoon. Now it looks like I may be headed back to one." He surveyed the room they sat in. "Let's face it, anything would be better than this."

"Maybe I can help. Let me ask around. I have friends who own the ranch where I board my horse. Maybe they would be able to use you. Have you ever worked on a ranch?"

Troy smiled. "Are you kidding? I've been working for wages since I was ten. Breaking horses was one of my favorite occupations. I'm sure I could round up a five-star recommendation from the King Ranch in Texas."

"That's good news. This is horse country, and there should be jobs available."

Looking her in the eyes, he pleaded, "Don't say you're sorry again. I don't blame anyone but myself for where I am. I got here all by myself. I'm a lot like the Apostle Luke, who did things without thinking of the consequences. I will appreciate anything you can to do to help get me out of here."

Carmela relaxed and nodded as she wrote the telephone number for Aviva and Tony Romero on the back of one of her cards. "Call these people if you're interested in the ranch job. I'll tell Paul you're doing well. He may have some ideas for jobs and living quarters also." She looked at her watch. "We have time left. Tell me more about your relationship with Paul."

Forty-five minutes passed as their conversation wandered into philosophical areas that Carmela had not expected. This man had a college degree in photography, but his intellectual interests were broad. She could understand why he and Paul became friends.

A guard knocked on the door to signal their time was up. Facing her, Troy said, "Show me the palm of your hand." He stared across the table at her lifted palm, his eyes following the long lifeline running down her palm. "Would you like me to tell you about your love life, and how you're going to become a millionaire? I'm pretty good."

"No. No. My love life is nonexistent, and one has to buy a winning lottery ticket to become a millionaire. I can't afford them."

"Show me again," he said, and she reluctantly lifted her hand. "You might be surprised. I see good things. There's love, there are children. Maybe you'll marry a millionaire." The guard signaled, with a jerk of his head, that Troy was to leave.

"Some other time, then," he said. "You will come back?"

"I'll talk to your lawyer about jobs and a place to bunk. Good luck." Carmela picked up her briefcase and left, wondering why she had allowed herself to become discombobulated by his predictions.

In her office, she scanned the answers Paul had written to her questionnaire. She found his life had been spent engrossed in the church of his parents and grandparents. He was baptized as a baby, again as a pre-teen when he was "saved in the blood of the Lamb," and he dedicated his life to serving his Savior as a church minister. He graduated summa cum laude from Bethany College in Kansas. Carmela frowned. Straight-A record. If he had so many brains, why wasn't he using them when this mess happened?"

She flipped through the information sheets, wishing her questions had been more precise. This was the first case she'd had with a man charged as a pedophile, and her questions had not been prepared for such a client. Oh well. It was a regrettable error, not irreparable, but embarrassing for a young attorney. She turned it over to Rosemary with instructions to do some googling on pedophilia.

Digging deeper into the pile of documents Harry had taken from Paul's office, she found the diary, which could hold a gold mine of information about this man. She found that Paul had suspected he was gay from the time he was a teenager. Had he confided in someone he trusted? His minister? A teacher? Best friend? What logic led him to continue his quest to preach to a congregation that he knew would oppose his leadership if they discovered his secret?

Chapter Thirteen

On the southwest side of San Carlos, off Highway 65, Travis sped northeast to the main road, Camino del Tierra, which led to Las Haciendas, a ritzy enclave filled with wealthy and often famous retirees. Commoners couldn't afford an estate in this high-desert oasis, nor could they pay the pricy stable fees or play golf on the Jack Nicklaus course. PT sat beside him, second in command.

Travis pressed harder on the gas pedal as they skidded about the narrow, unpaved roads and then came to a halt at the gate. An emergency ambulance from the fire department pulled up behind them, and the gatekeeper waved them through and directed them toward the address they sought. Travis slid to a stop beside the ambulance when they reached the adobe mansion. He led the way and knocked on the massive door intended to keep everyone out except the owners and invited guests. Two other police cars pulled into the driveway.

A nervous Hispanic maid motioned them to follow her. Loud voices echoed down the hallway, and Travis jogged past the servant, with the other detectives following, hands on their firearms. Inside the master bedroom, an imposing gentleman with a mane of gray hair and bulging shoulder muscles dropped a round, decorative pillow he had used to protect himself. Blood dripped from his nose, and he wiped it with the back of his wrist. His left eye was swollen shut, blood dripping from a cut above his brow.

A woman dressed in spandex exercise clothing stood across the bed, yelling at Travis, the first officer to enter the room.

"Who the hell called you?" She held a golf club and showed no signs of having been the victim in this encounter. Her tanned skin glowed against long, bleached hair, accenting the delicate features of a Mideastern descent. She looked years younger than the man she evidently had bloodied with the golf club.

"Put down the club," Travis ordered, and PT moved to stand behind the woman.

"I asked what you're doing here? Get out!"

PT grabbed the club from the woman and handed it to a third policeman. "Ma'am, we're just here to keep the peace," she said. "Let's go to another room, and you can tell me what happened."

The medical staff moved toward the bleeding victim, but he jerked his body from the medic's clutch and backed up against a Mexican armoire. "Thank you, but I don't need your help." He spoke to Travis. "Who did call you? This is between me and my wife."

The woman relaxed, confident that her husband could pull strings to get this matter settled without police interference. Travis felt his muscles tightening. The morning had already been frustrating. He hated domestic violence cases and felt lucky that his partner was still young enough not to be burned out, hearing the same garbage every day: "He hit me with his fist. I wasn't doing a thing." "Yeah? I found her in bed with another guy. This is the third time." The stories varied by which party was in bed with a second party, and who had the black eye. In this case, a golf club driver had done a good job of substituting for a gun that could have put an end to the fight.

As Travis stepped aside, another policewoman moved to assist PT in guiding the woman out of the room. The maid hovered in the background, wringing her hands. "I called them, ma'am. You said you was going to kill him, and I thought you might do it this time."

The woman struggled to free her arms from the female police officers, but gave up when PT pulled her arms behind her back, clamped on handcuffs, and then pushed her toward the door.

"Get out, Glorietta. You're through here," the woman shouted over her shoulder. "Go home and don't come back." The maid remained in the hall, shaking her head as if she'd heard that order before.

PT directed officers to take the woman outside and followed the maid to the kitchen.

The bedroom was cleared except for Travis, a second officer, and the husband. "What's your name?" Travis asked.

"Can't we talk about this? My wife and I just had a little disagreement. I'll move to a hotel for a few nights and everything will calm down. We can handle it ourselves."

"I asked for your name."

"Oscar Wright Whitney. Give Judge Salazar a call. We play golf together."

"You'll get to see Judge Salazar in person, Mr. Whitney, but it won't be on a golf course. From the looks of your eye, I'd say your wife is the one with a good golf swing. We'll book her for assault and take you to the hospital. Then you'll have to come down to the police station to answer some questions while we fill out a report. Let's go."

"I won't file charges against my wife, so just let her go. Let me call my attorney; he'll take care of things." He reached for the telephone and punched one button while he held the bloody cloth to his nose. "This is Oscar. Where's Farris?"

Art Farris? Travis raised his eyebrows. Oscar Whitney, bloody nose and all, no doubt retired from some big job in Washington or California, was now connected to the most prestigious defense law firm in New Mexico.

Travis waited while the two spoke for a minute. "Let's go," he said, and pulled handcuffs from his belt. Whitney slammed down the phone.

"For God's sake, I don't need those." He brushed past the officers and headed down the hall, where they could hear his wife screaming obscenities. He stopped in the hall as they passed the door leading to the kitchen and shouted to the maid. "Glorietta, tell Marvin to put the horses up and see to things till I get back. Brooke's over at Sherry Callahan's. Call Ms. Callahan and tell her it's okay for Brooke to spend the night with Sherry. I'll call them later and explain."

"Ms. Whitney said I was fired and not to come back."

"Pay no attention to her, Glorietta. She'll be over this by tomorrow." He led the way to the waiting cruisers.

Travis shrugged his shoulders. This man was used to being in charge of things, and since he was the victim, as long as he agreed to go to the police station to make a statement, there was no need to antagonize him.

Two hours later, with Ms. Whitney processed and in a cell and their reports filed, Travis and PT returned to normal patrol. PT drove this time, and Travis silently reviewed the morning's events. One problem remained. Mrs. Whitney had insisted that she be allowed to go home to make sure her daughter was safe, although she refused to say why she thought the girl was in danger. Her concern was enough to cause PT to call Child Protection Services to order an immediate investigation before allowing the teenager back into the home.

Mr. Whitney's offer to leave the house if they would allow his wife to return wasn't sufficient to get her out of jail, but it might be enough to satisfy the judge at her hearing. Travis relaxed when he learned that Aviva Romero was being assigned to investigate the child's case. He did still have one niggling worry.

He turned to PT. "Did you hear Mr. Whitney tell the maid to have Marvin take care of the horses?"

"Yeah. So what?"

"Remember when we went out to arrest the preacher, the kid's stepfather was there, and his name was Marvin? He was dressed in cowboy clothes."

"You going somewhere with this?"

"I don't know. If he's the same guy, it just seems strange to me that he'd show up in both these cases."

"He isn't the accused in either one."

"Guess you're right. Just seems too much of a coincidence."

They were on the outskirts of town when Travis offered another thought that bothered him.

"You'd think folks could work these problems out without swinging golf clubs."

"We wouldn't want that, pal. We'd have no excuse to visit Las Haciendas." She looked at her watch. "We have an hour to go before checkout. Why don't we stop for some coffee and donuts? My stomach doesn't recall having lunch."

"What I need is a beer. Coffee bothers me this late in the day."

"Yeah, well, you know a beer stop won't happen. Forget my suggestion. Let's get back to headquarters."

"You sound like a nagging wife."

"You would know."

"What's that supposed to mean?"

"Just what I said. If you didn't have a nagging wife, maybe you wouldn't be chasing skirts."

"Who says I'm chasing skirts?"

"A secretary I know says you spend a lot of time dropping into Carmela Jared's law office—through the back door!"

"So? Maybe I have legal problems."

"I can believe that."

Travis held his breath and stared out the window. He sighed, wondering how far he should pursue this conversation. Leaves on the trees along the San Carlos River, bordering West Alameda Street, fluttered like butterflies caught in a minor whirlwind. His life was becoming as jumbled as this scenery, with no clear lines marking a path.

As PT pulled to a stop in the headquarters parking lot, Travis reached for the car keys and turned to look at PT. "So what did Rosemary tell you?"

"She said a sexy cop was keeping her boss company."

"Well, that leaves me out."

PT's smile was beautiful. "You don't get away that easily."

Travis swung out of the car and slammed the door shut.

"Don't get mad at me. Next thing we know, you'll be taking a golf club to someone's head." She shook her finger at him like a mother would.

Travis leaned one arm against the car trunk. "Who all did Rosemary tell this to? Every damned lawyer and cop in town?"

PT laughed. "Calm down. She explained to me that your relationship with Carmela was a secret. I promised not to tell anybody and I haven't . . . except you. She talked because I tricked her into revealing why you and I spend so much time driving past Carmela's office building. I thought maybe they'd been having break-ins. We agreed that you're keeping your love life secret because legally you're still hitched." She cocked her head to the side. "How is Carolyn?" He didn't answer, and she walked away muttering something about dumb men.

By the time Travis reached the door, the receptionist had pushed another emergency call into PT's hand. "We gotta go back," she grumbled, bumping into him. "The lady who's supposed to be keeping the daughter overnight just called and said she thinks Brooke Whitney may be a sexual-abuse victim. She lives a few doors down the street from the Whitneys."

"Suppose that's what the parents were fighting about?"

"Could be. If the father's the perpetrator, we jailed the wrong person."

Travis looked at his watch. Damn, he'd miss eating with Carmela. He cussed under his breath.

"Shall I drive?" PT asked.

"Yeah, if you want to." It would give him time to think.

"I suppose Child Protection has been notified," PT said.

"Yeah, they're already on the case." He looked at the papers PT had been given. "We're just the backup on this one, so CPS might be out there with the point crew."

By the time they arrived at the Callahan home, another police cruiser had pulled in ahead of them. Inside the home, Aviva Romero sat on a leather couch near a stone fireplace that covered one wall of the cathedral-sized living room. Twenty feet above the floor of the south wall, a second-floor hallway disappeared toward the back of the house. The view from two directions was impressive. Travis and PT slipped down the hall, hoping not to interrupt the conversation between the caseworker and the child.

"What's going on?" Travis whispered to the officers on call.

"There was a report of possible sex abuse to a fifteen-year-old girl. We don't have a lot of facts, but an investigation is underway."

Travis groaned. "We just arrested the girl's mother for using a golf club on the father's head. Could he have been abusing the kid?"

"Maybe."

"She didn't name names?"

"Not yet. Aviva's talking to her. She'll no doubt be taking the kid into protective custody, since the mom's in jail, and we'll have to get her to the hospital for a rape kit."

Travis looked at his watch and spoke to one of the policemen who had arrived first. "I've got a dinner date. Can you guys handle this?"

"Yeah. Who's the date? If you want to take over here, we'd be happy to keep her company."

"Ha," PT said.

Travis bumped his fist against her shoulder. "Mind your own business."

Travis stared at the girl sitting with Aviva. She looked about fifteen, but she dressed like a college girl. He wondered how many daughters he and Carmela would be able to manage at that age.

PT placed her hand on Travis's elbow. "Looks like they've got it covered, and our shift ended an hour ago. Let's head back." Travis shook the daughter question out of his mind and headed for the cruiser.

Chapter Fourteen

The following morning, Bettina Whitney was brought from the jail to appear before the municipal court judge on the charge of domestic violence. Oscar and Aviva sat in the back of the court room. Bettina moved to the podium to stand beside a smiling Art Farris, the hot-shot defense attorney from Albuquerque. He was representing their joint interest in getting Bettina released from jail. Farris could care less who paid the bill.

Aviva listened while Farris urged the court to release his client and allow their daughter, Brooke, to return home, insisting that the parents had resolved their differences, that the altercation was the result of miscommunication on the part of the parties, and that it wouldn't happen again. He assured the court that Mr. Whitney would not pursue assault charges against his wife.

Judge Casey scolded the parties for acting like spoiled children and told them she would expect the police to arrest both parties if there was another call to their home. Bettina was released from jail on the condition that the parents were to attend parenting classes sponsored by the Child Protection Services. Bettina was reminded that the matter of Brooke's return home would be resolved in a district court proceeding, which would determine whether she had been sexually abused and whether she would be safe in the home environment.

Following the hearing, Aviva made a quick stop at Wendy's to pick up two large Frosties . . . vanilla for her and chocolate for Brooke. She found Brooke alone in her room at the foster home, watching television, wearing skin-tight short-shorts and a sleeveless tee that covered a small bust and revealed her navel. She fumbled with the Frosties on purpose, and Brooke reluctantly reached to retrieve the treat.

"Good catch," Aviva said. "I hope you like chocolate."

"I prefer Starbucks mocha lattes. These things are fattening."

"You're right." Aviva said, patting her stomach. "And when you get to my age, it's harder to lose those pounds."

Brooke sucked noisily on the straw.

"How old are you, Brooke?"

"What's it to you?"

Aviva paused. The kid was snotty. Spoiled might be a better word. It wouldn't be easy to win her trust. She sucked on her straw and lowered her chin, looking up below her brows. "I just came by to tell you, you won the lottery."

Brooke looked puzzled, but interested.

"Since you are over fourteen years old, you get your own special attorney."

Brooke's eyes widened, confused.

Aviva nodded. "It's true. I came by to tell you the court has just appointed Lucinda Trujillo as your personal attorney. She will represent you free of charge. That's almost as good as winning the lottery."

"Trujillo. She's Mexican. That's not who I was told would be my lawyer."

"Someone told you this already?"

"Yes, and she wasn't Mexican."

"Lucinda isn't Mexican. She's an American. Her name is of Spanish descent. What difference does it make?"

Brooke grimaced. "I don't need an attorney. My dad has plenty of attorneys. They're all men. They wear suits and drink hard liquor when they come to our house. They always win their cases."

Her disdain caused Aviva to grit her teeth to avoid returning the remark with a nastier one. "I doubt if they have time or expertise to represent kids who are in trouble," she said.

"Kids I know don't get into trouble. If I had been home, my dad would have taken care of this without the police."

"Not this time, Brooke. You were taken out of the home partly because your parents were fighting. You can't stay there alone."

The child was listening, no longer defiant. She was not used to having people question her father's beliefs.

"Lucinda won't be working for your father. The judge appointed her to work for *you*. She will explain to you what the court orders mean, and she'll tell the court what you want done about your case. How cool is that?"

Suspicion oozed from Brooke's eyes. She set her drink aside, stood up, and began gathering her scattered possessions. "Okay. Tell her I want to go home."

"You tell her yourself. She will be out to see you today. Next Monday, there will be a court hearing, and if you want her to, she can tell the judge you want to go home. I will then tell the judge whether the department thinks that's in your best interest. With this information, the judge will decide whether to let you go home."

Brooke plopped down on the bed. "What if the judge says I can't go home? Then what do I do? Stay in this crummy place?"

"If that happens, a guardian *ad litem* will be appointed for you. That's an attorney who, unlike me or Lucinda, would look at what he or she thinks is in your best interest and will either take your side or the social worker's. Then it's a toss-up for the judge. The judge appointed Lucinda to investigate your case, and regardless of what I or the guardian *ad litem* recommend, she will argue for what you want. The system may seem cumbersome, but it guarantees that the judge will hear your side of the story."

"Can't I talk to the judge?"

"Your attorney may be able to arrange that. But judges are busy, and they expect your attorney to represent your position. First you have to tell her what happened. Then she'll draw up a plan of attack."

"You make it sound like a game."

"It's not a game, Brooke. I'm in court almost every day, arguing for young people like you who have been abused. It's a very serious business, and you need to take it seriously."

Brooke jumped up from the bed and went to the window. "I wasn't abused. I've told everybody that. Sherry's mother made that up because she didn't want Sherry to be my friend."

Aviva relaxed. "Why?"

"How should I know? She just doesn't like me."

"There has to be a reason."

"I think it's because she doesn't like Connor."

"Who's Connor?"

"He used to be my boyfriend."

"Why doesn't she like him?"

"How should I know? She just doesn't like him."

"She seems to think you've been having sex. Is it with Connor?"

"No, but I told Sherry that he wanted to, and that I knew how, and she told her mother, who reported that lie to the police."

"You're saying you already 'know how'?"

Brooke leaned her head against the window and began crying. Aviva put her arms around the child and let her sob.

Several minutes later, Aviva waited while Brooke walked to the bathroom and washed her face. When she returned, she sat on the bed as if relieved. "It's okay if Lucinda wants to be my lawyer. But I can't tell you or her what you want to know, because he said he'd go to jail if I told anybody. My whole life would be ruined. Things aren't so bad now, and we won't do it again. He promised. Can't we just forget it ever happened?"

"Are you talking about Connor?"

"No."

"Tell me who."

"No. I promised not to tell. We'll never do it again."

Aviva felt like a soccer ball had landed in her midriff. "I'm sorry, Brooke. That's not the way things work. The court can't trust that the man involved won't abuse you again, and if not you, he will probably abuse other girls. You wouldn't want that to happen to your friends would you?"

"No, he won't. He promised."

"Who promised?"

"I told you I can't tell."

"You're seeing a therapist, aren't you?"

Brooke nodded.

"You can tell her."

"No. She told me she'd have to report it as a crime if I told her." Tears were forming in her eyes again.

Aviva's voice softened. "She's right. But you need to know that the truth usually comes out no matter how hard we try to hide it, and it's better for everyone if it does." She held out her hand. "Think about it, Brooke. Call me if you want to talk to someone." With the tears running down her cheeks, Brooke reached past Aviva's hand and held up her arms, asking to be hugged. Surprised, Aviva held her for a moment and then handed her a Kleenex. "Please discuss this with Lucinda."

"Do I have to?"

"You decide."

Brooke blinked rapidly and looked out the window. "My father . . . at least my father loves me."

"I'm sure he does. How do you know?"

"He takes my side when my mother yells at me for the way I dress. He tells her to lay off, I'm old enough to decide what I want to wear. He's right. I'm more mature than most girls my age, and I shouldn't have to dress like the nerds in my class."

Aviva held her breath. This conversation was about Brooke and her father, an opportunity not to be missed.

"How else does he show you he loves you?"

"He cheers me up when I'm sad. If I can't sleep for worrying about a test the next day, he hugs me until I go to sleep. That's really important, because my grades have not been good this year."

"Does he come to your bed or do you go to his?"

Brooke's eyes widened as she realized she had been lured into an area that frightened her. She changed the subject. "What kind of grades did you make in school?" she asked Aviva. "Were the teachers jealous of you, like they are of me? Teachers pick on pretty girls all the time."

"I guess I wasn't that pretty." Aviva understood she had been too abrupt and backed off. "I'll pick you up late this afternoon, after you've talked to your lawyer, and we'll go by your home where you can pick up more of your things. Okay?"

Brooke nodded.

Aviva had missed the opportunity to find out more about Brooke's relationship with her father. She hoped she'd get a second chance.

Chapter Fifteen

Across town, Carmela dialed her office from the courthouse to make sure there were no emergencies. Then she headed to an early lunch at the Wayside Inn, where she hoped to find an out-of-the-way table in one of the numerous, small dining areas. She ordered green chili stew at the counter, took her order number, and wandered down the hall to see if her guest was already seated. Dr. Barkley stood and nodded his recognition as she entered the otherwise empty room.

"How nice of you to come. Travis says I can trust you to help me on this case, and heaven knows I need all the help I can get."

Dr. Barkley's eyes surveyed her face as if he were reading a book. Satisfied with what he saw, he sat across from her. "I think you're being too modest. I've talked to lawyers who say they always worry when you're the opposing counsel."

Carmela shrugged. "This case is different. Many people charged as pedophiles are penniless and have to be represented by the public defender. Private attorneys are appointed when the public defender's office is over-loaded. That's why I was appointed. Problem is, it's difficult for the court to find attorneys who specialize in the area needed. For example, I've never defended a case like this before. In fact, I recommended to Paul that he find an attorney experienced in pedophilia defense."

"And he chose not to?"

"He said he couldn't afford a private attorney, and he was satisfied with me since I was the only one he knew personally."

"I'm told you're one of the town's busiest attorneys."

"That only means I take a wide variety of cases. Some attorneys, in larger districts, handle only sex offences, which would give them more experience in this area."

"Paul seems satisfied with your representation."

"That's what he keeps telling me."

"How about the judge he'll face?"

"Salazar is the judge on this case. He's getting old and sometimes grumpy, but he's fair." A waiter brought their orders, and the diversion gave both of them time to concentrate on hunger. Waves of steam, heavy with the odor of green chilies, surrounded the table as Carmela rolled a warm tortilla and dipped it into the stew. "How long have you been in San Carlos?" she asked.

"Six months."

"Like it here?"

"I can't say I do. This case has soured whatever good feelings I might have had when I arrived."

"I'm sorry about that. Did you know Paul before you came?"

"No. We met on a Sierra Club hike near Taos and discovered we had similar interests. However, he works on weekends, so we've had difficulty finding free time to hike. We went up to his cabin in the mountains once." Barkley concentrated on stirring his stew, his eyes shifting around the room, sliding past Carmela's face and back. She waited as he searched for words, wondering which of them would broach the subject of Paul's sexual orientation. She decided to take the lead.

"I assume you're gay?" Carmela continued eating, acting as if her question covered normal dinner conversation, but inside, her stomach roiled. She couldn't blame it on the green chilies. The answer to her question might make or break her case. On the positive side, if Paul were ensconced in a satisfying partnership with a respected doctor, it could be argued that he wouldn't be seeking sexual pleasures from children or other gay adults. She wasn't sure that was statistically true, but it could sway the jury.

"This judge. You say he's old and grumpy. Does that mean he's living in the dark ages?"

"Not at all. He's a smart man. He listens and he's fair. However, he's a tiger when it comes to protecting children, and that will hold sway in this trial. If the jury finds Paul guilty, the judge will throw the book at him. That's why I need your help."

"Your interest in me is limited to the fact that I'm gay, and you expect me to out a friend who chooses to maintain his privacy?" Jason's charges were uttered in an unfriendly tone.

Carmela had not expected this to be a particularly congenial encounter, but she had hoped Paul's friend would be cooperative. "I can't deny that if the DA makes Paul's sexual orientation the big issue in this trial, I will need witnesses to support Paul's position."

"Paul told you he's gay?"

"I can't reveal what Paul told me. My investigator found evidence that the two of you are friends and meet socially."

"Where did he learn that?" Jason's voice tightened with anger.

"He found notes on Paul's desk calendar. You attended ball games together . . . and such."

"'And such.' You're his lawyer, but you don't trust what he tells you! You want to use me to prove he's a liar?" He laid aside his napkin, as if he planned to leave.

"Jason, listen to me. I can't reveal what Paul told me, but I'm assuming you know his history, and you can be sure he has been honest with me. If the DA puts some guy on the stand to testify that he has first-hand information to prove Paul is lying, I will need counter witnesses to re-enforce his testimony." She shrugged. "Maybe you can direct me to other friends who will testify on his behalf."

"No. I will testify. Paul is an honest and beautiful person. It seems unfair to me that he would deny such an important part of his nature. We've met a couple of times for breakfast and dinner. Went to Isotopes games. Spent one painful weekend at his cabin in the mountains. Just friends." Jason blinked tears from his eyes.

Carmela relaxed. It was possible the calendar notations Harry had copied had no hidden meanings. The two were only buddies. The question that bothered her was why Paul had denied this friend's relationship? He had been quite specific that he wasn't seeing anyone. Breakfasts, dinners, and an Isotope game would be hard to forget. Or did he equate "seeing someone" with a sexual relationship, and his denial meant that?

Jason laid aside his spoon. "How do you plan to deal with this issue in Paul's case? He's not out of the closet, and there's no way he can remain in the ministry if he's exposed."

"It would be nice if we could avoid it, but the chances are good the DA suspects Paul is gay, and even if there's no proof, he'll find a way to get the suspicion before the jury. You seem much more open than Paul, and the DA will use your friendship to support his theory. I asked about your status because whether you're gay will determine how I use you in the trial."

"I guess it's a good thing I'm not crazy about living in San Carlos. While this city is not openly hostile to alternative lifestyles, if my status comes out, I doubt that it will be politically correct for the city to keep sending business my way."

"I'm sorry. I don't have to call you as a witness, if you prefer it that way. You can still be helpful in the background. However, I can't promise that the DA won't subpoena you if he finds out there's a connection between you and Paul."

"I wouldn't call it a connection. I've known Paul two months, and as you know, he's celibate. His argument is that this allows him to serve God in a church that teaches homosexuality is a sin. He's convinced he was born to fulfill his mission here in San Carlos, in this church."

Carmela paused, mulling over this new information. It was possible these two men were just friends. They met for breakfast, dinner, or a ball game—why not? Everyone has friends. Her relationship with Travis over the years served as a good example. Sex doesn't make the world go around.

Jason relaxed and seemed relieved to find someone with whom he could discuss this relationship. "We were attracted to each other the first time we met. However, he was honest from the beginning. He would not change his lifestyle. I feel like I'm caught in a Greek tragedy, with God pulling puppet strings."

"You haven't given up pursuing him?"

"Pursuit is too strong a word. I respect his position."

"He tells me these charges may be God's way of calling him to a prison ministry. Is it possible he'd be willing to go to prison to avoid coming out to his congregation?"

"I see his going to prison as a means of self-punishment—maybe suicide. He's too intelligent to believe gays deserve such punishment, but intelligence doesn't always overcome guilt."

"My impression of evangelical ministers is that they aren't among the free thinkers of the world. Those I'm familiar with teach the Old Testament scripture, where death, not imprisonment, is the proper punishment for sodomy."

"It isn't fair to judge Paul by your standards or your reading of the Bible. I know him as a wonderful, open-minded person, someone who would lay down his life for others. I suspect his reading of the Bible is that Jesus gave his life for all people. That would include gays."

"How does he reconcile that teaching with his church's position that homosexuality is a sin? How can he stand up in front of the congregation every Sunday, preaching one thing and living another?"

"As I said, he thinks if he doesn't enter into sexual relationships, he isn't a hypocrite, which may be illogical, but it works for him." Jason's cell phone rang, and he apologized before answering. He frowned. "I'll be right there," he said, and then turned to Carmela. "I'm sorry, but that was a call from the hospital. I have to go." He handed her his business card. "Call me any time."

Carmela cupped the card in her hand. "Thanks. I'm sure I will. I want you to know I understand your attraction to Paul. When I met him, I was moved by some of the same emotions you describe. I didn't know he was gay at the time, but there was something about him that made me want to connect—to be friends. That's why I can't believe these charges are true. It reflects on my judgment, I guess. That may be part of why I'm committed to proving he's innocent."

"Whatever works. And will you also help Troy Leader? He told me what happened at the jail. That crime was a setup. The San Carlos jail is no different from jails everywhere. Racism and homophobia grow like weeds in a manure pile, and jails are full of that shit. No doubt the guards are still laughing about how easy it was to frame a gay man and an Indian at the same time."

"I've talked to Troy's lawyer. He thinks there's an even chance of proving that Troy's innocent. You mentioned that it wasn't the first time this sort of thing has happened here. Do you have some factual information we can use?"

"I haven't researched it, but the story on the streets is that people who are 'different'—including gays, blacks, Indians, the homeless—are targeted by corrections personnel. I'm sure there are people who have witnessed it. I don't know about statistics."

"Thanks." Carmela pulled out a business card and wrote on the back of it. "Here's the name of Troy's lawyer. Give him a call as soon as you can."

"I will." He stood and held out his hand. "I'm going to be late. It's been nice talking, Miss Jared. I now understand why Paul trusts you." He hurried away, and Carmela sat musing over what she had learned.

She reached for her cell phone and dialed Harry's number. She had an hour before her next appointment, and that would give her time to exchange information with her private investigator, if he were in the neighborhood.

Harry answered immediately and said he could be there in ten minutes—order him a beer. She moved outside to the far corner of the patio and signaled for the waiter.

When Harry arrived, his Dos Equis was waiting, and Carmela was attacking the corn chips and red chili sauce as if she hadn't just had lunch.

"This is a *very* interesting case we have," he said.

"Good. I wouldn't want you to be bored. Heaven knows you're working for almost nothing, so you deserve all the entertainment you can get."

"I will ignore that sarcasm. Rosemary paid me the last half of my down payment plus a little more yesterday, which is why I can eat at the Wayside Inn instead of Bumble Bee's."

Carmela smiled. "This one's on me, Harry. I got paid yesterday, too. What have you learned?"

"Well, it seems that your client has a clean record, but as you know, a homo in the closet may have unwashed laundry hanging between the clean stuff. From what I can determine, the connection between him and that Dr. Barkley is innocent enough. I visited with Paul, and my gut feeling is that he uses the church and his faith to suppress the carnal desires most men feel free to indulge. In other words, since becoming a Christian minister, he's avoided gay bars and social events. At least, I haven't discovered any suspicious get-togethers, unless you suspect something between him and the doctor." Harry's bushy eyebrows rose to emphasize his point. "However, the fact that he doesn't have gay contacts doesn't mean he's innocent of the kid's charges." He paused, puzzling over the faraway look in Carmela's eyes. "You question that?"

Carmela shook her head as she re-connected to the conversation. "Yes. No," she said. "I guess we have to keep digging. Check to see what his relationship is with the women in his congregation. We can't have the DA bringing in disappointed women to testify against him."

Harry relaxed and settled back, enjoying this time with his favorite attorney. He'd worked for her from the time she set up her office, fresh out of law school, with a lot to learn. He'd been in the business of private investigating for twenty years, and there were very few secrets in this town that he didn't know or couldn't uncover. From the first case he'd helped her with, they'd felt the closeness of family.

"Funny you should say that. The church secretary says the pastor's good looks and charisma draw women to the altar like honey to a sopapilla. Says most of the hopefuls drop out when they discover he's just flitting among the flowers, not interested in marriage."

Carmela nodded and pursed her lips. "He admits that's true, unlike some other evangelists."

"Well, some of them are more devious than this one. They marry for the purpose of hiding their bi-sexual makeup."

"Yes, and I find that offensive. There is no concern for the women and children involved. However, some people say the wives know what's going on and go along with it." Carmela laid aside her napkin. "But you think Paul is on the up-and-up?" she asked.

"I've talked to five families who have young boys, and none of them believe the pastor's guilty. He's well liked. They invite him over for Sunday dinner, he plays ball with their kids, takes them fishing. They don't understand why he's being charged and are sort of waiting to see what happens. They would like to know what the kid said happened. You can understand the parents' need to get to the bottom of this matter."

"Of course. Have you looked into the stepfather's background? That man worries me for some reason."

"Now the case gets more interesting. This guy spent some time in the marine corps, left before his enlistment was up, with nothing good or bad on his record. Came back home, changed his uniform for a black hat and cowboy boots, got a job out at Las Haciendas, and started dating Cody's mother, after her first husband died. As you know, he got saved during a summer revival meeting, they married, and now he's rarely seen in church. Everyone says he and Cody get along okay, as far as they know.

"He hangs out in bars around town. My next step is to put on my cowboy boots and pony up to the bar with some of his friends on Saturday night. I hate those boots. They pinch my toes." He paused to allow Carmela time to appreciate the lengths to which he went to serve her. "When I was a kid and went to cowboy movies, the bad guys wore black hats. His dark Stetson makes me suspicious."

Carmela laughed. "Maybe you're jealous of his good looks, Harry. Suppose playing cowboy is just a ruse to get in with the visiting movie stars who hang out in the bars?"

"I doubt that Randy Travis or Val Kilmer are going to waste their star dust on a local wannabe."

"No, I guess not." Carmela picked up the check. "About Dr. Barkley, I think we have to keep him on our list of characters in this case. Although Paul declares he's not involved with anyone, Barkley is interested in making it a twosome. See if he's ever had contact with Cody, maybe as a doctor." She finished paying for their lunch while Harry added more notes to his little black book.

After they shook hands and went their separate ways, Harry sat in his car, watching her leave, unable to forget the sadness in her voice when they discussed Evangelical indiscretions. She gets too involved with her clients, he thought. She ought to spend more time analyzing her relationship with that cop.

Chapter Sixteen

Grim-faced Bettina and Oscar Whitney entered their six-thousand-square-foot Spanish hacienda from the garage entry, kicking off their mud-covered shoes. The rain had stopped. The only sound in the house came from the portico, where Glorietta sat shelling peas she'd purchased at the Farmers' Market that morning. She grumbled at the two dogs who began barking when they heard the car enter the driveway. As she carried the pan to the kitchen sink, Oscar went through the kitchen, yelling to quiet the dogs. Bettina stopped and spoke to the maid.

"Thank you for coming back, Glorietta. I was upset because you called the police, but it's turning out okay. You can take tomorrow and the rest of the weekend off. Oscar and I need to get some things resolved before Brooke gets home. Take the peas with you. I won't be cooking."

"Shall I come back on Monday, then?"

"Yes, unless you hear from me."

Oscar's voice boomed into the room, and Glorietta began shaking.

"When the policewoman came in here, what did she say to you?"

"I'm not sure I remember everything exactly. It was so confusing. She wanted to know if I was in the room while you were fighting, and I told her no. And did I know what started the fight, and I told her no."

"That's all she said?"

"Yes, sir."

Oscar seemed relieved. He looked at Bettina and smiled. "I think that's all we need, Glorietta. You can go now." He hurried toward his office.

Bettina swished her hand as if to sweep Glorietta out of the house.

"Will Miss Brooke be coming home this weekend?"

"I just got a call from the social worker, and she's bringing Brooke to get some of her things this afternoon. We have to get a court order before she can stay. I'm told that takes a while. I'll see you Monday."

"Yes, ma'am. Thank you, ma'am." Glorietta stored the peas in a zippered plastic bag and called her daughter for a ride home.

Bettina walked with her to the front door. "Is there anything else I should know, Glorietta? Has Brooke mentioned any names around you? Maybe some of her school friends?"

"No, ma'am." Her voice became belligerent and she added, "Except I did tell her last week that I didn't think it was right for her and that Connor to spend so much time by themselves down at the stables, when they didn't have lessons. And there's that stable manager too. I don't like the way he finds excuses to come up here when Miss Brooke is sunbathing at the pool."

"When does he do that?" Bettina's tone was harsh.

"Every time he sees her at the pool, he makes some excuse to come ask her something about what he's to do with Cedar—whether he's to exercise him or is she going to?"

"I don't see anything wrong with that. What did she say about it?"

"Just that I'm living in the dark ages and to mind my own business. So I did. Now look what's happened."

"Nothing has happened, Glorietta. Don't worry about it. Oscar is talking to the lawyer, and he'll work things out. I'll see you on Monday."

Bettina returned to the kitchen, where Oscar stood at the bar, pouring himself a bourbon, straight. He looked at Bettina. "The usual?"

She nodded, but added, "Make it light. We have some serious talking to do."

They walked to the east side of the portico, overlooking the ninth hole of the golf course, and settled into soft chairs.

"I've just talked to Art Farris and told him what Glorietta told the police. He thinks we can beat this rap if we keep our heads and cooperate."

"By 'rap' you mean we can keep you from being arrested for having sex with your daughter?"

"I haven't had sex with my daughter! That's your sick mind. I've been lying down with her since she was a kid, when she's upset and can't sleep. I hug and comfort her and that's all that's happened."

"What I saw was more than hugging."

"I told you that was a one-time happening. She told me Connor was pressuring her to have sex, and she wanted me to show her how. That's when you came in."

"Just in time it seems."

"She's becoming an adult, Bettina. She needs someone to talk to about these things. We don't have time to argue about this. Are you going to cooperate with Farris's plan or not?"

"What is he asking me to do?"

"So far, from what we've been able to find out, Brooke hasn't mentioned my name. Talk to her and make sure she understands the consequences of getting me involved. I could wind up in prison, in which case attorney and court fees will eat up our whole estate. She may never be able to come home again. If she's smart enough to keep her mouth shut, this can all blow over. Better still, Farris has a plan to clear my name if it comes up."

"What do you mean, 'if it comes up'? If Brooke talks, your name will come up."

"Not if you can get to her this afternoon. You need to let her know I'm moving to a hotel downtown, maybe even to Albuquerque. The court will have no reason to worry about a man being in the house with her. She needs to understand that I'm moving out in order for her to come home. There are two possible names where Farris can lay blame: Connor and Marvin Stokes. Connor's only sixteen, and there are no serious consequences involved if the kids did make out. He wouldn't even be arrested. Stokes is a different matter. His name has come up in his stepson's case, where their preacher's been accused of touching Stokes's stepson. Farris says there are rumors that the attorney hopes Stokes will be nailed in this case in order to make it look reasonable that he's the pedophile who also abused the boy. All Brooke needs to do is remain quiet when she's asked if Stokes did it—she doesn't have to lie about it."

"And what does she say if they ask if her father gets into bed with her?"

Oscar jumped from his chair and began pacing near the porch rails. "She'll say exactly what she always said to you—I lie down by her when she's too upset to go to sleep. It's never been a problem for you."

"Until I came in yesterday and found you kissing her on the mouth. I was in denial before. I didn't want to believe I'd married a pig. That's what you are, Oscar. A pig! You've ruined your daughter's life and mine. Things will never be the same."

"No, but they'll be a lot worse if you don't cooperate. Rape and incest are felonies. People convicted of either of them go to prison. Attorney fees alone will force us to sell this place. You and Brooke will be living in a garage apartment in some trashy part of town." He spoke over his shoulder as he returned to the bar for a refill. "You've got to do this for her sake."

Bettina pulled a linen handkerchief from her pocket and wiped tears from her eyes.

"Here's the plan." Oscar leaned forward in his chair, elbows on knees, waiting for Bettina to get control of herself. "When the social worker brings Brooke out here this afternoon, you tell her I've moved into a hotel in Santa Fe, and I won't have any contact with Brooke. That should reassure her and the court that Brooke can come home. Farris has talked to the police, and he says they're taking a closer look into the Vernon case to see if Stokes could have done that. If he's caught for abusing the boy, it'll take just a few smart moves to get him for abusing Brooke, also."

Though shocked, Bettina offered, "Glorietta did say that he comes up to talk to Brooke every time he sees her outside sunbathing."

"Yes, and he could have done it at the stables. She's down there every day. It will just take some cooperation from Brooke, and it's your job to talk to her ahead of time and let her know all she has to do is keep quiet when they ask her if Stokes ever touched her. She won't have to lie. If they get him on the Vernon case, he's going to jail anyway, so she doesn't have to feel guilty about it. Farris will see that she doesn't have to testify in court."

"How do you know she hasn't already told someone the truth? Glorietta has her suspicions, and Brooke may have told her more than she's admitting to us."

"We don't know for sure what Brooke said, but she didn't name names, or Glorietta would have told the police. Just make it clear to Brooke what her role is. She claims she's going to be an actress. This is a perfect place to start."

The telephone rang. "You get it," Oscar said as he pulled out a cigarette and steadied his hands to light it.

Bettina joined him after a brief time. "That was the social worker. She says they'll be here in an hour. I told her you were moving out. You'd better get going."

Oscar relaxed. Bettina had bought into the master plan, and no one was better at plotting a winning campaign than his wife. She had been the secret weapon furthering his career from day one. "I'll take my laptop," he said. "See if you can find Brooke's. If she took it with her, check it out when she gets home and eliminate any contacts that may discuss sex. Look for Connor's emails for sure, and leave them on there. If there is anything about me, get rid of it. And if she has a diary, find it before the police get it. And tell her to stay off the damn computer and Twitter until this is all over."

He hurried to his room to change clothes and pack. Leaving this place would be a relief.

At four o'clock, Aviva returned to the foster family's home to pick up Brooke and was pleased to see that the girl's attorney was just leaving.

"How did your meeting with Lucinda go?" she asked as they got into her car.

"She's okay. She said she'd try to get me back home now that mother's out of jail."

"Good. I just talked to your mother. She's home, and you'll get to see her right away."

"May I stay home now?"

"No. We have to get a court order for that. Possibly early next week. But we can go there now and pick up anything you need."

They headed for Las Haciendas, with the Jonas Brothers blaring from Brooke's cell phone.

Aviva was surprised at the change in Brooke's demeanor. She was now indulging in the bubbly, nonstop chatter one expected from most teenagers. Her mood contrasted sharply with the sullen, arrogant pose she'd exhibited that morning. She was obviously happy to be on her way back home, which was a good sign. She seemed pleased at the idea of seeing her father.

Aviva hadn't revealed to Brooke that her father was moving out of the house. She wanted to see her reaction when she learned he wasn't home.

When they arrived, the warm embraces exchanged by mother and daughter seemed sincere.

"Where's Daddy?"

"Honey, he decided it would be better if he moved out for a while. He said he'd call you tonight, and he'll be back as soon as he can." She turned to Aviva. "I understand you agree Brooke will be safe here. I can assure you she will be. Let's go look at her room and anything else you want to see."

Aviva watched the mixed emotions that flashed across Brooke's face when she learned her father wasn't home. Relief? Disappointment? Confusion? The child shrugged and dashed ahead of them to her room, whirling in a pirouette near the wall of windows overlooking a chamisa-covered arroyo. "I love it here," she said as her eyes skipped around the room from the bed to her desk. She stared at her mother. "Where's my laptop?"

Bettina's complexion blanched, but she turned away and smoothed the covers on the bed. "Didn't you take it with you to Sherry's?"

"Oh. I must have left it there." She looked at Aviva. "Can we pick it up when you take me back?"

Aviva nodded, wondering how she could get it turned over to the police, who should have secured it immediately.

Bettina waved her hand to brush the problem aside. "Don't bother. I'll pick it up and drop it off where you're staying. Why don't we go have some iced tea on the portico?"

"I don't remember taking it to Sherry's. Let me look some more." She began searching in her closet and then rushed out of the room, returning with it clutched in her arms. "I left it on the couch in the TV room," she said. "It was under some cushions." She snatched a suitcase, filled it with jeans and tee shirts, and grabbed a blanket from her bed. Arms loaded, she leaned over and kissed her mother goodbye, then headed for the car without looking back.

Aviva opened the trunk and arranged Brooke's possessions, hoping the computer would be overlooked when they got to the foster home. It might contain names of men or boys who had contacted Brooke. The police would have no trouble getting a subpoena to search it.

On the way to the foster home, pleased by the breakthrough with Brooke, Aviva pondered how to press for more information. "Maybe next time we meet, we can drive out to my ranch. I think you'd like Feisty. He's a lot like you."

Aviva darted a look sideways and smiled when she saw Brooke suppressing a grin.

After dropping her off at the foster home, Aviva called the police department and suggested they subpoena Brooke's computer, which the teen had taken with her. "Do it ASAP," she said. "She may be smart enough to wipe out contacts."

Chapter Seventeen

The Sunday newspaper thumped against the portal, and Carmela's eyes blinked sleepily. She heard the door open and close, followed by Travis's familiar footsteps coming down the hall. She pulled the covers over her shoulders and stared into Travis's amused mug.

"Goes to show who's important in your life. I've been trying to wake you for thirty minutes, and it took the newspaper boy only one thump to do it. What's he got that I don't have?"

Carmela chuckled. "If you'd come around early on Sunday mornings more often, maybe you'd find out. And if you've been here for thirty minutes, where is my breakfast?"

"The bagels are ready to toast and the coffee's hot. Would you like them in bed?"

"No. I'll get up." She pushed the covers aside and sat up, with the strap of her gown falling off one shoulder. "While you were fixing bagels," she said, "in my dreams I was beating you at a game of tennis."

Travis sat down beside her and reached over to replace the fallen strap. She placed her hand over his as it slipped downward and cupped her breast. He pressed her shoulders back to the pillow and bent forward, touching the nipple of her breast to his open lips. Surprised, Carmela guided his chin to her mouth, and they were kissing, like no kiss he had given her before. Shaken, she moved her head aside, and he sought her breast again, now tender beneath his touch. She lifted his cheeks between her palms. "What are we doing?" she whispered.

He grinned. "Playing doctor?"

She fell back on the pillow, laughing, shaking her head. "No. We did that when we were kids. We're not kids anymore, and you know this is breaching the boundaries we agreed to until you get a divorce." She adjusted the sheet over her breasts, but he continued to nuzzle beneath her chin, up to her lips.

"Travis, you aren't listening."

"First things first," he said as he pulled his sweatshirt off and threw it aside.

She gasped. "That's what I'm trying to get across."

"Spoken like the lawyer you are, for sure, yet I'm getting vibes from a beautiful woman who's in bed—not a courtroom—and they tell me she wants the same thing I do." He continued to disrobe. "Truth is, we've been talking to ourselves about this for a long time. Just not to each other." His hands began roaming over her body, and she felt muscles tightening across her stomach and below.

"This morning while you were dreaming of tennis, I was dreaming about bedding a beautiful woman who looked a lot like you. Why else would I break into your house while you're asleep?"

"You've never needed an excuse for that. Perhaps you came to discuss something with me?"

"Ummm. You didn't discuss tennis with me. You just went for it," he said, as he moved in beside her. He pulled her gown above her waist, and she helped slide it over her head. His hand returned to her flat, tight stomach, and then slid to the dampness between her thighs. He moved above her. "It's obviously too late for a discussion," he said. "However, I'm willing to beg."

Carmela was breathless at the touch of his nakedness and the odor of heated bodies. "You know you don't have to beg," she whispered, "but what if we're sorry later?"

"We'll deal with it then. Just tell me it's okay." Carmela relaxed beneath his body, her mouth sought his. No words were necessary.

By the time they dressed and went to the kitchen, an autumn shower had doused all hopes for tennis.

"There goes my chance of beating you while you're exhausted," Carmela said.

"I'm not that tired, woman. Why don't we go back to bed and wait out the storm?"

"Maybe next Sunday. I had plans to go to the office this afternoon."

"Maybe we should just forget the tennis on Sundays. What we did was more to my liking."

Carmela shook her head. "Travis, why do you suppose we didn't get serious in high school?"

"I know why. When I was fifteen, Dad sat me down for a birds-and-bees discussion, and at the end he told me if I ever touched you he'd thrash me within an inch of my life. In his mind, he felt responsible for you after your dad left and your grandpa died. And he went further. He told me to tell all the guys you dated that he'd do the same thing to them."

"He didn't!"

"He did. And you can bet none of the guys wanted to tangle with a cop." He paused while setting the table and searched her face. "Did they?"

"Are you asking me if any of my dates made serious passes? No. Which made me think there was something wrong with me."

"Dad must be up there cheering. His lecture worked."

"I'm not so sure it was good policy. Here I am, over thirty, and still an old maid."

"I have plans to take care of that, too. I told you I've got Raymond Ortiz starting on the divorce papers. How soon can you plan a wedding?"

"How soon?"

"Yeah. How long does a divorce take?"

"I thought you said Carolyn was coming home from the hospital."

"Well, I don't have to be there. I've been talking to her doctor, and her brother says he can drop by to check on her. I'll look for a place to bunk down for a while." He hesitated, waiting for Carmela's response.

She pulled the toasty bagels from under the broiler and transferred them to a plate. At the table, she poured cream into her coffee and watched as the color changed from dark brown to a pale tan, the color of her skin.

Travis pushed his plate away and leaned forward on his elbows. "Does your silence mean you don't want to marry me?"

"No, but how can we desert Carolyn if she's so sick?"

"I'll keep paying the mortgage and expenses until she decides what she wants to do. Her family will help take care of her physically. It will all work out."

"You're positive this is what you want?"

"We both know it's the right thing to do, Carmela. My marriage to Carolyn should never have happened in the first place. I've never told you this, but while we were growing up, I just assumed you and I would get married after graduation. When you went off to college, it pissed me off. I didn't think you'd ever come back. I dated practically every girl in our class, looking for someone to take your place. Carolyn was the first one who came close. We got carried away one night, and she convinced me that sleeping together meant we had to get married. Dad's dating rules seemed to support that. When we found out she was pregnant, I didn't have any arguments left. I confess, I married her hoping it would hurt you."

He finished his bagel, frowning. "Maybe if the miscarriage hadn't happened, things would have worked out better. But it didn't happen that way." He paused. "What I'm trying to say is, there's nothing left between me and Carolyn. I've turned off Mom's and Dad's voices telling me it was my duty to marry her and take care of her. After she left, I woke up and decided I didn't have to live by their rules. You and I should have married in the first place. It's stupid to let that first mistake ruin our whole lives."

"I hear what you're saying, but I have voices in my head, too. I learned what was right and wrong from Grandma and Grandpa, and their voices still come to me when I have to make moral decisions. If they were alive, they'd be horrified to know you and I slept together this morning, and they'd never approve of our moving in together while you're still married. It's hard for me to approve of that, either."

"Actually, I'll bet they'd be more than happy to know we're getting married. They loved you a lot. And we don't have to move in together until we're married, if that will make you happy. I told you, I'll find another place to live until the divorce is final."

Carmela laughed and replenished their coffee. "I got up this morning expecting to play tennis with you and instead we're talking marriage. Let me catch my breath."

"Let's set a date."

"Get your divorce and we'll talk about it."

"I'll take that as a yes."

"It is a yes—with reservations."

"What do you mean?"

"Divorces are complicated. They don't happen overnight."

"Jeez. That's why I'm still married—I don't like going to lawyers."

Carmela laughed at him. "If you hate lawyers so much, I'm surprised you want to marry one. I think you ignore the fact that I'm a lawyer, and you just think of me as that damn good soccer player you want on your team. Am I right?"

"I definitely want you on my team."

"I want that, too. But on another subject, you'll have to get used to the idea that lawyers work overtime, and my plan for this Sunday afternoon was to do some research while the phone wasn't ringing." She grinned. "I'll consider your proposal on one condition. I get to be team captain this time." She kissed him lightly, picked up the Sunday newspaper, and turned to leave. "You can leave the dishes. I'll clean up later."

Travis smiled at the confident swing of her hips as she disappeared down the hall. "You want to be captain?" he called. "That's fine with me. I'll be the coach."

She slammed the door behind her, not seeing Ms. Peña watching from behind the curtains in her dining room. She almost stumbled over Prissy, who jumped from the portal where she had been patiently waiting for Travis to exit and give her a scratch behind her ears.

At the office, Carmela opened the newspaper to a banner headline stating that the Southern Pentecostal Holiness Church was voting on whether to discontinue its Cub Scout program in view of the shocking event concerning their pastor. Brian Otis, a reporter from Albuquerque, was bylined on the story.

> Over fifty people gathered at the Southern Pentecostal Holiness Church in San Carlos last night to discuss whether the church should abandon its sponsorship of the Boy Scouts, which includes the Cub Scout program, in the turmoil following the recent arrest of Pastor Paul Morrison on charges of sexual abuse of a Cub Scout. No consensus was reached, despite the warning from interim pastor, Reverend Haskell Watkins, that the church could be held liable for damages if the former pastor is found guilty in a court of law. He compared the case to the situation years ago when a Catholic priest was accused of sexually abusing boys over a period of years. A

million-dollar settlement kept the sordid facts out of the
courtroom and away from public scrutiny. The priest
was sent to the Servants of Paraclete facility, known
as Via Coeli, a rehabilitation facility in Jemez Springs,
New Mexico, which the Catholic Church sponsors for
priests charged with sexual offenses.

The congregation listened to Pastor Watkins's recitation
of the criminal charges against Pastor Morrison, and then
a few parishioners rose as a group, shouting, "No, no, it's
not so!" The audience seemed split fifty-fifty on whether
their pastor was guilty of the crime.

This episode began last week when . . .

She skipped the five-paragraph explanation of what happened in the
church basement during a Cub Scout meeting. She was more interested
in how the congregation responded to the charges. People similar to these
would be on the jury, charged with finding Paul guilty or not guilty. Fifty
percent was a better prediction than she had expected. With new energy,
she began her research.

Chapter Eighteen

On Monday morning, Carmela settled into the comfortable porch swing on the Morrison's patio and heaved a sigh of relief. Her research had been encouraging, and Harry's investigation had turned up a number of witnesses who would support the minister, including church members, teachers, and Scout leaders. She looked forward to discussing all this with Paul, who was discharged from the hospital earlier than expected.

The sun's heat radiated over the patio. Paul sat with his legs spread-eagled on a folding lawn chair facing the mountains, away from the screened door that opened to the kitchen, where his mother rattled pans on the stove. He was dressed in navy shorts and a sleeveless white tee shirt that revealed bruises on his right shoulder and legs. His arm was still in a cast, which he scratched beneath as they talked.

Carmela smiled at Paul. "It's so good to see you taking the sun. You're not quite as pale as you were when I saw you last."

"Two days of sun will do wonders. Mom insists the best way to heal is to sit in the sunshine, commune with Mother Nature, and listen to the birds." He lowered his voice. "I've been fighting sunburn, watching the cat capture innocent baby birds, and cussing life in general. I trust Mother Nature won't reveal my true character to my mother."

"For an outdoorsman, you sound quite cynical. I agree with your mother. This looks like the perfect place to recuperate."

"Too much time to think. I used to meditate, but I'm not the same person I was before this happened."

"'This' meaning the false charges and the fall down the stairs?"

"For starters."

"Care to talk about it?"

Paul blinked. "No. I suspect they're things I should discuss with a therapist. If I told you or my friends what bothers me, we might cease being friends."

"You underestimate me and your friends, but I understand." She shuffled through papers in her briefcase and glanced through the door to the kitchen, where his mother stood with one ear turned their way. "Is it okay if I close the door?"

Paul nodded. "You'll have to forgive my mother. She can't comprehend all that's happened. Yesterday she was reluctant to let Jason in, until she learned he was a doctor."

"Oh, I'm glad he came. We had lunch last week. I like him very much."

"He said the same of you. Has he told you he's gay?"

Carmela's head leaned to the right as she dipped her chin to peer over her reading glasses. "As a matter of fact, I asked him directly. He avoided the answer, but I'm not a complete idiot, you know."

"I'm sorry. He doesn't hide the fact, but he's probably trying to protect me. I thought you should know."

"Thank you. It's no fun being blindsided in court."

Paul frowned. "Why would he appear in court? He has nothing to do with the abuse case."

"If the DA chooses to use your sexual orientation against you, which he will, then any gay person you know will be fair game as a witness."

Paul stared past the arroyo, and with a low sigh, leaned back in his chair. "This trial is going to be hell, isn't it? I don't mind it so much for me, but it's unfair to my friends."

"Friends will be honored to help you, Paul. You would do the same for them. And, speaking of Jason, I'm wondering if that relationship is such that you're thinking of making it public?"

"Coming out, you mean?"

"Yes. It's a major consideration for the trial."

"No. I've told you a number of times that I'm celibate. You obviously don't believe it."

"It isn't that I don't believe you, Paul. But a trial is like a chess game, where you move the pieces around trying to get into the best position in order to win. Each witness adds or subtracts from the final decision for or against the defendant. If you admit to being gay, the chess piece moves one way or disappears. If you don't come out, it moves another. I just need to know in which direction we're going."

"Right now, the answer is no, I'm not coming out. What else do you need to know?" Carmela was not surprised at his impatience.

"Before we start, we need to have another discussion about whether I'm the right attorney to represent you. I got a call from a national gay organization, saying they are very interested in your case and think it may have national repercussions. They suggested it would be safer to have a specialist in this area of the law take over, someone who has handled— even won—this type of case. They're offering to pay the fees."

Paul's eyes closed, and he leaned back in his chair and rubbed his forehead as if he had a headache.

"Perhaps from the world view, it would be better, but I don't see my case as a referendum between the gay versus straight world. I am a person who has been charged wrongfully with a horrible crime against a child. Whether I am gay should be irrelevant. If we invite the gay coalition to take over this case, I will be freed or found guilty because I am gay. I don't want it to be about that."

"Even if their expertise might increase your chances of being freed of the charge?"

"I don't think it will help, and it might hurt. You're well known in this small community. The people trust you. There could be a backlash against outside counsel, couldn't there, just like changing venues could cause?"

"I can't argue with your logic, but it may be misplaced. I hope you're right. If you change your mind at any time, let me know." She picked up her file. "Let's get to work. We'll start from the beginning. Tell me what you noticed about Cody when he arrived at the Cub Scout meeting."

Two hours passed while Carmela probed Paul's memory about the incident, going over the same material more than once to check for inconsistencies or nuances that might suggest the story was fabricated. Did he know other adults Cody might have had contact with? If he played teeball, were there coaches and parents who spent time alone with the players? Were there church parties, hikes, or choirs where he had other adult supervision? How about older boys who helped supervise the youngsters?

She left the meeting with a list of contacts for Harry and confidence that her client was telling the truth. Convinced that her strategy to free

Paul must include finding the perpetrator, she had to depend upon Harry to develop new leads.

At home, Carmela fixed a drink and settled into a comfortable chair on the portal, shaking her head at the squabbling of redheaded finches at the bird feeder and enjoying the arrival of ladder-backed woodpeckers whose red crowns heralded their royalty. Other than riding her horse, this was her favorite get-away from work, from stress, from people. It was her thinking place. Her hours with Paul, followed by a conference with Harry, had been tiring.

She looked above the tall coyote fence to the trees bordering the acequia, where two enormous ravens were perched on the same limb—no doubt, like her, enjoying their favorite resting place. The smaller one, likely a female, was hunkered near the tree trunk; the other was about six inches away, sitting tall, his head turned away as if he were uninterested in the body language coming from his companion. Carmela tried to ignore them and sweep her mind clear. However, the male moved the short distance to the side of the female, and their beaks met in several pecking kisses, their heads rubbed each other's necks. Carmela suspected he was ready to make his move and was surprised when he hopped back to his original perch, six inches away, and looked off in the opposite direction, showing complete disinterest. Strange action. Is this a male of Paul's persuasion, perhaps only interested in being friends? If not, who is pursuing whom? Is it a lover's rendezvous, and I'm spying on what should be a private moment between male and female?

Behind Carmela, the front door slammed, and she heard Travis wandering about looking for her, pouring himself a drink before opening the door to the portal. "Hi, babe. What're you up to?" He pecked her on the forehead.

"See those ravens?" She pointed across the acequia.

"Yep, they're ravens alright."

"They act like two people, out on a blind date, curious as to whether they can trust each other."

Travis watched the birds for several minutes. "You have a vivid imagination. They're just two birds doing what comes naturally."

"And you have no imagination. I'm positive the female is pursuing the other one, and he, like most males, is just leading her on."

"And what if it's the other way around?"

"You mean she's flirting and then giving him the cold shoulder?"

"It happens." Travis chuckled and emptied his glass. "Is this all you have to do? Sit around and psychoanalyze a couple of ravens? Why aren't you out at the ranch, riding?"

"Look. The male is flying away, leaving the poor female alone."

"Like I say, honey. That's life."

"Well, it's not over yet. See? She's chasing after him. Who's to say how it will end?" She turned her worried gaze to Travis's beautiful smile and teasing eyes.

He bent over her and kissed her lips. "I know exactly how it will end. Come inside and I'll show you."

Chapter Nineteen

When Carmela arrived home from work the next day, the table was set with her grandmother's nicest china. A bottle of champagne rested in an ice bucket. Travis was lighting tapers on each side of a water glass filled with red roses from her yard.

"My goodness. What are we celebrating?"

"Raymond filed my divorce papers today."

Carmela paused, dropped her briefcase and coat, and moved into Travis's arms. Had her worries been for nothing? Could Travis overcome all the stumbling blocks she'd envisioned when he outlined his plans to divorce Carolyn? Cautiously, she said, "That sounds like progress."

"Have I ever lied to you?"

Carmela shook her head and watched as he popped the cork from the champagne bottle.

"No, honesty is one of your strong points."

"Sit down," he said, and he began filling their plates with creamy pasta Alfredo. He set a salad beside each plate, and Carmela paused to admire this man her childhood friend had become.

She twirled her fork in the pasta to spin a perfect wheel. "This stuff is bad for your heart, you know. Too much fat."

"Nag, nag, and we're not even married, woman. Count your blessings." He leaned one elbow on the table as he lifted a forkful of pasta to his mouth and chewed slowly.

"How is Carolyn doing?"

"Fine. Why do you keep worrying about her?"

"I'm sorry, Travis. I feel guilty for my part in what happened to your life . . . and hers. After high school, I couldn't look at things from your perspective. I had no parents to show me that a good marriage and children were a worthy goal in life. I should have gone to school here in New Mexico while you pursued your career. I just wasn't into marriage at that stage in my life."

"And I could have gone to college with you, but I didn't."

"So we have to live with the choices we made."

The phone rang and Carmela answered, but there was only agitated breathing before a click on the other end of the line.

"Who was that?"

"I don't know. Just a crank call. Sounded like a woman. Lawyers get lots of those."

Travis frowned. "It could have been Carolyn trying to find me. She's been calling off and on all day. I finally quit answering. Did she sound okay?"

"Well . . . no."

"Her brother was supposed to take her to his place today. Let me call him." He pulled out his cell phone, dialed, and filled his mouth while the phone kept ringing. He pushed his plate aside and dialed Carolyn's number. "No one's home. I'd better run by and see if she's okay. Save this. I'll be back."

When Travis arrived home, no lights were on. Carolyn was nowhere to be seen. He heard a muffled groan and opened the door to the guest room, where she insisted on sleeping. She was in bed, moving restlessly in a troubled sleep. He approached to retrieve the light cover she had tossed aside, and recoiled when he saw his hunting rifle leaning on the chest of drawers. He knew he hadn't left it there. Alarmed, he took it out to the garage and hid it under a tarp, then called Carolyn's brother and asked if he could arrange for an emergency appointment the next day with her psychiatrist. They agreed that Travis should spend the night to make sure she was safe. He called Carmela, asked her to save his dinner for lunch tomorrow, and she agreed that he should watch over Carolyn.

Carolyn was asleep, breathing peacefully when he left for work the next morning. Her brother called and assured Travis that he would come by late in the morning to take her to her appointment.

Rain splattered on his newly shined shoes as PT picked him up. He grunted hello, his mind still on the gun hidden in the garage.

"Where the hell were you last night?" PT asked, as she pulled out into the street.

"Where was I supposed to be?"

"There was a fight at Cowboys, and everybody else was busy, so we got the call. What gives you the right to choose which emergencies you answer?"

"I, uh. I must have slept right through it. Come to think of it, I left my phone in the car."

"It was pretty damned early in the evening to be dead asleep. Maybe you were doing something besides sleeping."

"What happened?"

"I just about got killed by some drunk."

"Hey, I'm sorry. Why didn't you call for backup? You know not to take on a bar fight by yourself."

"I depend on you, Travis. I left you a message and thought you'd show up. I don't trust some plebe just out of training. It was a good thing Harry Rodriquez was there. He covered my back."

"God. I'm sorry, partner. I was in the middle of something. It won't happen again."

"Was it alcohol? Drugs? How about sex?"

"You're way off base."

PT waved the issue away. "Forget it."

"What was Harry doing at Cowboys?"

"He was there investigating Marvin Stokes's activities. Carmela's got him checking out the kid's stepfather. I understand Harry was asking some personal questions of a man who'd been drinking with Marvin, and it got back to him. Marvin took a swing at Harry, and by the time I arrived, the whole crowd was either fighting or cheering it on."

"Why didn't you wait for help? Even when we're together, we have sense enough to do that."

"I admit it was dumb, but those guys all know me. I was in the neighborhood and thought if I got there quickly it wouldn't amount to anything. But Stokes was mad. He'd just gotten word that he's being called in today for some questions on that case up in Las Haciendas about the Whitney girl. Can't blame him for being hot, I guess, but he should know better than to get drunk in public when he's already in trouble."

"Was Harry hurt?"

"Got a black eye, which he's bragging about."

Travis shook his head and looked over the assignment sheet. "What's on for today?"

"Things seem pretty quiet out here. We can stay in the office unless there's an emergency. Since you took the night off, you should be rested. You can drive." She slowed down and pulled over to the curb. "On second thought, you don't look like you had much sleep. I'll drive."

Travis reached for the keys. "Thanks, but I can handle my job and my personal life without your help."

"Is Carolyn still in the hospital?"

"I think her brother's taking her back to the hospital today. They discharged her, but she fell apart again."

Well, PT thought. That should make things interesting. Maybe that's his problem. Keeping one woman happy is hard enough. Two could be a reason for oversleeping. PT decided to drop the subject. Travis needed sympathy, not nagging.

Rosemary's car space was empty and her desk unoccupied when Carmela arrived at the office. She shook the rain off her hat, made the coffee, and sat down at her desk, prepared for a pleasant catch-up day. However, a note, "Call the DA, ASAP," lay where she couldn't miss it. What catastrophe had happened now? Questioning her compulsion to return calls promptly, she dialed the DA and put him on the speaker phone so that she could takes notes. Sedbury had a history of forgetting exactly what he said to her.

"I understand you've been appointed to represent the Whitney girl. I wanted you to know I'm going to object to that appointment, unless you have the foresight to withdraw."

"Really, Roman? On what basis?"

"I just learned that Marvin Stokes is being sought as a person of interest in that case. You're well aware that he will be an important witness in the Cody Vernon case, also."

"He does get around, doesn't he?"

"This is not a matter to joke about, Carmela. It's obvious that, as the attorney for Reverend Morrison, you'll be trying to find someone else guilty of abusing the child, especially if that person is his stepfather, who just happens to be a suspect in the Whitney girl's case. I'm sure the judge will see his mistake and withdraw your appointment, but you could save us all some time by volunteering to withdraw."

"Gee, Roman. How nice of you to lay out a strategy for my winning two cases at once. I would never have thought of it. I'll take your advice under consideration." She smiled, anticipating the slam of his telephone.

She should have told him that Yolanda had already called to see if Carmela anticipated any conflict between the two cases. Carmela had assured her there was no conflict and that she would be happy to represent the girl. However, she'd added that she would not be surprised if the DA objected, and if the court wished to avoid hearings on the matter, Carmela would be happy to withdraw. She didn't say so to Yolanda, but she was willing to bow out knowing that Aviva would still be on Brooke's case, and she could unofficially keep up with what was going on as it related to Marvin Stokes.

Carmela had a court appearance scheduled for 10:15, and it was raining cats and coyotes outside. She searched the front office, but Rosemary had probably taken her umbrella when she left to run errands. Her search for a substitute plastic sack to ward off the rain was interrupted by the noise of Rosemary's yellow bug parking near the back door. She watched as her secretary hurried inside, dressed in a short skirt, knee-high boots with four-inch spike heels, and a fuzzy sweater that covered, yet emphasized, her bust. Carmela had learned long ago that Rosemary's sexiness was an asset in the office equal to her computer skills. Every male lawyer in town managed to drop by, insisting to his gofer—a high-school or college student hired to run errands—that the drop-off was on his way to court. The gofers guessed that Carmela was the drawing card, but she knew better.

"Did you see the message from Yolanda yesterday that the court had appointed you on another sexual-abuse case? If this keeps up, you'll soon be an expert in criminal defense. It's a fifteen-year-old girl this time."

"Well that appointment is being withdrawn. I talked to Yolanda this morning while you were out and told her there was no legal conflict in the appointment, but if the court wished to pacify the DA, I would withdraw. Sedbury called, too, just to make sure I knew he was aware I'd be looking for *the real* abuser and his belief that I would use the appointment to pursue that strategy in the pedophile case.

The buzzer sounded as Carmela closed her briefcase and lifted the umbrella. Rosemary asked if she had time to talk to Ms. Peña.

"Is her cat up another tree, in this rain?" Carmela's loud response needed no intercom assistance, and Rosemary backed away from the bark.

"No. Just calm down. She wants to tell you how pleased she is that you and the nice policeman are seeing each other socially." There was a long pause.

"My personal life is not something I wish to discuss with Ms. Peña or anyone else, Rosemary!" She unfurled the umbrella and headed for the back door. Ms. Peña must be doing more than bird watching with her binoculars.

"Don't lose my umbrella. It was a gift!" Rosemary called after her, disappointed that she didn't get to hear the story about what Ms. Peña thought was socializing. But then, she knew an "off limits" order when she heard it.

Fallen rain was running like a small creek down the side of the street, and Carmela hopped over it, holding onto her floppy rain hat and the umbrella at the same time. At the courthouse, she shook water from the umbrella and took the back stairs to avoid the possibility of meeting someone who knew Travis. Heaven only knew how far Ms. Peña's gossip had flown. Carmela headed for the downstairs cafe, frowning as she checked the time. Aviva was probably already there.

She relaxed when she caught Aviva's smile. Most social workers were special people. Their DNA allowed them to deal with the trauma involved in healing broken families and the crushing disappointment when all efforts to save a child failed. Aviva was one of the best. They had become close friends the week after Carmela moved back to San Carlos from law school. Getting her own horse was a first priority as she began her career. She'd shown up at the Las Cabalas ranch, where the horse auction/adoption of wild mares was taking place, intent on adopting one of the free-bees. Aviva moved beside her as she leaned on the corral, began asking questions, and without being pushy, let Carmela know which mare would best meet a novice's needs. She signaled a wrangler to cut a beautiful dun mare from the herd, and they watched as his mount nudged the mare against the fence so that she could be roped and bridled.

"What do you think?" Aviva asked him.

"She's a keeper." He patiently described her good features and potential problems to the women. For Carmela, it was love at first sight. The horse's color was a perfect, soft sandy-gray, with a black tail and mane. She had no idea what her other good features might be.

"Can we put a saddle on her?" she asked. The wrangler suppressed a smile and shook his head. "She'll have to be gentled, ma'am."

"How do we do that?"

Aviva slapped her hand on Carmela's back and pointed to the wrangler. "Carmela, this is Chuck. He knows as much about horses as you know about the law. I suggest you spend some time with him and Bella, that's what we named her, and he'll have you riding in no time at all. When can you work her into your schedule, Chuck?"

The cowboy ran his hand down the mare's rump and slapped his hands together to scatter the horse hair clinging to his glove. "She needs to be dressed." He looked at Carmela as if she might fail this first test. "That's your first job. Horses love it, and it's a good way for her to learn to trust you."

"When do I start?"

"Right now, if you're ready." He dipped his hat toward the stables and led Bella to the gate.

"I like a man of few words," Carmela said to Aviva and climbed the fence to follow him.

"Come up to the office when you've finished, and we'll make arrangements to break and board her."

So began Carmela's friendship with Aviva. Today, Carmela admired Aviva's beautiful head of gray hair, which spoke to the number of years she'd been a social worker and ranch owner with her husband, Tony. She wore no makeup to hide the crow's feet around her eyes and needed no lipstick to embellish her smile.

Carmela dropped her briefcase on a chair, hung Rosemary's umbrella on the back of it, and ordered coffee at the counter. When she returned, Aviva began. "You didn't come out to ride this weekend."

"No. Something came up. I should have called."

"No problem. I rode Bella down to the river and back. She's developed into a wonderful pleasure horse. Her gait is beautiful. Oh, and we hired Troy Leader, at your recommendation. Chuck says he's working out well."

"Good. And thanks for exercising Bella." She sipped her coffee. "I see you have the Brooke Whitney file. You know I was appointed the girl's attorney, but I withdrew my appointment from that case because one of the suspects in her case is the stepfather of Cody Vernon. No legal conflict, but the DA is upset that it would give me access to information about Marvin Stokes. He may complain about your being on both cases, too."

"I hope not. The department gets away with overlaps sometimes because we are so short-handed. Depends upon whether the DA is on his toes."

"Believe me, he's living and breathing this case, plus my pedophile case. He expects them to influence his re-election this fall."

"I was hoping we could compare notes on the Whitney case, but if you aren't representing Brooke, I guess we have nothing to discuss."

"Seems that way," Carmela replied. She raised one eyebrow and gave Aviva a meaningful look.

"I see Rosemary running errands over here frequently. Tell her to meet me for coffee when she has time. I always carry an extra copy of my reports." She left abruptly and Carmela smiled. Rosemary would love to do undercover work. That reminded Carmela to call Harry about what he might have learned about Marvin Stokes. There was no answer, and she left a message: "Come by this afternoon if you want to discuss it. I'm in a rush."

Without warning, a sharp pain shot through her forehead, behind her eyes. She reached in her briefcase for medication. She had no time for headaches.

Across town, Carolyn Hawk shook a plastic bottle holding twenty or more pills that were prescribed to ease the pain in her head and return her life to normal. They weren't working. Her fingers tightened around the bottle to control the tremors that had increased after she left the hospital. She felt nauseated and leaned low over the toilet, hoping to reduce the splashing on the spotless rim. Travis was such a damned neatnik. This place had never been this clean when she lived here. She rose and tried to focus on the bottle of pills. Chances were good she would vomit them if she took the whole bottle, and a failed effort to overdose would do nothing more than put her back in the hospital.

She stumbled to the bedroom. Where was that damn rifle? She banged into the dresser, and her wedding picture fell, face up. Travis still looked pretty much the same. He was a cop now, instead of a football hero. He'd no doubt hidden the rifle she'd left by the dresser. Maybe he had a hand-gun somewhere. It wouldn't be so heavy. He was used to bloody messes in other people's homes. He saw them all the time. Mess or no, she couldn't think beyond the need to end her misery.

Halfway through rifling the second drawer, she was overcome with weakness and fell backward on the bed. She had a distant awareness her thinking was crazy. Maybe she should go back into the hospital.

The thought of positive action stirred an impetus to find her car keys, but she couldn't remember where she left her purse. She wandered, aimlessly looking for it, and returned to the bedroom empty-handed. She blinked rapidly. Travis always left his truck keys on the bureau when he drove the police cruiser. There they were. She hadn't properly appreciated his obsession for putting things in the right place. She picked up the keys and shuffled in her house shoes to the dark garage, where she struggled with the heavy pickup door. She had difficulty pulling herself up on the running board. Inside she slumped, slowly straightening her body behind the wheel. She turned the key and shuddered at the noisy roar of the engine.

This truck was Travis's baby, and he treated it with the same love and attention he'd give a child. She felt safe inside it. Her head fell forward to the steering wheel, and she breathed in the smell of oil and gasoline mingled with the odor of her husband's shower soap and shaving lotion emanating from his overnight kit on the front seat. Must keep it in the car for nights he spends with Carmela. Tears dripped unbidden down her cheeks. She reached for the garage door opener on the visor, but it seemed too high, and her hand fell uselessly beside her. She reached out in an effort to find his body next to hers, but the space was empty. He must be working late. She relaxed and went to sleep.

Chapter Twenty

Downtown, Travis and PT were leaving Bumblebee's, where they had gotten lunch, when the police chief pulled up beside their cruiser and motioned for Travis to join him. Travis handed his clipboard to PT and slid in beside the chief, who leaned out and asked PT to report back to headquarters for a new assignment.

"What's going on?" Travis asked, as the vehicle sped into traffic with the lights flashing.

"We've got an emergency out at the hospital, Travis. Your next-door neighbor called and asked me to pick you up. Carolyn's out there."

"Yeah, her brother was going to admit her. Did something happen?"

"They didn't tell me. Just said to get you."

Travis tensed; his blood felt chilled, sluggish, slowing his heartbeat as it solidified the muscles in his body. The chief didn't make runs like this unless the situation was the direst of emergencies. What had Carolyn done? Could she have found the rifle? She must be badly hurt. He began shaking, and he clasped his hands and dropped his head backward, closing his eyes. The chief rolled up to the emergency room entrance and parked behind a fire department medical unit, empty, with the doors open. Travis jumped from the cruiser before it stopped and ran inside. Betty Wadley, their neighbor, huddled in a chair near the hallway leading to the medical facilities. She was pale and frightened.

"What happened?" he asked.

Tears flowed down Betty's cheeks as she shook her head, unable to speak. The chief stood at the registration desk, barking orders, and a doctor appeared, as if by magic. Frowning at the uproar, he asked them to follow him to a private room. Travis was familiar with that room, and with the canned message doctors gave to grieving relatives. "I'm sorry to tell you that Ms. Hawk had been dead for several hours when her body arrived here. There was nothing we could do."

"How did it happen?" Travis asked.

"Probably carbon monoxide. I understand she was in a truck with the garage door closed."

Chief Garcia turned to Travis. "It looks like an accident, Travis. The hospital address was on the GPS, as if she was on her way here. She got the truck started, but for some reason the garage door didn't open."

An accident? Suicide? Does it matter? Travis wondered. Why hadn't he answered her telephone calls? She had looked so peaceful when he left that morning. He turned to the doctor. "Where is she?"

The doctor led the way down the hall.

Travis's mind went blank. Later he couldn't remember how he got to her side, what she looked like, who led him away, or how he got home. He vaguely remembered leaving a message on Carmela's phone: "Call me. It's important."

It was seven o'clock when Carmela reached home. She punched the play button on her telephone message machine and discovered she had two messages. The first was from Travis. She had difficulty hearing the second. It was Rosemary's voice, speaking loudly over a cacophony of noises. She must be partying. "Carmela, I'm at Cowboys having a drink with friends. Harry is here, and he asked if we'd heard about Travis's wife. Did you know she died today? I wasn't sure Travis would have time to call you. Harry says it looks like suicide. I was afraid you'd read it in the paper tomorrow and that's always . . . so shocking. It's not the way to find out about things that bad." Her voice trailed off. "I guess there's no good way." The message stopped.

Carmela's knees weakened and she hurried to a chair at the table. Could this be Harry's and Rosemary's drunken idea of a joke? There had been too many deaths lately. Too many rapes of children. Too much loss of love. And there was the message from Travis. She laid her head on the table and sobbed over whatever part she may have played in this tragedy. And she wept for Travis, who had tried so hard to help Carolyn through her problems. He was bound to blame himself for this tragedy.

She dialed his number, but there was no answer. She showered and followed her instincts. No matter what happened, she and Travis were family. She needed his arms around her, and she wanted to smother him with her love. Surely no one would find it inappropriate for Carmela to stop by his home to offer condolences. She drove quickly.

Carolyn's sister answered the door. "Travis is asleep. He told us he didn't want to see anybody. Try again after the funeral."

After the funeral? Carmela couldn't believe her ears. She'd believe that message only if Travis said it to her face. Why hadn't he connected with her?

At home she sat immobile, wondering how long he would sleep, when he would call.

At eight o'clock the next morning, she dialed his number again. There was a new message on his cell phone: "Sorry I can't return your call. Please check with police headquarters if this is an emergency."

An emergency? Yes, it was an emergency, but not one the police could solve. Why hadn't Travis taken the time to come by or call? He should have known how upset she would be. Was it possible that he really did not want to see her?

She drove past the police station, but Travis's vehicle was not there. She parked her car half a block away from his home, hoping he would come out so that she could see that he was well. There was no sign of him or his family. Florists, neighbors with casseroles, and his buddies from the police department all came and went. He obviously was seeing people.

Over the next few days, she read and re-read the newspaper articles about Carolyn's death, and she waited for his call.

He entered her office a week later, dressed in blue jeans and a sweatshirt. He was unshaven, his eyes swollen from too much sleep or not enough. He entered through the back door without knocking. Carmela gasped and waited for him to speak.

"How are you?" he asked.

"How do you think I am?"

"I'm sorry, Carmela. You have a right to be angry. I just haven't been thinking straight. I wanted you to know I'm getting out of town for a while."

She had no response.

He stared at her angry eyes as if he'd never seen them before. "This has been very hard. The only reason I can think of for Carolyn's death would be something I did or didn't do . . . mostly with you. And seeing you would have made it worse."

"That doesn't make sense. Carolyn was depressed over Brian's death. It wasn't my fault or your fault that she fell in love with Brian. And it was his death, not something we did, that triggered her relapse. Also, the paper said her death was likely an accident. Maybe she didn't intend to kill herself. How can you blame us for that accident?"

He began blinking away tears. "She knew I loved you when we got married. If I'd done my duty as the husband she needed, she'd never have run off with Brian."

"I don't believe that for a minute, and you don't either." She paused, but he didn't respond. Softly now, she added, "We talked about your going to see a therapist not long ago. Maybe now's the time."

Travis shook his head. "I've asked the chief for some time off. I've got three weeks coming. I'm leaving town. I need some time to think." He turned and walked to the door. "Raymond called and said he'd withdrawn the divorce petition."

She talked to his back. "You no longer need a divorce to get on with your life."

He paused with his hand on the doorknob. "I don't see myself going anywhere."

"If this is goodbye, Travis, just say so. Don't leave me hanging." The angry edge had returned to her voice.

"Why don't we talk about it when I get back?" He was talking to the door, which he opened and closed carefully.

Carmela felt transported to the acequia where she had hidden while her parents loaded the van, preparing to leave without her. That day, Travis's father had rescued her. Today, she had no one. She slammed her chair against the desk and yelled at the door: "If you don't fix your head while you're gone, then don't bother me when you return."

Across town, Paul stood in front of his bathroom mirror and pulled at the bandage over the stitches on his head. The itching was killing him. His mother used to tell him that itching meant the wound was healing, but he doubted it. He was due at the doctor's office to have the stitches removed, but he questioned why the doctor hadn't used thread that melted so he wouldn't have to go through this procedure.

"Paul?" His mother called as he moved to the bedroom to dress.

"Yes, Mother."

"We'd better hurry. I'll be late for my meeting."

"You go ahead. I'll drive myself."

"But I don't mind, dear. It's on my way."

"No, please go without me. I may drop by the church on my way home. Thanks, anyway."

Mary appeared at the door of his room and quickly averted her eyes as her son buttoned his shirt and reached for his pants. She stared at his hairy legs, blushed, and turned away.

"Oh, I'm sorry." She retreated down the hallway.

Zipping his pants, he wondered if all mothers were embarrassed to see their sons half-dressed or whether his mother was an aberration. His brow wrinkled as he heard the front door close. How many times had she backed away from him when a hug or kiss seemed the natural thing for a mother and son to share?

He hadn't forgotten the last time she held him in her arms and said, "I love you." It was his tenth birthday, and his father gave him a push away from her arms and told him to blow out the candles on his birthday cake. "You're a man now. No more of this mother-hugging stuff needed." Paul didn't feel too old to be hugged by his mother. His sister, Ginny, who was much older, often received hugs from their mother. As he bent over, the heat from the candles caused tears to blur his vision, but he blew angrily and the candles began smoking where the fire had been. He looked up and relaxed at his father's thumbs-up sign of approval.

Why had he found it impossible to tell his parents that he was gay? Maybe because there would have been no thumbs-up sign of approval, and living a lie was easier.

He reached for a tie and then tossed it aside and undid the three top buttons on his shirt. No longer representing his church, he could dress comfortably. He wondered if the new pastor would welcome him. He didn't look forward to seeing another man behind his desk. He shrugged, resenting the idea that he should have to make an appointment to go inside his own church, and he refused to do so. If he wasn't welcome, he'd leave and drive to Carmela's office, where the atmosphere was less judgmental. She never indicated disapproval of his lifestyle, nor suggested that his calling to the church ministry was fake or misguided. Her philosophy seemed to be "live and let live." He wondered what her parents were like.

Rosemary was tired and ready for the day to end. When Paul called and asked if he could drop by to see Carmela, she grimaced and told him that Carmela was already booked until four o'clock, hoping he would delay his visit until tomorrow. Cases as complicated as his usually took hours of work, and if he came late in the afternoon, Rosemary could expect to find her desk piled high with new work in the morning. He informed her that a late appointment would be fine.

Despite her desire to leave early, Rosemary greeted the minister with her loveliest smile. She blushed when he apologized for the late appointment, sure that her disappointment at having to work late was obvious. While he sat across the office reading *Money* magazine, she let her eyes wander his way and thought what a shame it was that he wasn't an eligible bachelor.

Carmela appeared from her office, greeted Paul with a warm handshake, and then turned to Rosemary. "You can check out now if the files are ready for court in the morning. See you tomorrow."

Rosemary loved her boss.

"Sooo . . . you're looking great," Carmela said to Paul as they sat. "No bandages. No black eyes. By the way, we must have ESP. I had just picked up the phone to call you when Rosemary informed me you were dropping by."

"Extra sensory perception? You believe in that?"

"Yes, I do. I don't have it with everybody, but it's kind of spooky when it works."

"Almost as if a greater power is busy connecting people and ideas?"

"Ummm. Some sort of vibe connecting people. Like lightning striking from one brain to another, I guess."

"That isn't quite what I was thinking of, but it will do. Why were you going to call me?"

"It was about your case. Two issues. First, you know I've had Harry looking for the person who is guilty of abusing Cody. That would be our best hope for winning your case. We may have gotten a break. We don't have confirmation, but Marvin Stokes works at the stables where the fifteen-year-old girl who was raped boards her horse. If he's found guilty of that crime, who's to say he isn't sick enough to injure a child?

"Cody's stepfather! You can't mean it."

"Yes. I hesitate to hope, but it appears to be good news for your case."

The room was quiet except for the noise of birds outside the window, fighting over grains in the feeder.

"When did it happen? The girl's abuse?"

"We don't have all the facts. She didn't report it. Her girlfriend's mother did, and Brooke still refuses to discuss it. On Monday, the court refused to let her go home. I understand the police are still questioning the parents."

"I feel like this is my fault. If I'd known about Cody sooner, perhaps this one could have been avoided."

"Don't feel guilty. I suspect this has been going on a while. The good news is that we may be able to get your case dismissed before we go to trial, if they get a confession or if the girl identifies Stokes as the perpetrator."

"This is unbelievable."

"Stranger things have happened." She picked up the damaging copies of the church calendar with dates marked where Paul and Dr. Barkley had met and tapped them absentmindedly on the edge of her desk as he blinked tears away. "Outside of legal problems, how have you been feeling?"

"Almost human. I'm anxious to get back to work, but I went by the church this afternoon and was told I've been put on indefinite leave. I guess there's nothing I can do about that."

"Who put you on leave?"

"The Board of Elders. They hire and fire. I guess I'm lucky they didn't fire me."

"You should ask for a hearing. Bring me your contract, and we'll see what your remedies are."

Paul shook his head. "I don't have a contract. Just a welcoming letter from the board. Our congregation is a voluntary gathering of believers. I'm just one of them. I get paid a percentage of the tithe. It's an effort to live as the early Christians did. Can you imagine the twelve disciples having a contract to preach?"

"You must not have any lawyers on the board, or there would be a contract. Maybe I should apply for the job."

Paul laughed again. "That's kind of you, but they don't allow women on the board either."

It was Carmela's turn to laugh before she added, "I don't know why we're being so jolly about this. Will you get your job back if we get these charges dismissed in court?"

"Maybe." Paul shifted in his chair. "But I'm not sure I want it. I don't look forward to confronting the questions everyone will have about my beliefs—which I'll have to address if I go back. It would be easier just to quit. Maybe it's time I move out of my mother's home. Go back to school. Start a new career." He stared at Carmela and waited for her reaction.

"That sounds like positive thinking, which is good. You're young. Future possibilities are wide open for you . . ." She paused, not sure how to enter the discussion of cautioning Paul against pursuing a relationship with Jason before the trial was over.

"The second thing I wanted to discuss with you is the importance of sticking with your church relationship throughout the trial. You have friends in the community who believe in you and the good work you have done here. We don't know what their reaction will be if you challenge their conservative beliefs. We have to prepare for this trial under the assumption that we haven't found the real perpetrator. That doesn't mean we won't stop searching, but it does mean we have to fight as if you are the only suspect."

"I'm not sure what you're suggesting, but I assume you're saying I should be careful who I associate with." His voice was tight and a little angry.

Carmela said nothing.

"The positive thinking you just praised happens to have developed since this whole mess started. I have allowed myself to meet with friends I would have avoided before. Jason and I have gone to ball games together, done some hiking, and I'm beginning to feel like a normal person. We have a bike ride and hike planned this weekend. You're telling me I have to stop that until this stupid trial is over."

"No, but I think it would be better if you didn't move in together."

"That's right. Don't try to live a normal life like other people do." There were tears in his eyes, and he stood, ready to leave.

"Paul, I can't imagine how hard your life has been or will be, but the world for gay men and lesbians is changing for the better. Slowly, but it's changing. All I'm asking for is a few months."

He stood. "Do what you have to do." He looked at his watch. "I have to go."

Chapter Twenty-One

It was Sunday, three weeks from the time Travis had left San Carlos. Carmela went to the office, where there would be no telephone interruptions, no clients, just time to plan, do research, and enjoy the possibility that her client might not go to prison. She'd have time to prepare a Foulenfont motion, showing that the state lacked the necessary facts to prove Paul was guilty of pedophilia. Judges rarely approved such motions, but an attorney should never pass up the opportunity to put the idea of dismissal for lack of evidence into the judge's mind.

Carmela was aware that there was no New Mexico case law supporting her position, but that wouldn't keep her from falling back on favorable case law originating in other states—not binding on New Mexico courts but persuasive for jurists who believed the New Mexico courts were behind the times on certain social issues. She could only hope that Judge Salazar fell in that group and that, when his decision was appealed, the New Mexico Supreme Court would likewise move with the times.

Reviewing *The State vs. Foulenfont* took only a brief time, and Carmela used the case to set the standard for what evidence the state would need to support its charges. She then turned her attention to searching for favorable cases from other jurisdictions that she could use to support that standard.

It was one o'clock before she found on the Internet the case law she'd been hoping for. The Gay and Lesbian Alliance was celebrating the winning of a case in California favoring a gay teacher. The State Supreme Court had ruled that a child's testimony—that he was touched inappropriately by a teacher—must be supported by physical evidence, witnesses, or prior offences!

She stood up, raised her arms above her head, and yelled, "Yes!" It fit her case exactly. First, doctors had found no physical signs that Cody had been touched. Second, no one had come forward as a witness of the abuse. And third, her client, the Reverend Paul Morrison, had no prior offenses. Surely, Judge Salazar would dismiss her case on that precedent.

A second case she found declared that a person could not be found guilty of the charge of pedophilia unless the victim named him directly. Cody had steadfastly refused to name the person who abused him. He certainly had not named Paul, and based upon this case, the court should dismiss. The only problem was that a few judges had refused to follow that precedent because the judge who made the ruling was a close relative of the person charged with the crime, which was an outright conflict of interest. The only bright spot in using this case was that a few judges had ignored the obvious conflict and followed the precedent. Perhaps Judge Salazar would, also.

Her euphoria at finding the cases supporting Paul's innocence was further tempered by the knowledge that case law was just case law, subject to appeal, and this new case certainly would be appealed to the US Supreme Court, where it might be overturned. However, that would take years, and Paul's case would be settled by then. It was law until it was overturned, and she hoped her judge would hold the DA to that standard. If he did not, Carmela might have grounds for appeal. With these cases in hand, Carmela could push for an early court date, which would please her client.

And while she might no longer need to find the man who did abuse the child, she felt sure that might happen as a result of the police investigation of Marvin Stokes's military records. Collecting and watching child pornography was not proof that the voyeur was a child molester, but such a person was abetting the child molesters who took the pictures. It was a criminal act, and it went a long way toward raising a reasonable doubt. The police might even charge and arrest Stokes before Paul's case was heard.

She filed her motion the following day, and the DA responded with an argument that emphasized the unethical and biased ruling of the judge in the second case, and he re-asserted the possibility that Cody might still identify the perpetrator.

Judge Salazar responded quickly in writing. "I do not believe this case represents good law, and it has not been affirmed by the appellate court.

I also support the state's position that the child should have every chance to identify the perpetrator. The case is not dismissed. Get it set for trial."

Carmela would appeal his decision, but her chance of success was small. She chided herself, knowing that the case she relied on was tainted by the fact that the accused predator was a relative of the judge. Nevertheless, the ruling should remain precedent until it was overturned. Instead, Judge Salazar, and judges before him, had chosen to look the other way and pretend it didn't exist, suspecting their decision would never be appealed.

Chapter Twenty-Two

The weather was beautiful, and the sun, shining through cumulus clouds, promised a perfect outing. Jason hurried to adjust their bikes while Paul fretted because he was of little help, still protecting the arm that had been broken in the jail fall. This was the first time in weeks Paul remembered smiling with real happiness. Satisfied with the task well done, the two men slapped hands, mounted their bikes, and Jason led the way down to the arroyo. The trail rose and fell through fields of chamisa and cedar bushes, until a half hour later the men arrived at the foot of Atoka Peak, where the bike trail ended.

"See that tree?" Paul pointed upward where a tree, growing from a split boulder on the side of the mountain, hung etched against the clear, blue sky like a skeleton.

Jason nodded.

"We can leave our bikes here and hike to that spot in only thirty minutes. There's a great view of the town from that ridge."

"Let's go."

"Bring your bike over and we'll hide them. We won't be gone that long."

Fifteen minutes later, Paul left the main trail and waved Jason to follow. "This is a nice rest stop, with a view of the east side. Let's sit down for while. I'm not as in good shape as I thought I was." He breathed deeply and pulled his water bottle from his lunch pack.

"Hey, this is beautiful," Jason said. "Why don't we eat lunch here?" He laid aside his backpack and started unbuttoning his shirt. "And we can work on a tan. Did you bring sunscreen?"

"Yeah. But it's a little late in the season to be sunbathing, don't you think?" He rummaged until he found it and handed the plastic tube to Paul.

"Sunbathing is never out of season—even when there's snow on the ground."

"Open it up for me and turn around. I still have one strong hand," Paul said.

It took some time to rub in the sunscreen, but neither man seemed in a rush. When he had finished, Paul handed Jason the tube. "Your turn."

"Turn around. I'll help with your shirt." Finished, he tossed it beside his own, on a nearby bush. Paul turned his back to the sun, and Jason massaged the cream over stiff shoulder muscles, down his spine and around his rib cage. Finally, his arms surrounded the chest and dropped below the belt line. He leaned his head against Paul's shoulder and continued massaging tight stomach muscles.

Paul uttered an embarrassed laugh. "Thanks. That's enough."

"Not for me it isn't." Jason's arms tighten around Paul, and his lips dropped to his neck. His teeth nipped the skin, ending in kisses along the hairline.

Paul moaned. "Please don't. This place already has bad memories for me."

"What do you mean?"

"I can't talk about it."

"That's bad, man. We could trade those memories for something good." Jason continued to hold Paul close, sliding his tongue to his earlobe.

Paul forced Jason's hands away. "I'm sorry, but I was crazy to come up here with you."

Jason backed away and tossed the sunscreen toward Paul's backpack. He moved to sit against a boulder, facing the sun, turning away from Paul. He covered one hand with sanitizer to remove the sunscreen, and with dry hands he removed a sandwich from the plastic bag and began eating.

"I should have known better. Please don't be angry. I should have said 'no.'" Paul paused. "I won't lie. I did know what would happen, and believe me, I wanted to be a part of it. For years, I've managed to be happy hiding in my church. Now, that hiding place is gone. My heart tells me I could find peace with you better than there, but I can't do it until this court case is completed. Does that make sense?"

"Considering where you're coming from, I guess it does. I don't like it, nor do I think you're making the right decision, but you have to do what you have to do. Maybe when this court business is over . . ." A chipmunk peeked from beneath the boulder, and Jason threw a crust of bread in his direction. Paul, thankful for Jason's kind words, lowered himself to sit beside his friend, shoulders touching, and tossed some chips to the rodent.

Jason frowned and moved away, turning his back to the sun, putting space between them. "Don't push your luck, fellow. You can't have it both ways. It's much easier to dodge a lightning strike than to survive one. Avoiding temptation is how you've made it this far in life—you'd better stick to it until you're ready to go all the way."

Paul bowed his head. "You're right. You're wiser than I am."

"You know as well as I do that the closet is a very dark place. As long as you're in there, you won't be able to move."

"I feel like I'm being pushed out, whether I like it or not."

"I hope you don't blame me for that."

"No, I don't. It's this criminal charge against me. I'm innocent, and it drives me crazy to think I can't prove it. I'm angry because of what it's doing to my faith. It's frustrating not to be able to forgive people for lying about me, but I can't. My instinct is to fight back. But you're right. I can't fight unless I tell people who I really am."

"What does your lawyer say?"

"She says the DA probably knows already that I'm gay, and even if he can't prove it, he will try to convince the jury that evidence points in that direction."

"What evidence do they have?"

"Circumstantial. I'm not married. I don't date women. I live at home with mamma. All the clichés."

"Well, let's see. You don't have a feminine voice, you don't hold your little finger up when you drink tea, you don't flick your eyelashes when you talk. These are other clichés that might help you."

They both laughed, and Paul stood to retrieve his shirt and tossed Jason's his way. "Thank you, friend. You almost convince me I'm not weird. But if the day comes when I walk out, you'll be the first person I come to. That's a promise."

They slapped hands and walked back to the trail.

Across the canyon, on a neighboring ridge, Marvin Stokes rested his horse at the same time Paul and Jason arrived at the lookout. He continued to sweep his binoculars across the landscape, in search of a deer herd he'd been stalking weekly, in anticipation of hunting season. He cussed under his breath at the sight of movement at the rest stop on Atoka Peak. Hikers were out today and would be scaring the deer deeper into the valley. He continued swinging the binoculars across the mountainside, hoping the deer would not have changed ranges. As his focus again returned to the rest stop, his breath caught, and he frowned, squinting to get a better view. He choked on his laughter. Forget the eight-pronged deer. This was more exciting. It was the preacher consorting with another man! What more would the DA need to support Cody's identification of his abuser? The guy was queer. He whipped his horse into a dangerous gallop toward town. Maybe he'd even get paid for what he'd seen.

Chapter Twenty-Three

Stokes arrived outside the district attorney's office Monday morning before the doors opened. He paid no attention to the looks of curiosity and admiration his Stetson and cowboy boots attracted from the secretaries and legal assistants arriving early. The security officer unlocked the doors, and Stokes rushed into the building, heading directly to the receptionist's desk.

"I'm here to see Mr. Sedbury."

"Do you have an appointment?"

"No, ma'am. But I've got to see him right away. I have some important information for him."

"Mr. Sedbury is scheduled for court at nine, so he won't have time to see you this morning. You can see his assistant, Mr. Gomez. Or you can make an appointment."

"I think he'll take time to see me, ma'am. I've got some firsthand information about that minister's case. I don't plan to talk to anybody else."

The secretary shrugged and lifted the telephone, turning her back to him. Marvin couldn't hear what she said, but he knew he had been successful when she rose and directed him to follow her.

Roman Sedbury was busy and not happy about the possibility of being late to court. However, the pedophile case might make or break his coming re-election to office, and he couldn't afford to pass up any information Stokes might have. He rose and pretended to be happy to see the man. "What can I do for you?"

"It's what I can do for you, Mr. Sedbury. I've got some information that will help you put that criminal preacher behind bars, where he belongs. But first, I need to know how it's going to help me."

"What it is you want?"

"According to rumors, that preacher's attorney is accusing me of being the one who abused my stepson. I want that lie wiped off my record. The kid truthfully told the police it was the preacher who did it. I got proof of it now."

"Really? Then we need to talk. Sit down. I'll have to record this." He called an assistant DA as a witness and told him to record the testimony.

"Do you have an attorney?"

"I don't need an attorney. I haven't been arrested. The kid says the minister did it. I have information that will seal the case against him one hundred percent."

Sedbury spoke into his intercom, directing his secretary to send an assistant DA over to Judge Salazar's courtroom, to substitute for his appearance and to plead an emergency excuse for Sedbury's no-show. He nodded to his assistant, who turned the recorder on, and Sedbury began speaking.

"This is District Attorney Roman Sedbury. The date is October 6, 2014. Mr. Marvin Stokes is in my office to make a statement about case number two zero three four, *The State of New Mexico vs. Paul Robert Morrison*. This case involves the charge that the Reverend Paul Morrison sexually abused Cody Vernon in the basement of the Southern Pentecostal Holiness Church of San Carlos, New Mexico. Mr. Stokes, is that a correct statement of your intent?"

"Sure is."

"And you have stated to me you are concerned you may be accused in this case—correct?"

"Correct."

"It is, therefore, necessary for me to read you your Miranda rights, which include the right to remain silent."

Stokes frowned at this unexpected turn of events as the DA continued. "You have the right to remain silent. Anything you say or do can be used against you in a court of law. You have the right to an attorney. If you cannot afford an attorney, one will be appointed for you. Do you understand these rights as they've been read to you, and do you want to waive those rights and proceed with your testimony?"

"I do."

"Sign this waiver, please, and we'll proceed." He placed a paper before Stokes. "Do you wish to have an attorney present before we go any further?"

"No, sir."

"Have you been advised of your right to have an attorney present?"

"You just read it. I don't need a lawyer."

"Do you understand and agree to have this information recorded and used as evidence if needed in a court of law?"

"I do."

"Let's get on with it."

Stokes shuffled his feet and tossed his hat onto an adjoining chair. His voice quivered and his face flushed as he related his story, which sounded memorized because he had gone over it numerous times in his head.

"On Sunday, October 12, I was riding up on the mesa past Solana Heights, looking for a herd of deer that I know roam up there on Atoka Peak. There's an eight-point buck that I've been following for some time, and I wanted to know where to find him when the season opens. I was looking through my binoculars, and I saw these two men stopping at the lookout on Pine Tree Trail. I didn't pay any mind at first, but as I watched, one of 'em seemed familiar, and I started paying better attention. I could see it was Preacher Paul Morrison and some other man I didn't know. I figured they were going to eat lunch. When I looked back the next time, I saw it wasn't just lunch they were having."

Stokes coughed, cleared his throat, and waited. Sedbury perched on the edge of his chair and leaned his elbows on his desk, never taking his eyes from Stokes's face. "And?"

"While I was watching, they stood there and took off their shirts and started rubbing oil on each other, and then I noticed this guy that I didn't know put his arms around the minister and started kissing his neck. They stayed there, hugging and kissing for some time."

"You said you didn't recognize the man. Describe him."

"He was a little shorter than the preacher. He had dark hair. Dark complexion. Wore glasses."

"By dark complexion do you mean Negro, Mexican, Indian?"

"Wasn't black, just dark. I couldn't tell for sure."

"Do you think you could identify the man you saw, if necessary?"

"I'm pretty sure I could."

Sedbury's voice was tight. "What else happened?"

"I don't know for sure, because they left their shirts where they hung 'em on a bush and walked off the cleared area, behind some boulders where I couldn't see 'em. There's some heavy underbrush around there, and I suppose that's where they went. I couldn't see what happened after that, but they didn't pick up their shirts for twenty minutes or more, and then they left."

Sedbury leaned over and turned off the recorder. "Why are you bringing me this information, Mr. Stokes?"

Stokes seems surprised. "Well, it proves the fact that that preacher is queer and was the one who abused my son."

Sedbury shook his head. "It doesn't prove anything, I'm sorry to say. But it does give us some leads, and I thank you for coming forward with the information. I'll get some people on it right away and see what we can find." He shook Stokes's hand and ushered him toward the door. "Oh. We'll probably call you as a witness in this case, so be sure you don't talk to anyone— and that means *no one*—about what you saw. Not even your wife."

Stokes found himself on the street, wondering what happened. He'd broken the case for the DA, and Sedbury was acting like it was nothing. Bam, bam, thank you, ma'am. Stokes headed for his pickup and sped toward home.

Inside his office, Sedbury was sharing victory slaps with his staff. "We've got that damn preacher! Now we've got to identify anyone he sleeps with. Get one of the investigators—Leon Sparks is the best one—and let him hear this tape. Tell him to get busy." He looked at his secretary. "I can't wait to see Jared's face when she hears about this witness."

Chapter Twenty-Four

Harry was seated in his car outside Carmela's office when she arrived for work. "Got a minute?"

"Sure. Come on in." Carmela tried to sound cheerful, but Harry's face was stoical, unlike him. She stopped by the coffee cabinet, poured two brews, and then watched as Harry doctored his own cup with two sugars and a quarter cup of half and half.

"Slow down or I'll have to get another cow!"

He added a few more drops of the rich cream and followed her to her office.

They savored the coffee, reluctant to begin a conversation.

"Is this news I don't want to hear?" Carmela asked.

"I doubt that it's news. From what I hear, you already know it. We just need to talk about it."

Carmela frowned. It wasn't like Harry to beat around the bush. "What is it I already know?"

"Marvin Stokes went to the DA with a wild story about how your client and his doctor friend had a rendezvous—if you know what I mean—up on Atoka Peak on Sunday. I asked a few questions and was told you knew they were out there together. So I figured you could tell me what happened."

"I know they went bike riding on Sunday and then hiked up to the first rest stop on the peak. What's so bad about that?"

"According to Marvin, riding bikes wasn't all they did."

Carmela set her cup down, splashing coffee on her desk. She stood and leaned over her desk, shouting. "How the hell does Marvin Stokes know what the two men did? They were getting some fresh air and sunshine. Riding bikes, for God's sake." Her face flushed.

Harry relaxed, glad their cards were on the table, hoping Carmela could rebut the story. "According to Stokes, he was riding his horse on the mesa, stalking a herd of deer with his binoculars. He looked across the valley to the hiking trail on Atoka Peak. He says he saw Paul and another man, half-dressed, rubbing each other with oil or sunscreen."

"What do you mean 'half-dressed'?"

"They had their shirts off."

Carmela grasped for straws. "Having one's shirt off is not half-dressed. And how else does one get a suntan without taking off his shirt?" She realized she was fighting for the tiniest bit of positive interpretation of Stokes's story. Her effort to keep the issue of homosexuality out of the trial was probably lost. The nightmare had been released from Pandora's box.

There was no way a jury would believe her argument that the two men weren't in the process of undressing, which obviously would have preceded an intimate encounter; and in the jury's minds, homosexuality and child abuse would go hand in hand. Nonplussed, she dropped into her chair behind the desk.

"What else did he say?"

"Next time he looked, they were gone, but their shirts were still hanging on the bushes. He figures they walked off to a more secluded spot, where he couldn't see what happened."

"That's at least half good. "

"How do you figure that?"

"Marvin Stokes didn't see anything except two hikers working on their suntans. He's adding intrigue to the story because he's desperate. He's now a suspect in the Whitney girl's case."

"How does that affect your case?"

"I've been looking for the real culprit in my case. He is the most logical target. It makes sense that he would want to point the finger at the minister to take the pressure off himself. But it also challenges Paul's reputation as a beloved minister whom nobody would believe abused little boys, which is what I have to convince the jury of."

"How come you knew they were going bike riding? Where were you while this was going on? Not taking off your shirt, I hope."

"That's not funny, Harry. I didn't go with them, but I did suggest sunshine and exercise was a good idea. I didn't even consider whether it was safe to leave them alone together. Who could have dreamed Marvin Stokes would be out with a pair of binoculars right at that time?"

"Or that they'd take the opportunity to 'sunbathe' instead of hike or ride bicycles?"

Carmela began pacing. "You're jumping to conclusions. This story is irrelevant as to whether Paul abused Cody. I can possibly get his testimony excluded if I can get the judge to agree that it has nothing to do with the case. It certainly should be excluded on the basis of irrelevance and the fact that it may prejudice my case. More than ever, though, we need the truth about what happened to Cody. Have you learned anything new from people you've interviewed?"

"No. And as soon as this gay stuff gets out, the jury pool will be so contaminated, there's no way your guy can get a fair trial."

"You're just full of good news today, Harry. I want the truth about what happened to that kid. He should be in play therapy classes now, where the truth may come out, but we won't be privy to that information for months. The truth is, he didn't tell a story about what happened. He merely nodded when asked if he agreed with what Marvin Stokes said. Nods are not sufficient to prove a positive. See if you can't find someone he spends lots of time with, someone with whom he actually talked. Maybe another Scout or school friend. Do whatever you have to, but it's important that we get that kid to talk."

"I didn't hear that, Counselor." Harry lowered his chin and was looking at Carmela over the top rim of his glasses, adjusting the height to avoid the interfering nose.

"Then I'll say it again. I'm not telling you to tamper with a witness, Harry. I just said I'll bet he's told somebody out there the truth. I want the truth. And the truth is that somebody other than the pastor abused this kid. I'm looking at Stokes because he's in the house with the boy, he's the one who shaped the story told to the police, and he's also a person of interest in the Whitney girl's case."

Harry nodded and rose to leave. "Okay, so we're going to play down and dirty. That's fine with me." He touched the still-sore yellow streak under his right eye, a reminder of his fight with Stokes in the bar. He smiled. Now he had leave to take his revenge. "I'll do what I can," he said, nodding his head in deep thought. At the door, he turned, rubbing his hand over a two-day-old beard.

"By the way. I ran into Travis this morning."

Carmela stiffened. "So?"

"He don't look so good. I guess his wife's death was a real blow. But we didn't talk about it. Men are no good at that sort of thing. He said that the police department had opened a file on Marvin Stokes and wondered what we knew. He may have information you need to follow up on. I suggested he talk to you directly, since you've been discussing the matter with the DA."

"And he said?"

"He said it wouldn't be a good idea for him to meet with you here in the office, since he'll probably be a witness for the DA if it goes to trial. He said to forget he mentioned it."

"And you said . . ."

Harry opened the door. "I said it shouldn't be all that hard for a policeman to find a secret meeting place. A good cop should know lots of rendezvous spots suitable for exchanging private information, drugs, or even sex. He gave me the finger."

Carmela smiled and watched Harry leave. That sounded like Travis alright. She stared at her telephone. She could think of no good reason Travis and Harry couldn't have shared their information, leaving her out of the equation. But no, Harry preferred to meddle in her personal life. She also knew Harry hated having a middle finger be the last word in any conversation he had, so he was challenging her to respond to it. She was sure she had no interest in meeting secretly with Travis. However, she did have an interest in winning this case. She called Harry on his cell phone.

"What did I forget?" he asked.

"Pass on to the detective that I'm a very busy attorney, but if he has information worth sharing in private, he can find me at the Romero's ranch Friday evening about six o'clock. I'll be riding down to the picnic area on the river, and if the mood strikes me, I'll pack a supper for two. Tony and Aviva go to the movies on Friday nights, and all the cowboys will be leaving work early to hit the bars. You should tell the dumb ass not to wear his uniform or drive the police cruiser to the ranch."

Harry chuckled. "I'll do that. Thanks, boss."

Was she making a mistake? Travis had made it clear that their relationship was on long-term hold, if not dead. It still shocked her to find that Carolyn's death had affected him so tragically. His earlier statement that he did not love his wife must have created a sense of guilt that kept him from turning to Carmela for sympathy. She could see some reasoning in that, but not much. Even though she, too, had felt guilty at first, it soon became clear to her that it was illogical to assume blame for what a mentally ill person did. Her lifelong friendship with Travis was not the reason for Carolyn's death. If he chose to believe it was, then he'd have to deal with it alone.

She put the issue aside and turned to her immediate problem, unwinding the mess made from her suggestion that Paul get some sunshine and exercise. Should she confront him on this issue? They had talked about the damage his homosexuality could do to his case. He'd sworn he was celibate, which appeared to be a lie. She punched the intercom button and directed Rosemary to set up an appointment with the minister.

"How soon?"

"Yesterday."

"Yes, ma'am. Shall I tell him what's it's about?"

"No. And Rosemary, clear my calendar after four o'clock on Friday. You can take off early that day, too, if you want." She loved Rosemary's giggles. Thank God somebody was happy in this world. A few minutes later, her secretary called back and said that Reverend Morrison would arrive at three o'clock the next day.

The big hand on Carmela's grandfather clock, sitting between two picture windows in her office, ticked to forty minutes after three. It wasn't like Paul to be tardy for a meeting. Was he finding it impossible to face her? If so, his instincts were on target. Her impulse was to shout, scream, and throw things. She decided it would lower her internal furnace and calm her mind if she pressed a cool washcloth against her temples. From the bathroom, she heard Rosemary announcing Paul's presence over the intercom. She tossed the wet cloth, dried her face, and swallowed, reminding herself that this was not about her and her unrealistic hope of winning a case. It was about a man caught between the needs of his God-given body, his love for an improbable career of teaching people to love God, and the homophobia of the community. What made her think she was capable of resolving such monumental problems?

"Send him in, please." Her words were clear, confident, and helped to hide the roiling of her stomach. He entered, smiling, with no apology for being late.

"You look well," she said as they took seats near the windows.

"Time heals, as the saying goes."

She wondered. "The bike ride must have helped. Got some sunshine and fresh air, a little tan?"

Paul nodded, suppressed a smile, and looked out the window.

"Why don't you tell me about it?"

Paul frowned, unsure of where the conversation was going. "It was fine. No problems. Weather was good. We left our bikes at the turnaround and walked on up the trail to the first oversight. We ate lunch there."

"And?"

"And what?"

"And you took off your shirts. Rubbed sunscreen—or some kind of oil—on your bodies. Go on from there."

Paul's face flushed an angry red. "You've been talking to Jason behind my back?"

"Not Jason. But I'd like to talk to him, with your permission, after we're through here. My information comes from Marvin Stokes, who had his binoculars trained on the two of you while you ate lunch. I have his story. I'd like to hear what really happened."

"Marvin Stokes? What is he doing, following me?"

"He wasn't following you. He evidently was riding horseback in the mountains across the valley, looking for a herd of deer, planning to shoot a certain eight-prong stag this fall. His binoculars accidentally rested on the overlook area where you and Jason stopped for lunch."

Paul sprang from his chair, crammed his fists into his pockets, and leaned his head forward, banging it against the glass.

"Be careful. You've already had enough stitches to last a lifetime."

He whirled around. "I wouldn't care if it cut my throat. What better way to end this craziness?"

"I'm sorry, Paul. Had I known your plans, I'd have advised against it."

"Why would you think to do that? I swore before God we'd never done anything. I still swear that!"

"I'm not so naïve that I don't know what happens when two people who love each other find themselves alone and both willing. God set it up in Genesis, didn't he?"

"Let's leave God out of this. You're making some wild assumptions. And so did Marvin Stokes—similar to his story about what happened between Cody and me. What did he tell you?"

"Tell me your side of the story first."

"Yes, we rubbed sunscreen on our upper bodies. We sat down, leaned against a boulder and ate lunch. That's it."

"That's all?"

"By 'all' do you mean did we have sex?"

Carmela didn't respond.

"No, we did not."

Carmela relaxed, but neither she nor her client moved to invade the dark, quiet cave of silence in the office. Birds outside the window hopped and scratched in the mulch beneath the rose bushes, but they, too, worked silently. Finally, Paul returned Carmela's gaze. "I must be honest. He asked me to, and dear God, I wanted it more than he did. It's been so long since I've allowed myself to admit that I have these needs, to acknowledge that I have a physical body, separate from my mind, from my career. But I'm burdened with a conscience, too. I've always been a man of my word. I told you I was celibate, and it's important to me to be trusted. That said, I wish I could tell you I feel good about my decision to say no, but I can't. The whole concept seems so unfair. At that moment on the mountain, I became aware that I haven't closed the door to the possibility of sharing my life with someone other than God—unless He strikes me dead first."

Carmela focused on the face of her client. This case was about Paul, but the man sitting before her was not the man she sat with in the interview room at the jail, nor the man who dropped out of the spinning class when the atmosphere became charged with sexual overtones. He had changed from the man she was appointed to represent. He no longer wore the robe he'd worn behind the pulpit, which served to protect him from the temptations of physical love, from the dangers of touching a body that caused the skin to tingle, from responding joyously when a loved one called— that robe had slipped from his shoulders. Before, it had seemed so clear who he was: a man of God, a fisherman of men, sacrificing his own needs to spread the Word, baptizing penitents, serving mankind. That man she could have sold to the jury as a person who would not abuse a child.

Now she saw a tormented soul who questioned whether he fit the role he had been called to fulfill. One who was not turning to God for strength to overcome his trials and tribulations, but one who wanted God to walk beside him as he searched for his own way to live a life that was true to himself. Would the jury rejoice with this new, freer man, or would it judge him as a person who thought it was his right to fulfill his sexual desires?

Carmela shuddered. Her core beliefs required that she support the new Paul. She just wished he had waited until this trial was over to seek his freedom. "I expect Jason will tell me the same story about your hike?"

"You should talk to him. No two people experience the world the same. He may see what happened in a much different light than I do. Tell me: what effect is Mr. Stokes's version of what happened going to have on the trial?"

"I'd like to keep this trial from being about your sexual preferences. I'm filing a Motion in Limine, asking the judge to rule that Stokes's story can't be used in evidence because it proves nothing about whether Cody was sexually abused, and your sexual orientation has nothing to do with the elements of this case. Rightfully, it should be about whether you touched Cody inappropriately that day in the Cub Scout meeting room. However, some jurors won't be able to separate the two issues, so the district attorney will try to emphasize homosexuality. Stokes's story will be the lynch pin that holds his theory together."

"Is there no way I can talk to Cody?"

"No. He has been interviewed on video by Social Services. I was present to make sure they didn't put words into his mouth. He refused to respond to questions about who touched him. That's in our favor, and I've now decided it's too risky to depose the child. Even if the court allowed the deposition, there is the chance that questioning him would backfire. He could say something that might solidify his prior assents to what his parents asked. If he did, we'll be helping the DA's case, not ours."

"Where do we go from here?"

"The DA has already set a date next week for Stokes's deposition. That will be our opportunity to put him on record that he didn't see anything incriminating, in case the judge lets the taped story in. I'll go over your version of the story, talk to Jason, and we'll go in prepared. Also, I have my investigator seeking evidence that will tie him to the rape of Brooke Whitney. I have other sources who may help. I know you won't approve, but we need to delay this trial as long as possible. Let some of the outrage cool, give people time to consider all the possibilities. Give Cody a chance to re-consider his charge. Give Stokes time to make another mistake. The danger with that approach, of course, is that it gives our side time to make mistakes also."

Paul stood and held out his hand. "Take all the time you need. I'm in no hurry to go behind bars again." He stared at her. "I'll be good. I promise."

Carmela watched him leave through a film of tears. Never before had she felt so alone. This case would kill her if he went to prison. For the first time, she was taking a case to court, afraid she wasn't seeing all the angles, afraid she wasn't good enough to convince a jury that they should believe in Paul's innocence, as she did. Emotions wouldn't do it. She needed evidence, evidence like the police are good at finding. What did Travis know that would be worth trading for what little she knew? What would she learn on Friday?

At the Mestas Baseball Park, Harry eased his ancient automobile next to a well-cared-for Ford Escort on the unpaved parking lot. The regular Thursday tee-ball game was underway. Coaches were on the field, surrounded by six- to eight-year-old boys and girls. He'd come late on purpose, so he could take his choice of seats among parents from Cody Vernon's neighborhood who had come to support the Bears. His luck held. Cody's mother, Lucille Stokes, was sitting on the second row up on the west side of the field. The row of seats above her was empty. He climbed up the steps at the end of platform, choosing a seat behind her, not conspicuously invading her space but close enough to hear any conversation she might have with neighbors.

On the field, the coaches yelled instructions to the boys, the referees took their places, and the tee-ball game began. Harry searched for the Vernon boy. He was seated on the end of the bench, his shoulders drooping, showing no excitement for the game. On the far end of the field, leaning against the front of a Camry in the parking lot, was the Reverend Paul Morrison.

Harry had trouble restraining a compulsion to express his shock— and possible good luck. He crossed the fingers on each hand that clasped his aching knees. The preacher was sure to be recognized and discussed by the women sitting near Cody's mother. He felt certain Carmela would have advised her client to stay far away from six- to eight-year-old boys until his trial was over—who knew when or where another abuse charge might surface—but here he was. Harry could hardly wait for some mother to recognize the figure leaning against the car and to start the conversation.

It happened during the second inning. A lady with short brown curls and horn-rimmed glasses leaned over to Lucille Stokes. "Isn't that Reverend Morrison?" she asked, nodding her head in his direction.

"Where?"

"Leaning against the car. I'm surprised there isn't a court order that he can't be around children. Especially at a children's playground."

A grandmother sitting below them chimed in. "He has his nerve. I'd never appear in public if I was accused of what he is."

Her neighbor, who appeared too young to have a son playing little league, looked up at Lucille. "He hasn't been proven guilty, has he? Is Cody still saying he did it?"

"We don't talk about the reverend when I go to the foster home." She paused. "I'm not supposed to discuss it."

"Well, I, for one, don't believe it. His sermons were so wonderful. I miss him. Pastor Waters is okay, but he's dull, dull." The young mother's declaration silenced the others. Someone hit a ball that rolled to the back fence near the parking lot, and while it was being retrieved, Harry decided to escape to a place behind the batting area, where fathers were lined up. Harry stopped where the backdrop curved around home base and where he could partially hide while he viewed this line of past little leaguers, now nervous fathers.

The father nearest him muttered out of the side of his mouth. "Bobby says that Vernon boy is worthless on the team. Every time the coach yells at him, he cries." He snorted and shook his head.

His neighbor answered. "The coach shouldn't be yelling. These are just kids having fun. If you want your kid to develop into a big leaguer, you should take him to the private leagues. My boy, Louis, plans to join the Tigers next year."

"There may be no 'next year' for little league. I hear the church is dropping its team."

""Hell, this is a lot of bunk, if you ask me. Some people are saying Marvin did it. I know Marvin, and he's no pervert. I've seen him pick up a whore more than once at the bar. Why would he mess around with a kid?"

"Maybe the whores don't fully satisfy him?" Everybody laughed.

"I heard this week that the police department may be taking sides in this case, too."

"How so?"

"Handing what they know over to the defense attorney."

"Jared?"

The speaker nodded.

"Hell, everybody knows Carmela and Travis have been like family since they were kids. What would you expect?"

No one responded as the third out was called and the teams ran to change places on the field.

"Well, if I had any information, I'd be more than happy to give it to that gal. Can't blame Travis." There was laughter and winks all around.

"Dammit, though. It's a matter of principle. She's defending that pervert minister, and he's just like them Catholic priests. They ought to hang him, I say."

Harry memorized the faces in front of him and made a mental note to get a list of the tee-ball team members. These parents could hold the key to Paul's future jury. He ambled off behind the stadium seats and casually leaned against the car parked next to Paul's Camry. They nodded, but neither spoke. With his back to the field, Harry placed his hands on the car's hood. "Who you rootin' for?" he asked.

Surprised at Harry's intrusion, Paul stared long enough to remember seeing him in Carmela's office. "The ones who come to my church."

Harry nodded. "I've been eavesdropping at the cheering section. Some of the mothers have nice things to say about you."

"Which means some of them don't?" Paul's eyes squinted at the ball field.

"That's to be expected. That's why we have juries. Anything new turn up since you saw Carmela?"

"Not that I know of."

"Your parishioners had a few things to say about Marvin Stokes, too."

"Such as?"

"He evidently picks up willing ladies at downtown bars. Made me wonder if your doctor friend ever treats STD cases. Maybe he could point me in the direction of some of Stokes's girl friends—see what else we can learn about his sexual habits."

"You're asking for privileged information."

"How else would you suggest I get it?"

Paul refused to respond and clamped his lips tightly, as if to make sure they didn't betray him. He straightened away from the car and stared at Harry. "Carmela should have legal ways to get that kind of information."

"Yeah, but it takes time. I'm faster, and that's what I get paid for. I'll pay Dr. Barkley a visit, but it might help if you talked to him first."

Paul frowned. "What do you want to know from him?"

"Whether he has any patients who may have passed on their diseases to Marvin Stokes. You know, when a doctor treats patients for STD diseases, they're required to get the names of people the person may have infected, or who may have infected them."

"I'll ask Jason to talk to Carmela."

Harry smiled and tipped his hat. "Just a little advice—it don't look so good, your hanging out where little boys are playing. Wait till the trial is over." He looked at his watch and hurried to his car. He had important information, which Carmela could share with Hawk. No one answered at her office, so he left the message on her cell phone. "People are talking about how you and a certain cop may be sharing evidence. Maybe the picnic isn't such a good idea."

Chapter Twenty-Five

Carmela left the office Friday at four, exhausted. Why had she agreed to go riding at the end of a long, trial-filled week, especially knowing that a meeting with Travis would add to her tensions instead of helping her recover? Then there was Harry's warning that people were talking about the close connection between the defense attorney and the police department. How serious was the gossip? Perhaps he was right that a meeting out on the ranch was ill advised.

She stuffed a leather bag that fit behind her saddle with ham sandwiches, two apples, a bottle of pinot noir, and a bottle opener, before reaching into the freezer for a slice of Travis's favorite chocolate cake, left over from happier times.

When she arrived at the Romero ranch, a blue Toyota was parked by the corral. Travis must have taken seriously her warning not to drive a vehicle that could be traced to the police department. Troy came from the stalls, leading a saddled Bella to the gate. She nickered and shook her head impatiently as Carmela rubbed her nose.

"She's eager to get going, ma'am. Don't let her get away from you. She didn't like being left behind." The black horse Travis usually rode was missing from the corral, and Carmela realized Troy knew she was following Travis to the river. So much for anonymity. At least the others had left early for an evening in town. Perhaps she could trust Troy not to mention this rendezvous.

"Thanks for saddling Bella. I could have done it. Are you liking your job?"

"You bet! Thanks again for recommending me."

"I was delighted to."

"I'll be here when you get back. Is there anything else I can do?" He frowned as if genuinely concerned.

Carmela smiled and lifted her foot for a boost into the saddle. "No, thanks. I'll be okay." She trotted past the corral and then let Bella speed into a fast gallop toward the river. When she arrived fifteen minutes later, neither of them offered a greeting, but Travis lifted his arms, and she slid to the ground, glad for his help.

"I brought sandwiches and wine." She pointed to the bag. He untied the straps and dropped the bag near the trunk of a large cottonwood tree that hung out over the river. He unrolled a blanket he'd tied behind his saddle and spread it in the shade. Carmela pushed the wine bottle and opener toward Travis, who popped the cork and looked around for glasses. She handed him plastic, and he poured a small amount in a glass and handed it to her.

She looked at it as if she disapproved, tipped it up, and handed it back to him. While Carmela unwrapped the sandwiches, Travis filled her glass almost to the top and handed it back. She drank half of it.

This was not the woman who usually commented when he drank too much. She seemed oblivious to the world as she nibbled her sandwich and then emptied the wine glass. She coughed, and wine dribbled down her chin. Travis resisted the urge to catch it with his thumb. "You're making a mess," he said, and picked up his sandwich. "Harry said people were talking about us. That has to stop."

"Don't blame me. He's the one who set this meeting—at your instigation, I understood. You told him you had some information to share. You wouldn't give it to him, so I'm here."

"That's not quite how it happened. I offered to give it to him, and he suggested that I should meet with you personally. I assumed that was with your approval."

She might have known—Harry was always matchmaking, and he'd seemed particularly upset at the recent chilling in this relationship.

She blinked tears from her eyes and held her glass out for more wine.

"Are you driving? I'd hate to have to arrest you on the way home."

"You and who else? What is this important information you told Harry you'd share?"

"First, I'd like to know what happened between your client and Dr. Barkley."

"It isn't what the DA thinks happened. The story he's pushing isn't true, and you won't find any witnesses to confirm what Marvin Stokes says he saw that day." She wondered how much he knew. "There isn't much to tell. Paul is still recuperating from the jail fall, and as you can imagine, he's very depressed. He's been cooped up in the hospital and the house too long."

"Very convenient, having a gay doctor for a hiking companion, wouldn't you say?"

Carmela wadded her sandwich wrapper into a ball and threw it for a direct hit on Travis's nose.

"I wouldn't start something I couldn't finish, if I were you." He threw the ball in her direction, but she dodged the attack.

"Since when have I started something with you that I didn't finish? Seems to me it's the other way around."

"Let's not get into that," he said and picked up the wine bottle, filled his glass half full, and set the bottle down near Carmela. "Come on. Tell me, what happened between the preacher and Jason Barkley on Saturday?"

Carmela's eyes squinted and she looked away, talking to the open space around them. "Paul was out of shape and tired quickly, so they stopped at the first scenic rest stop and decided to eat lunch there." She swished the wine in her glass and took a long look at it before tipping it high.

Travis frowned. "Go on."

Relaxed, the wine beginning to affect her more than expected, she lay back, propping her head on a tree root that protruded toward the river. She shouldn't drink when she was so tired. Maybe sipping would have been wiser, but she'd never admit it to Travis.

"They decided to work on their suntans, so they pulled off their shirts and applied sunscreen. That's evidently what Marvin Stokes saw, and from that he wove a fairy tale," she smiled at the pun she'd accidentally created, "the tale of two gays having at it. The truth is, he saw nothing because nothing happened."

"I don't suppose they have witnesses?"

Carmela laughed at the incongruity of the suggestion, but her response was that of an attorney. "Proving they are innocent isn't our obligation. People are innocent until proven guilty, remember?" Unfortunately, her words were beginning to slur. She closed her eyes and wished she could sleep. "Ssyourturn. What do you know about Marvin Stokes that I don't know?" She hadn't given much information, and she didn't expect to get much in return.

"His reason for leaving the marine corps isn't as clean as the record shows." Travis watched to see the surprise on her face and was pleased when the news seemed to sober her.

Her eyes opened wide. How could Harry have missed an irregularity in the discharge papers?

"I thought you'd be interested to know he was pushed out of the military for spending work time on the computer looking at child porn. The military was having enough problems with Don't Ask, Don't Tell at the time he was serving, and they didn't want to add porn cases to the bad publicity they were getting. So they resolved the problem by giving offenders a 'less-than-honorable' discharge and kicking them back out into society."

Carmela sat up, loosening the top button on her shirt as if she needed air. "Where did you get this information? I need some proof." This could be enough to swing the jury's opinion of Stokes over in Paul's favor, even if they found no solid evidence that Stokes abused Cody or Brooke. She wondered again how Harry had missed reading the discharge papers.

Travis's smirk drove her crazy. He had indeed given better than he got, but if he were a gentleman he wouldn't crow about it. She tried hard not to slur her words. "How'd you learn about this?"

"I can't reveal my sources. You know that."

"So you brought no proof. That's okay. Harry will run it down."

"Also, the judge gave us a subpoena to search his house for evidence of porn surfing. If they find contacts with children, they'll arrest him."

The news shocked her sober. She stared at the piercing brown eyes that tried to cover the glimmer of a "gotcha" smile. He leaned down again, resting on one elbow, nearer her level.

"Tell me how you got the discharge information."

"No. I think we're even. Maybe I'm ahead," he said as he reached for the dessert. He dipped his little finger deep into the chocolate icing. "Is this the cake you baked just for me?"

She opened her mouth to deny his suggestion, but his chocolate-covered finger slipped between her lips, pushing between her teeth, and the chocolate frosting melted on her tongue like warm butter. He sat up and licked the remainder from the finger that had touched her tongue. The old Travis would have followed that with the kiss she longed for, but he seemed disinclined. She felt dizzy from the wine, and by the time her head cleared, Travis was watering the horses and returning the leather picnic pouch to its place behind her saddle, as if nothing had happened between them. And little had.

She rose and stumbled to her horse, where Travis clasped his hands into a stirrup and boosted her into the saddle. He slapped her mare's rump, as if Carmela weren't capable of guiding her back to the barn. Halfway there, she spurred her mount to a gallop to prove she was sober.

At the corral, Troy hurried from the bunkhouse and took Bella's reins. Before he could help Carmela dismount, she slid to the ground and sat down with a thump.

"Are you okay?"

"To tell you the truth, I'm not," she said as he helped her to her feet. "It's been a hell of week, and I drank too much wine."

"Why don't I take you home, ma'am? These country roads can be tricky at night."

"No." Carmela stared toward the river. Travis was nowhere to be seen. She couldn't give him the pleasure of stopping her on the way home, so she'd let him go first.

She looked toward the ranch house, but there were no lights on in Aviva and Tony's house, and Aviva's vehicle was still missing. "I don't suppose I could get some coffee around here?"

Troy hesitated. "Come on into the bunkhouse. There's some left over from supper. I can warm it up."

He took her arm, and they disappeared into the bunkhouse.

"Maybe I could lie down for a few minutes," Carmela said after gulping the coffee.

"Yes, ma'am. I hear the other horse coming. I'll be right back." He returned to the corral and took the reins from Travis's mount.

Travis surveyed the area, frowned at Carmela's car and her saddled mare. "Is she okay?" he asked.

"Yes, sir. Just having some coffee. I'll see that she gets home alright."

Travis obviously was not happy with that solution, but what could he do? He stared at the bunkhouse, glared at Troy, and stormed off to his rented car.

Troy frowned as he unsaddled and bathed the horses. He leaned against the corral, one foot propped on the bottom rail, and lit a cigarette. What would Tony and Aviva say when they discovered Carmela went to sleep on his bunk? Blame him, for sure. He threw his cigarette away and headed for the bunkhouse. He would find a place to read until she woke. He wondered if anything else could go wrong with his life.

It was eleven o'clock when he shook Carmela awake. "Carmela. I'm sorry, but the guys may show up anytime now. Let me take you home."

She sat up, surveyed her surroundings, and pushed herself upright. "My God. What time is it? I'm so sorry this happened." She dropped her head into her hands. "I'm really not a drunk. I was just so tired. I shouldn't have been drinking at all."

Troy smiled. "Hey, you're welcome to sleep in my bed anytime. I'll bet you're the prettiest, smartest lady this old bunkhouse has ever had the pleasure of entertaining." He leaned against the door jam, waiting for her to rise. As she dropped her hands and looked up, she saw a long corkboard hanging on the wall opposite the bed, filled with numerous thumb-tacked snapshots. Beautiful pictures he'd taken, no doubt. She reached out and touched one of a couple standing near a van. "Who are these people?" she asked.

"That's Mom and Dad. It's pretty old, but it's the only one I have."

"Your mom and dad? What are their names?"

"Marcus and Angel Leader."

"Are you sure?"

Troy laughed. "Why wouldn't I be sure? They're my parents."

"I'm sorry. They remind me of my parents. A long time ago. They had a van, too."

"Really?"

"I know it sounds crazy. When I was little, we traveled around the country, wherever they could find work. I loved it, but . . ." Her voice trailed off as she moved to the door. "Funny the things we remember," she said, as Troy trailed behind her.

"Confusing, too," he said. "These people weren't my birth parents, but they reared me. I've searched the county property records here for their names and came up with a blank. Paul says I should try the Indian records, even though they weren't Natives. My mother was Indian, but she died when I was born. I don't know who my real father was."

"So they really weren't your parents?" She tried to make light of her observations, but all humor disappeared from Troy's countenance, and he rubbed his thumb over the back of one hand, jerked his head away and turned to open the door. "We'd better get out of here. The guys will be coming." Carmela reached for the picture, wishing she had better light, but she knew he was right. She had to hurry.

She drove away, totally confused by the conversation with Troy and hoping she could remember what Travis had told her about Marvin Stokes's military history. Her brain seemed to have shifted into neutral, refusing to move in either direction.

Chapter Twenty-Six

Saturday morning, Carmela opened her eyes at 4:00 a.m. She was lying on top of the covers, still in her jeans, with the wine- and chocolate-stained shirt sweaty against her body. Her boots lay flopped over on the floor between the door and her bed. This made twice she had slept on top of the covers without undressing, once with a headache and once with too much work. Neither was a good sign. Too much wine. That was Travis's fault. She felt a little horny. That was Travis's fault, too.

The needle pricks of hot water exploded the suds in her shower gel, combining with a fragrant shampoo to leave her feeling clean and new. She was ready to take on the world, but only after she had poured her coffee and carried it with a toasted English muffin to the patio did she allow herself to think about her meeting with Travis last night. She could still taste the chocolate frosting he'd left in her mouth, and it irritated her to realize she had wanted to taste his kiss. She remembered Paul describing what had happened when he walked to the overlook with Jason, and his admission that he wanted it to happen. He wanted to be a part of something bigger than life, more exciting than anything he'd known before. That's what Carmela felt when she was with Travis, but for some crazy reason they had lost that contact, and deep inside, she wondered if Travis was now in the process of cutting all connections with his past in an effort to find peace. That probably meant saying goodbye to her forever and finding another woman to love. With him gone, she would be left without a connection to her past—her grandparents were deceased and she had no picture of her parents. Troy had more memories than she had.

She went to the office, forced by a feeling of guilt if she didn't spend her weekends working on her cases. Outside, the sun was shining on the tiny garden where her bird feeder attracted sparrows, finches, flickers, towhees, and sometimes woodpeckers. She walked to the window and closed her eyes, thankful for the sunshine, irritated that the memory of Travis's finger touching her tongue last evening kept bugging her.

She felt alive, too energetic to spend more time in the office. It was Saturday afternoon, and she deserved some time off. She was only an hour away from the mountains. Or she could go to the ranch and ride Bella. She stuffed her research into a carry-on and threw it in the back of her car. If she got bored in the mountains, she could work on the case. She'd drive by home, pack some food and a sleeping bag, in case she decided to spend the night. She felt a weight lift from her shoulders.

She pulled up in front of her house, frowning. Travis's truck was parked there, and he was carrying an armload of what looked like clothing he had left in the laundry when he moved out. Good. Let's cut all the ties that bind us.

She sat in the car, waiting for him to leave. He was taking his time, and she finally pulled into the driveway and walked to the back door. Inside, she began filling the ice chest with leftovers, water bottles, and beer.

"Going somewhere?"

She looked up, wondering why he cared. "No, I just pack food and sleeping gear in the car to keep in practice."

"You shouldn't drive that old Cadillac on mountain roads."

"There's no need to insult me or my car, Travis. I haven't said a thing about your trespassing into my home."

"I don't mean to insult you, but you know that car is too low to the ground to be safe on mountain roads. Maybe you're going to stay on the highway?" He leaned against the cabinet with his legs crossed and his arms across his chest, as if he planned to stay a while and discuss this matter. She didn't respond.

"Where are you going?"

"It's none of your business."

"It becomes my business when I have to come rescue you."

Carmela sighed. He was incorrigible. "Travis, what makes you think I would call you to come rescue me? You made it very clear that our association was over. Done with. Dead." In retrospect, she regretted using the word "dead."

"I don't understand why you got so upset when I left. All I said was that I was going on vacation for three weeks."

"And, that *maybe* you'd get in touch with me when you got back. Well, guess what? I'm changing my telephone number and the locks to my house. And you can leave those keys you just used to trespass into my home on the counter when you leave."

He put on his heartbreaking smile. "You're still awfully pretty when you get mad."

"Travis, don't mess with me. I'm in a hurry."

"I won't keep you, but we need to talk." He sat down and stared at her.

"I see the vacation did nothing to improve your communication skills."

"Oh yeah. It did. I just haven't had the opportunity to use them on a sharp attorney lately."

Carmela chewed her cheek and stared at him.

"I've missed you," he said. "Am I to believe that feeling wasn't reciprocated?"

She surveyed her closed bag while she thought of a response. There was no way she would admit that there were times when she had missed him. She hadn't allowed those thoughts to dwell in her memory. "I've been pretty busy."

"That's not what I asked. See? I do have trouble making you understand me. I asked if you missed me."

"Rarely."

"On Sunday mornings?"

She blushed. "On Saturdays . . . my car needs an oil change. On Sundays . . . my tennis game is getting a little rusty. But don't worry. I'm working on finding a new partner."

"You've had three weeks. That's a long time for a pretty woman like you to be still looking. I didn't realize my talents were so specialized."

"Think anything that boosts your ego, Travis. I'm sure you haven't had a problem replacing me."

"I'm not here to fight, Carmela."

"No, you came to get the rest of your clothes. You have them. Why don't you leave?"

"I thought you'd talk to me."

"You hurt me worse than I've ever been hurt, Travis. I'm recovering from that injury, and I won't let it be repeated."

"I'm sorry. Very sorry. I wanted you to know I took your advice and am going to a therapist. He's helped me gain some insights into what happened in my mind when Carolyn died and how to deal with the trauma I underwent that day with Billy. It's all getting clearer to me. I was advised that mending fences is part of the healing process."

"Evidently he didn't tell you how to do that."

"He told me it might take more than words. I thought maybe I should come around on Saturday and give that old Cadillac a checkup. Change the oil, as you say."

She breathed deeply, but didn't respond.

"Or I could climb that tree and rescue Prissy again. Is she staying home now?"

Carmela knew she should tell him how much Prissy missed him, but it seemed like giving ground, which she refused to do.

"I don't suppose you need a tennis partner to trounce on Sunday?" He wasn't giving up, and he remembered how to touch her soft spots.

Carmela refused to smile. "I think we should see how Saturday goes before planning more."

"You're a hard woman to bargain with. I'll have to tell my therapist the fence is still broken, but I'm working on it." He walked to the door and turned on his sexy smile, knowing he was making progress. "I miss you like hell."

"Therapy will help, I'm sure."

"I don't suppose you have any more of that chocolate cake in the freezer? I could use some right now."

Carmela slammed the lid on the ice chest. "I wonder what would happen if I called 911?"

"I'd be right here."

Carmela gave up. Why was he being so obstinate? This was not the man who had left her office with more than a slight suggestion that their relationship was over. He was not the man who had withheld his kiss when she was vulnerable at the river. This man was asking her to open the door and let him back into her life. Did she dare give him a toehold?

"Travis, if you want to share a ride with me to the mountains, just say so."

"Only if we go in my truck. Romo offered to lend me his cabin up on Mirror Lake this weekend. He says there are three-pound browns up there."

"I have to be back tomorrow."

"I'll call Romo. When can we leave?"

"I'm ready."

"I like a woman who's always ready."

"I still hate you, Travis."

"I know, honey. My therapist says if I'm lucky, you'll get over it."

The lake was as smooth as glass, reflecting the mountains, sky, and clouds. Travis claimed squatter's rights to a flat boulder extending into the water at the far end of the lake and had whipped his first fly within fifteen minutes of their arrival. One beautiful brown already stirred in his basket. His promise of a grilled fish dinner their first night at Mirror Lake was halfway fulfilled.

Carmela watched from the front porch of the log cabin, arguing with herself about whether she should open her briefcase and study the research she had found this morning or if she should relax and do some hiking, as she'd promised herself, by following the trail she'd discovered behind the cabin. The chirping birds and chattering chipmunks reminded her that she had come here to get away from work. She looked toward the lake and saw that Travis was having more fun on her time off than she was, and that settled the argument. She warmed a cup of coffee and carried it with her down the trail that led through a heavily wooded area of aspen and ponderosa pine.

A half hour later, she was delighted to find a resting place where a large pancake rock overlooked what she imagined to be a replica of the Garden of Eden. Hidden deep in a bowl-like canyon, horses, cattle, and sheep grazed in the meadow, and young calves bawled, searching for their mothers who were contentedly chewing their cud in the shade. Ponies bucked and kicked as they played near the mares. A small number of ewes grazed near the river, and she marveled at the herd of deer stripping leaves from the bushes on the opposite side of the canyon. She wondered if Marvin's eight-pronged buck laid claim to these beautiful does. How nice it would be to live here, where there were no pesky lawsuits or noisy neighbors. She rolled her jacket into a pillow, lay back on the smooth rock, and went to sleep.

The sun was low in the west when she woke, took one last look at the valley where the animals were heading to the river for drinks, some splashing in the water to cool off, the young ones simply playing. She rose and headed back to the cabin, suddenly very hungry. Travis had moved farther around the lake, but he seemed to be packing his gear to return to the cabin. She opened the wine bottle and carried a plate of veggies, cheese, and crackers to the porch as he climbed the steps, showing her three beautiful fish on his way inside.

"Did you bring something to go with the fish?" he called.

"What's left of a three-bean salad I made yesterday—and some fruit. Canned goods if we're still hungry."

"Sounds good. I'll clean the fish."

When he returned, he carried an unused ashtray filled with peanuts.

"We won't get cancer eating peanuts out of an old ashtray, will we?" Carmela asked as they settled around the table.

"Lady, you're camping out. Be glad Romo quit smoking a year ago, and his wife is too frugal to throw away his ashtrays. Otherwise, you'd be eating peanuts out of the can."

"You like Romo a lot, don't you?"

"Yeah. And his wife, Liz, is great. They were made for each other."

"Happily married."

"Yeah."

Flames began rising from the grill. "Oh God. I forgot the fish. Well, we weren't going to eat the skin anyway."

An hour later, they settled on the porch swing again and watched the rising moon peek over the mountain. They heard masculine voices, laughter, and footsteps on the path around the lake. They had seen no other campers since arriving, and hikers were unexpected at this time of evening. They watched as two men came into sight. Suddenly, Carmela sank back as if to hide, and Travis moved in front of her, his back to the trail. Paul and Jason walked past, deep in conversation.

"Did you know they were going to be here?"

"Of course not. I didn't know we were going to be here either."

He couldn't argue with that, so Travis walked inside, letting the screen door slam behind him. He returned with a beer.

"It's a dammed small world," he said.

Carmela nodded. "I knew Paul had a cabin somewhere in the mountains, but I had no idea it was *this* mountain. I wonder if he's decided to come out."

"'Come out?' Like admit he's gay? Right now, before the trial? How stupid can he be? You told him not to, didn't you?"

"It's not my business to make that decision for him."

"It damn well is. Look at all the time you're putting into this trial, and this jerk could lose it for you before it starts." Travis paced across the porch, muttering under his breath.

"They're coming back, Travis. Why don't we invite them over tomorrow?"

"Are you serious?"

"I am."

"I was going to ask if you were crazy, but that goes without argument. I thought you came here to get away from people." He paused. "You knew they'd be here, didn't you?"

"No. I did not. But it wouldn't have mattered if I had known. It was my idea to come to the mountains. You are the one who picked the site."

Travis shook his head and watched as the two men returned. He stepped forward and Carmela was shocked to hear him yell, "Hi, guys. Catch any fish today?" He stood with legs spread, both thumbs in his pockets. Carmela wondered if she was watching Gary Cooper get ready for a high-noon showdown. She realized she had stopped breathing and choked down some air.

Paul and Jason stopped, waved, and turned in toward the cabin. "We didn't come to fish, but we're loving the peace and quiet." Jason looked at Paul for confirmation. Paul was staring at Carmela, who rose and slipped her arm around Travis's.

"Hi, how are you doing?"

"Having a great time. It's beautiful here," Paul answered, and all four stood waiting for something to happen.

"We saw you go by and wondered if you'd be around tomorrow? I'm catching some keepers, and we'd be pleased to have you come for early lunch. That is, if you don't mind my being the chef." He pointed to Carmela. "She's a lousy cook." Embarrassed, he added, "But she's a great lawyer."

"We wouldn't want to impose on you," Jason said.

Carmela dropped her hold on Travis's arm and went down the steps holding out her hand to Jason. "It's no imposition, really. You know Captain Hawk. He loves to cook, and as he says, I'm not much good at it."

She turned to Paul. "I've been working your case this week and found some encouraging case law I'd like to discuss with you, if you don't mind mixing business with pleasure. It'll save some office time later on. Of course, we don't want to impose on your weekend either."

The men exchanged quick glances. "We'd love to. We could bring some blueberry muffins," Paul said.

The incident was over quickly, and Carmela and Travis returned to the porch. "Thank you. You're a trooper," Carmela said.

Travis turned away. "I'd better get up early. I'll have to catch some more fish." He walked inside, and Carmela heard him setting up a cot in the hallway. So he wasn't being a trooper. He was acting like a spoiled child having a tantrum, and she had no intention of becoming his mother figure. So much for a resolution of their personal problems.

Late the next morning, Paul and Jason arrived with the muffins, a box of nougats, and a bottle of Irish whiskey. Carmela smiled at the unexpected treats, and the initial tension melted away over the remains of last night's peanuts and the whiskey. For the most part, Travis busied himself at the grill and in the kitchen.

"Are you two married . . . or partners?" Paul asked, smiling at Carmela and then glancing toward the kitchen, where the noise of chopping paused.

The whiskey had created a lively flush to Carmela's cheeks, and she felt the warmth spreading unreasonably to her throat and chest as she glanced away. "No. We've been friends since grade school." The chopping resumed, and she asked, "What are your plans?"

Paul frowned, but Jason spoke with authority and a touch of anger. "This lawsuit doesn't give us much choice. We'll leave here when the trial is over. Any idea when that might be?"

Carmela shook her head. "That's one thing I wanted to discuss with you. As I said in our earlier discussion, there is no statute or case law in New Mexico that defines the requirements the state must meet to find a person guilty of child abuse. My hope is that this court will follow the direction other states have taken on the issue of charges against gays in mentoring positions. A new California case defines exactly what facts must be present in order to find an accused person guilty of sexually abusing a child. The court ruled that a child's testimony that he was touched inappropriately by a teacher must be supported by physical evidence, by witnesses, or by proof of prior offences by the accused. This case has facts very similar to ours. We know the DA has no physical evidence that Cody was abused, there were no witnesses to the act, and Paul has no prior offences. While such a ruling in California is not binding in New Mexico, there is no reason not to put the facts of this judgment in front of the court and ask that New Mexico make its own comparable case law, which will then encourage the legislature to act on this subject. I believe Judge Salazar might be brave enough to take that step."

"Then you think there's no need to ask for a change of venue?" Jason asked.

"I considered that, but the downside is losing the potential local jurors who might be sympathetic to us. It's a toss-up, but these people may be able to influence the rest of the jury. And with this potential support in case law, I don't think it's necessary to change venues. The judge's interpretation of the law will be important, and I trust Judge Salazar to read it the way I do. He may be more apt to approve the motion to dismiss that I filed earlier."

Travis came from the kitchen carrying a salad. "Don't you think you'd have a better chance with the jury if you held off this . . ." He waved his hand. "Whatever you're doing, until after the trial?"

"Travis!"

"It's okay," Paul said. "He's right, of course. The safe thing to do would be to deny that I'm gay. As you can imagine, I've weighed the pros and cons, but I'm still undecided." He stared at Carmela. "You no doubt question how this weekend fits into my claims of celibacy—and maybe you won't believe it—but Jason agreed to accept my insistence on remaining true to what I pledged to God when I became a minister. In exchange, I've decided to give up my affiliation with the church as soon as this trial is over. It is important to me that I remain true to my pledge to be celibate and honor my vows as a minister. I know the jury needs to trust me and what I stand for. Whether I touched a child inappropriately has nothing to do with whether I'm gay or straight."

He turned to Travis. "As a policeman, you deal with perverted people all the time. They do abuse children, and I share your anger at this largely ignored cancer in our society. But all gays are not perverts, not even to the degree that straight people are. The two issues have to be separated. I've never improperly touched a child. I've never even thought of it.

"As for my trial, there is no evidence, other than the false statements from the stepfather, that I abused Cody Vernon. If I allow the state to proceed based on the district attorney's insinuations that I'm gay, therefore guilty, I will have done a great injustice to society at large. In the past, I haven't chosen to be an active member of the gay community, but I've decided I can't forever continue lying about who I am." He looked at Jason and smiled.

A cloud moved over the lake and the sun disappeared, leaving them in a shade that emphasized the silence spreading over the campsite. Only the light splash of feeding fish in the lake and the distant howl of coyotes suggested there was life beneath the canopy of trees.

Travis cleared his throat. "I guess I owe you two an apology—or something. I don't pretend to understand what makes your world turn, and I'm not sure I'll ever feel comfortable about it, but I'm willing to accept what I don't understand and live with it. It does get my hackles up when your actions threaten what's best for Carmela. I know how much she wants to win this case, and she thinks she can do it. But," he paused and looked away from Carmela, "it may be impossible if you guys come walking out of the closet right in the middle of the trial."

Carmela's throat tightened from the tension between the men. Why hadn't she discussed this before with Travis? Come to some understanding that they could agree to disagree on an important social issue? She understood the isolated, small-town environment that informed Travis's view of the world, and she was tolerant of what she considered his weaknesses. People are products of their environment. Travis had still not come to terms with the fact that one of his best friends in high school was gay. Although his work as a policeman forced Travis to deal with divergent lifestyles, he accepted them only conditionally.

Listening to him, Carmela understood why she had felt compelled to leave New Mexico after high school. Now she questioned what had brought her back. It must have been her attachment to Travis. She pulled her sweater closer around her shoulders and reached for Travis's hand. "Travis, I appreciate your concern for me, but, please, it's important that I resolve this. Why don't you go take a walk? We'll be through in just a few minutes."

He left, kicking aside a chair, heading out behind the cabin on the trail to Carmela's Garden of Eden.

Paul leaned forward, his elbows resting on his knees. "I'm so sorry. I didn't realize how he felt. His invitation seemed sincere. I guess he was doing it for you."

Carmela shook her head, as if to clear her thoughts. "Don't worry about him. I'll take care of it." She looked at Jason. "He's right that it would help me to plan trial strategy if I knew what the two of you intend to do publicly between now and, say, the first of the year. I think the trial will be set then."

The two men were silent. Finally, Paul asked if Carmela believed he had a chance of staying out of prison.

"Right now, I'm optimistic. We've had new twists and turns every few days. Once we've completed interviewing witnesses, I'll have a better idea. We need to see what happens in the teenage girl's case. And strangely enough, the lawsuit filed against the jail by the lawyer representing you and Troy may have a residual effect on this trial. The DA is in a hurry to get this trial held before the civil case is heard for fear you will win that one, and it will influence the jury in the criminal case. He hopes if our case goes first and you're found guilty, it will help the state win the jail case. Like I said, I can't guess the outcome of either case, but Travis was right when he said our chances of winning would be better if we kept your relationship quiet."

"I was pretty sure that's what you would say."

Jason intervened. "We realize our wish to stand up and be counted will be pretty sterile if Paul winds up in prison because of it."

Paul nodded, and the men shook hands with Carmela. "Let us think about this, and we'll talk tomorrow. Thank Travis for the great meal," Paul said. Carmela looked toward the woods where Travis had disappeared. She should go find him, but wondered if he needed time alone to think this through. She didn't look forward to a fight.

Chapter Twenty-Seven

Alone at the cabin, Carmela began clearing the table. Her cooking skills might not be the best, but she had learned to do a good job of cleaning up messes others made. Travis did not return, and against her better judgment, she decided to find him. He was seated on the same pancake rock she had rested on, and she slipped down beside him.

"Are they gone?" he asked.

"Yes. They said to thank you for the good food."

"Cooking is easy. Controlling my mouth is harder."

"Why didn't you come to bed last night?"

"After you sent me away? I thought you made it quite clear that you could get along without me. I may be dense, but I'm not dumb. I shouldn't have imposed on your weekend." He stood as if preparing to leave. "It's hard to believe we're no longer friends."

"We tried to be more than friends, Travis. Maybe your therapist can help." She pointed to the scene below. The noontime sun was hot, and the animals were hunkered beneath the shade trees, sleeping or nudging each other affectionately. "I wonder how they get along so peacefully?"

She turned to check a soft rustle in the grass beside the rock where she stood, and froze when she heard a snake's rattle.

"Watch out!" Travis yelled, and she leaned into his arms. An unlucky mouse became the victim of the attack, and they watched, not breathing, as the mouse disappeared and the bulging snake slithered away, dinner complete. Carmela buried her face on Travis's shoulder and gazed down at the valley. "That's the trouble with paradise," she said. "Snakes live here, too."

They walked back to the cabin, holding hands.

"I'm sorry about what I said to your friends. I'm used to your being on my team, but it seems pretty clear to me whose side you're on now."

"If that's the way you saw what happened—that I was taking sides—I can see why you were angry. But, Travis, there aren't any sides. Paul is my client. I am required by law to do what I can to win his case. That's totally separate from my personal life, and I learned long ago not to mix the two. Maybe I haven't been careful enough to keep our jobs as separate as I should have, and that's a problem we have to deal with. I can't allow our personal differences to interfere with my profession."

He dropped her hand. "In other words, if we find ourselves on different sides of a question, your profession wins and our relationship can go to hell, which is what it seems to have done."

Carmela's hope for a reconciliation disappeared, but she wasn't willing to take all the blame. "Isn't that exactly how you feel when you discover your ethical duty as a police officer interferes with your obligations to me?"

"How can you say that when I just gave you the information about Stokes's military discharge?"

"Okay. We both know that was over the line. You did choose to help me instead of abiding by your code. However, I suspect you did it because you thought it was right and would protect children, rather than because you had an obligation to me. I admire you for that."

"Yet when I tell two guys off for doing something that may cause you to lose a case—when I'm trying to protect you—you call it 'butting in.'"

"I'm afraid I was weighing what you said against my understanding of how you feel about gay men. There has to be some middle ground where we can meet to discuss issues we disagree on."

They arrived at the cabin, and Carmela picked up her cup to see if there was a sip left of her drink. Travis looked at his watch. "I doubt there is a middle ground. I'm going back to the lake for an hour. Then I'm ready to go home."

"Can't we finish this discussion?" Carmela's voice was louder than she had intended.

"The only time I've ever won a debate with you, Carmela, was when we were on the same team. Otherwise, you always kick my ass. We're definitely not on the same team this time, and I concede before we start. Have things your way. I'll be back by four o'clock." He threw the truck keys on the table. "You can do the packing this time."

Carmela turned, and with the strength of a high-school softball pitcher, threw her empty cup at him. It hit a tree and splintered in all directions. Travis turned, his eyes wide. "You ought to stick to soccer, Counselor. Cup ball's not your thing." He sauntered off, whistling.

"I hate you, Travis!" Her words spit out in a rush, but Travis paid no attention.

He was happy to hear them, she thought. They would make it easier for him to end their relationship. She spent the next half hour packing their camping gear into the pickup, angry that he hadn't bothered to ask if she was ready to leave—just like a man! The work helped to dissolve the tension that bound her chest muscles. She stared at the vehicle keys and considered driving away, leaving Travis with the unpleasant task of hitching a ride back to town with the men he disrespected, but then decided that was not in her best interest.

With Travis a lost cause, she looked toward the campsite of her client. The only way to get some benefit from this trip was to find out what the two men had decided about their future. If she and Travis were leaving early, she shouldn't wait for them to come and tell her their decision. She pocketed the keys so that Travis couldn't leave without her, and headed up the path.

She found the men lazing in front of a campfire nursing coffee and cigarettes.

"I guess you've already applied sun tan oil," she said.

Jason roared with laughter and Paul grinned. "I'm sure that's supposed to be funny."

"Sorry, I'm not all that good with joke telling. Travis and I have decided to break camp soon, and I wanted to find out what conclusion you'd come to before we leave. Sorry if I'm rushing you."

"That's alright. We've decided." They laughed again as they stumbled over each other's words. Paul continued. "What you said earlier makes sense. I don't want to go to prison. Being separated that long would be torture. So, lofty principles aside, we've decided to face facts. I will not deny in court that I'm gay, but we will stop socializing until the trial is over in order not to support the charge that I've broken my pledge to remain celibate. This time you can trust us." He reached for Jason's hand and placed it on his thigh as they sat silently waiting for her response.

"Good. Travis will be pleased. We both appreciate your help, and I'll do everything I can to win your case." She left, sad that the world of legal battles had won over a man's wish to set an example for the world, and relieved that this one issue was resolved. Why was it so easy for these guys to communicate, and so hard for her and Travis?

Back at the cabin, with the camping gear packed in the truck, Carmela decided she had time for one more hike before Travis quit fishing. However, as she walked down the path, she found it impossible to wipe the events of the weekend from her mind. Their brunch with Paul and Jason had been both a disaster and a success, if that were possible. If the men had hoped to get approval of their plan to live together, they must have been disappointed. She wondered how she could have handled it better. Travis had seen her criticism of his input into the discussion as an insult, which had put an end to whatever hope she had of a reconciliation with him. However, if her goal had been to make progress with her trial preparation, the trip had been a success. She felt more confident that she and her client were communicating well, but her hope that she and Travis could revive their love affair and possible marriage was now doomed for failure.

At the end of the trail, she was relieved to see that peace among the animals still existed, and there was no sign of the snake. The cattle and horses were stirring from their afternoon naps, their offspring nursing or playing tag in the meadow. The deer herd had disappeared. Carmela's pain began slowly dissolving. She had never been one to allow losses to take over her view of life. What she couldn't have, she had learned to live without. As she stared at the valley, she summoned the will to return to the world she had inhabited during Travis's marriage. She had lost her parents and lived; she had lost her best friend when he married another woman and lived; she had lost her grandparents and lived. She could live without Travis again, if that's how it had to be. She mentally waved goodbye to the occupants of Eden and went back to the cabin.

Travis didn't speak when he returned but picked up the wrapped sandwich waiting for him on the table.

"Want a beer?" Carmela asked, as friendly as she could muster. He surveyed the area and saw that their supplies were packed in the truck, ready to leave. He walked to the ice chest and chose his own, popped the lid, and sat down at the table, staring at the lake.

Silence was not something Carmela was good at living with. "I talked to Paul and Jason. They agree with you that they should hold off making their relationship public."

"Did they come down here again?"

"No. I walked up to their cabin. You were right about my need to get that matter settled before I go any further preparing for trial."

Travis turned from the peaceful view of the lake and stared at her. "Is that an apology?"

"An apology for what? Telling you that I'm the one who has to make decisions related to my trial? I still believe that, and I don't apologize for saying it."

The campsite was quiet except for the chatter of magpies, hopping on the perimeter, waiting for the campers to leave so they could scavenge the crumbs from Travis's sandwich. He stood and tossed the napkin into the sack of trash in the pickup. "Let's go."

She stared out the truck window on the way home, silently criticizing Travis for overtaking a sheriff's van that may have been going five miles under the speed limit. If they stopped him for speeding, she was sure all he would have to do would be to show his police badge. He probably wanted to do it, to show off his power. She smiled. She bet she could talk her way out of ticket without that badge.

As the truck sped ahead, she felt herself withdrawing further from the battle with Travis. By this time next year, she promised herself, she would have forgotten him. He dropped her off, helped unload the camping equipment, and left without speaking. She watched as he gunned the engine and disappeared, exactly as her parents had done. So much for them. So much for Travis.

Chapter Twenty-Eight

While Carmela and Travis were at Mirror Lake, Marvin had returned to the site where he'd scouted the large buck throughout the summer; he bagged him with one shot. His triumph was overshadowed when he returned to town and learned in the Sunday morning newspaper that the police were expanding their interviews of "persons of interest," in the case of alleged sexual abuse of a fifteen-year-old girl in Las Haciendas, reported last month. Marvin knew he was one of those, and in a panic, he informed Lucille that he had to get out of town for a while. He quickly stuffed a small bag with a change of clothes and toilet articles.

"You tell Cody when you see him that I've gone out of town to find work, but I'll be back. Tell him not to worry and to stick with what we talked about."

Lucille stared. "What did you talk about? What did Cody tell you?"

"It doesn't matter. The main thing is for him to be a man. You tell him that."

"I don't understand, Marvin. Why are you leaving?"

"Didn't you read the story about that girl up at Las Haciendas who reported a rape last month? It was all over the front page. Nobody's named, but I can tell from the story it has to be Brooke Whitney. She rides up at the stables, so I'll be the one they're after. The police may be out here tomorrow to question me about it, seeing as how I used to work there. I'm being blamed for everything bad that's happened at that place. I can't afford to wait around till someone figures out the girl is lying."

"What do you mean, the girl is lying? How do you know her? What is she lying about?"

"She was messing around with one of the boys who kept his horse up there, and what if she's pregnant? I figure the police will be looking at everybody who had anything to do with that place." He picked up her purse and dumped the contents on the table, taking all the money from her billfold. "Is this all you got?"

"You can't take that, Marvin. That's my whole month's check. Where are you going? Take your credit card."

"I can't use credit cards. I might as well tell them where I'm going. You must have enough stuff in the pantry to last a month. Plan to wire me some more money next time you're paid, in case I don't find a job right away. I'll let you know when I find work. Hurry up."

"Marvin, this is crazy. Why are you running if you're innocent? I need you here."

"We don't have time to argue about it, Lucille. I can't take my truck—they'd catch me before I got to Raton. You just drop me off at the gas station out by the freeway, and I'll hitch a ride east."

"You've got this all figured out, haven't you? Without even talking to me!"

He hurried to the door. "I'll let you know when I get somewhere. Let's go."

Blinking away tears, Lucille replaced the contents to her purse and followed him to the car.

Harry sat waiting for Rosemary to open the door to Carmela's office. He knew he was early, but Rosemary made good coffee, and it was cheaper than Starbucks. He tipped his hat as she pulled into her parking place.

"What are you doing out so early?"

"Just checking in with your boss and looking for a cheap cup of coffee."

Rosemary unlocked the door. "You mean a free cup of coffee. Anything new?"

"That's what I came to find out."

Carmela pulled into the parking lot and came toward them, loaded with her briefcase and the box of research she'd taken to the mountains and never opened. She nodded her head toward her office, and Harry followed her inside.

"I wondered what you learned from Travis on Friday—and if it had anything to do with this morning's article about the police investigation in the Whitney case."

"Well, I don't know much about the rape case. You know I withdrew as the girl's attorney. We'll have to see how it develops. However, what I learned from Travis may help us win this case. And I'm curious as to why you didn't find out that the man received a less-than-honorable discharge from the military. He was caught using his office computer to view child pornography sites."

"He what?"

"That's what I learned from Travis. Stokes could be the perpetrator we need to win our case."

"Holy Moses! How did I miss that?"

"I don't know, but follow up. We may have missed other stuff. I hear they're bringing Marvin in for questioning."

Harry pushed himself out of the chair and ambled toward the door. "I'll talk to Travis again—see what evidence they find in the house. It may take another meeting between you guys to get this thing settled. See you later."

"Harry! Travis is no longer willing to pass along information, so stop talking to him."

"Is that an order?"

"It is. Get your information some other way."

Across town, PT and Travis left headquarters, headed for the home of Marvin Stokes, carrying a warrant for his arrest in case he refused to come in willingly to discuss his activities as the manager of Las Haciendas Stables. Voluntary interrogation would be a routine endeavor if Stokes had an attorney or was dumb enough to agree to proceed without an attorney, but they never expected things to go without a hitch. They also carried another warrant to search for evidence incident to that arrest.

When they arrived, a pickup was parked in the driveway, which was a good sign. "Maybe he hasn't left for work," PT said. "His wife will probably be here, too." She knocked on the door, and it was opened by a man too young to be Marvin Stokes.

"Who you looking for?" he asked.

"A Mr. Marvin Stokes or his wife, Lucille Stokes. Are they here?"

"No. They were gone when I got up this morning. I guess they're at work."

"Is that his truck out front?"

The man looked surprised and pushed the door further open to view the driveway. "Yeah." He threw up his hands. "I don't know what's going on."

"What's your name?"

He hesitated. "Rusty. Rusty Thompson. Lucille's my sister."

"Do you live here?"

"I've just been here while I looked for work. I'm moving out this week."

"Found a job or leaving town?"

"A job. I'm working at McDonald's."

Travis held out his card with the warrant to search the home. "Is it alright if we come in? We have an order to search the home, even if Mr. Stokes isn't here."

Rusty paused but spent little time looking at the warrant. He pulled the door open and Travis stepped inside.

Both officers placed their hands near their guns as they entered the home. PT stayed near Rusty while Travis made a quick sweep through the house, looking for Marvin or Lucille, picking up mail that lay unopened on the hall table, bills, and a checkbook.

"Marvin won't be happy about this," Rusty said.

"You know where he is?"

"Nope. He was here last night."

As they proceeded through the bedrooms, PT noted that Cody's room was unoccupied, with all his toys in place. A cot in the room, which Rusty admitted he was sleeping on, was unmade; clothes were piled on chairs or the floor. The master bedroom appeared to have been vacated in a hurry— the bed still unmade, a man's clothing scattered as if discarded hurriedly. PT searched underneath each bed and pulled a locked overnight bag from beneath the king-sized bed. She shook it and determined it was filled with papers worth investigating.

As the officers left, carrying items they'd confiscated, PT handed Rusty a card with her telephone number. "Give this number to Mr. Stokes or his wife, and tell them to call us as soon as possible."

Rusty nodded and watched as the officers retreated.

Travis sat musing before he started the vehicle. "Let's park up the street for a while. They may be back if they went out for breakfast. Then we'll swing by headquarters before we go to the library. Why don't you call the library now to find out whether the woman's at work, before we waste a trip. She could have left town with her husband."

Chapter Twenty-Nine

Lucille Stokes pushed a cart half-filled with returned books down a cramped aisle in the history section of the community college library. Her hands shook, and she had trouble focusing on the letters and numbers she must follow to find the correct space for each book. Rusty had just called and informed her that the police were on their way to the library to talk to her about Marvin's disappearance. As she worried about what to do and say, she reached up to place a well-worn *History of New Mexico* on the almost-empty shelf and found herself face to face with Pastor Morrison. Surprised, neither spoke. The history book fell sideways and both reached to lift it upright.

"Sorry," Paul said and hurried back to the carrel where he had been writing.

Lucille looked toward the checkout desk. Maybe the pastor would give her advice on what to tell the police. She followed him and sat in an adjacent carrel.

"Please, can I talk to you?"

Paul was speechless. Carmela had made it clear to him that he should have no contact with Cody or his family. Did she also mean that he could not talk to them if they contacted him? It was too late to worry about that.

"My brother just called and said the police are on their way here to talk to me. Marvin ran off this morning because he thought they were going to arrest him for a rape that happened up where he worked. I don't know what's going on."

"I can't help you, Lucille. I'm not even supposed to talk to you."

Tears filled her eyes. "I'm sure what Cody said about you isn't true. If he raped that girl, he could have abused Cody, also. If he did, he'd want to put the blame somewhere else."

"But why me?"

Lucille blushed. "Marvin's always resented the fact that I go to you for counseling when I need help. He accused me of loving you more than him. He seemed happy that Cody accused you of hurting him. Later, when I had time to think about it and tried to talk to Cody, he said, 'It's a sin to lie, Mamma,' and that's all he'd say." Tears ran down her cheeks and Paul handed her his handkerchief.

"What if they take him away because of this?" She smothered her sobs, unable to continue talking.

"Lucille, I can't tell you how sorry I am to be a part of this. I didn't touch Cody, nor did I ask him to touch me. I don't know what he means by telling you it's a sin to lie. If he said I touched him, it was a lie. When he said someone hurt him, I told him what happened to him wasn't right, but God would understand it wasn't his fault. He didn't become hysterical until I told him I had to talk to you and his stepfather and that I had to report it to the police. Now that he's lied about what happened, maybe he's worried that he's still sinning."

"Because Marvin ran this morning, I'm afraid he must be the one who is guilty, and he could have told Cody to accuse you. I hope the police do catch him if he did that to my child!"

"Lucille, be careful what you say. We don't know for sure who hurt Cody. Let the courts figure it out."

Lucille looked toward the checkout desk, where police officers now stood talking to the librarian. She jumped up and ran for the back door. Paul's handkerchief fell from her lap.

PT paused to pick up the fallen handkerchief and looked at Paul, whose attention was buried in his work. He pretended not to see them as they began searching the aisles for Lucille. PT stopped and asked Paul if he had seen the aide who was stacking books on the shelves. He shook his head, "'Fraid not." He could hear Cody's tiny voice saying, "It's a sin to lie."

PT examined the damp handkerchief she held and then dropped it on the table and walked away. Paul murmured, "God loves us and forgives our sins." He watched as the police left the library, gave them time to drive away, and, clutching his note pad, headed directly to Carmela's office.

Rosemary informed him that he was in luck, since Carmela's court hearing for the hour had been canceled because somebody didn't show. Carmela smiled her usual greeting when he appeared at the door of her office, but instead of sitting, Paul walked to the window and leaned both hands on the window seal, contemplating the beauty of the woodpecker, chipping away at the seed bar hanging from the tree limb.

"Did you come just to watch the birds?"

"No. I'm trying to decide how to tell you of my latest faux pas." He turned. "Perhaps this will do: forgive me, Counselor, for I have sinned."

"Not again! And you were doing so well. Only one dinner, a couple of lunches, and one sunbath on top of the mountain."

"You won't find this one so amusing. At least the court won't."

"What happened, Paul?"

"You told me not to talk to Cody or his family."

"You didn't." Carmela sat shaking her head in disbelief.

"It wasn't my fault. I was sitting in the college library this morning, minding my own business, when Lucille Stokes came over to my carrel. She was weeping. What could I do?"

Carmela held her breath while Paul finished his story, including the information that he had lied to the police officer about not seeing Lucille.

"Your biggest sin may be lying to the police," she replied. "They hate being led up the wrong trail by a lie. If I were you, I'd be thinking of another whopper to get you out of this first one."

"You don't seem to be taking this very seriously."

"The lying, no. Your conversation with Lucille, yes. What else did she tell you?"

"Not much, except she wonders whether Marvin is the guilty person."

Carmela jumped up from her chair. "She what?"

Paul shrugged. "I don't think we can trust what she says. She was angry at her husband for leaving town and for maybe having sex with a teenager. Accusing him of touching Cody inappropriately could be her way of getting back at him."

"And we haven't talked about her attachment to you. Could she be lying to save you from the charges?"

Paul didn't respond to her question.

"It really doesn't matter!" she said. "Her testimony will be powerful evidence in court."

Paul sighed and sat down. "I guess we have to consider her reasons. I did a lot of counseling with Lucille after her first husband was killed and again when she was considering marrying Marvin. I've told you there was talk about me and Lucille—I'm afraid she wanted it to be true. I finally sent her elsewhere for counseling."

"She's obviously not angry with you if she's willing to accuse her husband of falsely charging you. I do worry about her safety, though. If Marvin finds out what she told you. He could harm her—he's known to be a mean drunk."

Carmela began pacing behind her chair. "This whole thing is beginning to make sense. Lucille may be our best witness, but it makes her vulnerable. How can we be sure she remains safe? Let's hope the police find her husband. If you hear from her again, please let me know. There's the possibility she'll take Cody and flee. "

Paul was already on his way to the door, shaking his head. "I don't know how you stay sane in this job."

Carmela grinned. "I don't have time to be insane."

Lucille Stokes rushed from the library to her car and sped toward the foster home where Cody was being kept. She'd pick him up and drive to her parents' farm, only twenty miles away. However, the more she thought about it, the crazier it seemed to try to hide there. It was the first place they would look for her. She slowed down, wondering why she was running. The police probably only wanted to know where they could find Marvin, and she didn't know. If she did, she would tell them. It was because of him that Cody was in foster care. And the bum had practically admitted he was involved with a fifteen-year-old girl where he worked. Why had she ever believed he was a Christian? How stupid had she been! Now she could see that fleeing from the police was a short-term solution to her problems. They probably would have no trouble finding Marvin without her help. What she needed was a way to be sure that she and Cody never fell into his hands again. That meant a long-term plan.

She pulled over, turned around, and headed back to San Carlos. She knew Cody would be frantic if she didn't show up for visitation. She had only two hours until five o'clock to come up with a solution. Gritting her teeth, and knowing she had no right to impose herself further on Pastor Morrison, she concluded she had to resolve this problem by herself. First she had to take Cody out to her parents' house.

Chapter Thirty

Friday morning, Carmela stood by the river walk, waiting for Shetland ponies to trot by at the end of an early morning parade down Sanbusco Street. A homeless man sat on the end of a concrete bench, alternately watching the parade and the clear water splashing over the rocks in the stream. It was a favorite spot of Carmela's when she found time to meditate.

Schools had been dismissed so that children and teachers, dressed in cowboy costumes, could skip and dance for five blocks to the music of school bands and military honor guards. Senator Manny Chavez, the mayor, and members of the city council had waved to the crowd from vintage cars, followed by horses and riders competing for best-costume prizes.

Chavez had just been re-elected, and cheers from the crowd indicated that he had been a popular choice. That point had been made in the morning paper, along with information that he had asked the mayor to support a special parade next spring for the local Gay Pride organization. The mayor had refused to nod his approval, and there was speculation that the mayor was misreading the local sentiment in the community, which seemed to be more open-minded.

Carmela felt some relief that the issue had even come up in the local news. It could only help in the search for a jury pool that might be unbiased about a gay minister. As the parade ended, Carmela dropped a dollar bill in the outreached hand of the bench rider, crossed the street, and hurried to her office. Rosemary and Harry sat on the office portal, nursing cups of coffee.

"Did you see the parade?" Rosemary asked.

"I didn't see much of it. I came late and got caught on the other side of the street, so I couldn't get to the office. I stood there, jealous, knowing you two had the best seats in town."

"Harry's been entertaining me with tales of his grandfather's military service years and years ago. The soldiers rode horses back then."

Carmela smiled at the childlike wonder in Rosemary's voice. Oh, to be young again. However, the difference in their perspectives on history might not be rooted in age. Only seven years older than her secretary, she had always been fascinated with New Mexico's history, including tales about the National Guard. A cavalry unit was not news to her.

Harry chuckled and followed her inside. He wandered around, surveying her law library, while Carmela unpacked her briefcase and poured cups of coffee.

"So, why are you working this holiday?" he asked.

"I can't believe the town is closed down all day for a rodeo parade. Only San Carlos would think of such a thing. Anyway, Rosemary wants an extra day off next week so she agreed to come in today, to catch up on filing before she leaves."

"What new leads do you have for me?"

"Have we followed up on Dr. Barkley's patients who were also Marvin Stokes's lady friends? And did you find out whether Cody Vernon was ever one of his patients? If so, how often did he see him, and what for?"

"Any special reason?"

"I want a list of every person who has had access to the kid's body for the past few months, including family members, teachers, doctors—you name it. We need to take a good look at them. Pedophiles come in all shapes and sizes."

Harry scratched his head. "Okay. So you think it wasn't Marvin who abused the kid?"

"I didn't say that. If we get Lucille to testify to what she told Paul, he's our man. But she's not reliable. And I don't want someone else to escape scrutiny because we're so sure we've got Marvin. What if he didn't do it? We'll be left high and dry."

"This case is getting complicated. Maybe I should raise my fees."

"You know who divvies up the office income around here. Talk to Rosemary."

Carmela searched in her little black book and jotted Glorietta's name and telephone number on a piece of paper. She handed it to Harry. "This is the Whitney's housekeeper. I understand that if there's a connection between Marvin Stokes and Brooke Whitney, she will know about it. You may have trouble getting her to talk, but she knows everything that goes on in that house. She keeps a close eye on Brooke, and you can probably get more information from her than her mother. See what she has to say about Brooke's sexual escapades, if any."

Harry nodded and pocketed the address.

"While you're doing that, we need to add Cody's best friend, Lonnie Scarborough, to the potential witness list. If Cody told Lonnie that Stokes touched him, the jury will believe it. If necessary, I'll talk to the parents and see if they'll agree to let me talk to him. He may want to help Cody. The DA will object, of course, because of the kid's age, but I believe I can get the court's approval. I'll put his name on the witness list and take it up with the court."

Rosemary cautiously announced over the intercom, "Troy Leader is here. He doesn't have an appointment, but he thinks you might see him."

Harry stood, saluted the boss, and ambled out the back door.

"Send him in," Carmela said and moved to the office door, praying this was a friendly visit, not a legal problem. They hadn't met since her embarrassing behavior at the bunkhouse.

"How nice to see you," she said, but he failed to smile.

She wished they could sit in the comfortable chairs by the window, but since his business might require the distance of a desk between lawyer and client, she motioned him to sit in front of her desk. He laid the snapshot of the young couple standing by their van in front of her.

Reluctant to look at it, she stared at him instead.

"I figure it's more yours than mine."

Carmela picked it up, afraid to believe that this was really Savanna and Buck Jared. "What makes you think so?"

"That night at the ranch, I was shaken by the comparison of your parents to this picture of mine. I've suspected ever since I joined the army that their name was not really Leader, and that there was something screwy, as you hinted, about my birth family. The government had trouble finding their records. I asked Tony for a few days off last week and started hitting the pueblos around the state. I wound up in the mountains east of Taos where the commune used to be. A few stragglers remain. I found an old grandmother who remembered my family. Her story is that a young Indian woman, Rosita Herrera, showed up at the commune one night, saying she was the victim of a rape at the Taos Indian Pueblo several miles east. Buck and Savanna volunteered to take her into their home. Free love was part of the movement from the beginning of those days, and this old woman says Buck had been pressuring Savanna to let him add another wife to their home for a long time. Granny said Savanna told her Buck wanted more children, and that she was unable to get pregnant after your birth." Troy's eyes lowered to slits and a muscle kept jumping near his jaw.

"Rosita died in childbirth, eight months later. I was that baby. It seems pretty obvious from that picture that I look like Buck. I'm haunted by the idea that he may have been the one who impregnated her even before the marriage."

"I'm so sorry," Carmela whispered and picked up the picture. "I loved my mom and dad. I was a little afraid of him, but I think he loved me, too. I never knew why they stopped coming back to Grandpa's and Grandma's to see me, and I wasn't able to find them after I got old enough to search. How did you find out their real name?"

"I discovered they changed their names to Angel and Marcus Leader, which were of Indian origin, when I was born. Old Grannie said they were afraid the Indian government would take me away if they discovered I was Indian and the parents weren't. "

"Could the name change be why they quit coming to see me?"

"I suspect so. They were protecting their new family. The Indians were very strict about not letting their blood children be adopted. Too many mothers went off the pueblo or rez to have their babies and then sold them to white people for adoption. The tribes often stole them back."

"But you said Buck might be your father."

"That's true, but still—he wasn't Indian."

"And you haven't been able to find them?"

"There's one more thing I have to tell you," Troy said. "Records show Angel and Marcus Leader were killed in a car wreck two years after I left home."

The room was so quiet they could hear the wind outside.

Troy searched Carmela's sad expression. "If you don't want the picture, I'll keep it." He slipped it into his billfold. "I don't know how to feel about what they did. I'll never know what really happened between the adults. Grannie said Rosita lived happily with them until I was born, and as I said before, she died in childbirth. I grew up thinking Savanna was my mother."

"Have you traced your blood relations?"

"I'm going back to my mother's pueblo to see if I can trace that line a little further. Her folks may have pursued her disappearance."

"Troy, it looks like we could be blood relations—we should have DNA testing. Then we'd know for sure."

Troy shook his head. "Do you really want to know?"

"Of course I do. I've been looking for my parents for years. I didn't dream I might have siblings." Tears began flowing down her cheeks, and as she cried, she stood and moved into his arms. "Come home with me. We have a lot of catching up to do."

The two talked far into the night, and Carmela became convinced that the people Troy described as his parents were indeed Savanna and Buck Jared. He had Buck's features. Savanna had taught him to tell fortunes. The story was mind boggling, but it gave her a sense of closure on the loss of her parents. What she needed now was to go back to the area where they had lived when Troy was born, but that trip would be impossible until after the trial was completed.

Troy left, promising to send her pictures and updates on each discovery he made.

Chapter Thirty-One

"Did you hear?" PT was eager to share the latest news with Travis. "Marvin Stokes was caught in Denver this weekend after a truck driver, who had stopped there for the night, saw on television that Stokes was under investigation and there was a warrant for his arrest. He recognized the photo as the man he picked up at Allsup's here in San Carlos. It took only a little while for the police to find him at a homeless shelter. He's been in jail there, fighting extradition. He lost, and we're expecting him back in a day or two."

Travis smiled, and PT was relieved to see it. He seemed more like his old self.

"Have we gotten the reports back on whether the evidence we picked up at his house showed that he'd been dealing in porn?" he asked.

"Other than the porn magazines, no. It takes a while."

"How about the lab tests concerning the girl's rape kit?"

PT shook her head. "Only that she was sexually active. We may hear something more at the briefing this morning, though." She looked directly at him. "Travis, it's good to have you back. It was like you'd disappeared into a dark and gloomy place, and you wouldn't let anybody in. Maybe all you needed was a long rest."

"Maybe." Travis wondered how long it would take before the whole department knew he was seeing a psychiatrist. He followed PT to the briefing room, which was chaotic, with desks scattered every which way to form talking areas. The coffee and donut line was long, the place noisy with jokes and storytelling. The walls were papered with missing person flyers, announcements, and wanted posters. A dilapidated Formica table pushed against the wall was piled with old training books and outdated memos.

The din settled as the shift supervisor banged for quiet. He closed his file when the police chief entered, and silent attention spread through the room. Travis listened carefully while the chief praised the work they'd been doing and offered help in the cases that needed a little push. At the end, he asked Travis and PT to come to his office after the briefing. They sneaked looks at each other, and PT shrugged her shoulders.

The chief was blunt. "Guys, I'm worried about these pedophile cases. Marvin Stokes is one of the suspects in the Whitney girl's rape case, and the DA says he'll be questioned in his stepson's abuse case. He ran on Monday but was caught in Denver, and he's being returned here tomorrow. Obviously, if he's found guilty of child abuse, it will leave the pastor innocent and make it harder for us to win the jail case against him." He turned to PT. "What kind of evidence did we get at Stokes's house?"

"We've bagged and filed the porn magazines, but we haven't gotten the report back on what was found in the documents we confiscated."

Travis chimed in. "The crime lab report is inconclusive about whether the Whitney girl was the victim of rape. She was dating a sixteen-year-old boy, and if he's involved, that isn't rape."

"Let me know if anything new develops. These are both hot cases, and we don't want to come out burned." The chief looked at Travis. "Glad to have you back, Captain. You deserved a break."

Travis thanked him and followed PT back to the office. He scanned his clipboard for the assignments in his district and covered the information from the "hot sheet."

"Look at this," he said. "Lucille Stokes didn't return her son to the foster home after visitation. Her name has been added to the arrest list. We need to bring her in. Where do you suppose we'll find her?"

"Let's run by her home first. It doesn't make sense for her to leave. She needs her job. Wonder if she has a lawyer?"

"Maybe not. That probably won't happen until she's arrested." Travis looked at his watch. "Call the courthouse and see if she has an attorney."

The call took only a minute. "Ross Barney. Wonder how she could afford him?"

"He does a lot of pro bono work for people he thinks are being railroaded. And he belongs to a Catholic church, too, so he may be familiar with the pedophile cases they're fighting. He won't let her go to jail. Let's drive out to the house."

They headed out to her residence, with little hope that she would be there. A bigger surprise was the sight of the old Karmann Ghia belonging to Harry Rodriquez. Travis pulled up beside it.

"Dadburn," Travis said. "I wonder where that man gets his leads."

PT eyed him, to see how far she could push. "Maybe from his boss, who gets hers from a certain policeman she knows."

"Are you accusing me of leaking information about police investigations again? I'm getting a little tired of that."

"You should be careful with your pillow talk. That's all I'm saying."

"It's none of your business, but for your information, there's no pillow talk going on."

"Oh, I'm sorry."

Travis slammed the car door and headed for the house. PT passed him and knocked on the door. Harry greeted them but didn't invite them in.

"We're looking for Lucille Stokes."

"Sorry, you just missed her."

"Did she take the kid?"

"What kid?"

"Stop playing dumb, Harry—although that's probably not hard for you."

"Sorry, she wasn't home when I arrived. Her brother said she left and didn't say when she'd be back." He scratched his head. "As for the kid, he's in foster care. I thought you knew that."

"You probably know she took him out and didn't return him. I want to make sure she isn't leaving town. We're here to bring her in, and if you interfere with our job, you could be next on our list."

"If it helps, Captain, I hear Ms. Stokes has an attorney. Why don't you contact him?"

Warm blood flushed Travis's face. Getting advice from Harry Rodriquez was tantamount to admitting that the private investigator knew more than the police department. In this case, it seemed he did. He turned on his heels and nodded to PT. "Let's go."

Across town, Dr. Barkley shuffled through a stack of patient files with blue stars beside the names. These patients were women who chose to go to private doctors instead of the county health department for treatment of

STDs. They came in, usually angry enough to kill their contacts—sometimes husbands or their best friends' husbands—people they trusted. Each patient who tested positive was required to name all her sexual contacts so they could be notified and encouraged to have themselves tested for the disease. The information was rarely complete, but it usually carried the names of men they now hated.

Complying with Harry's request to look for Marvin Stokes's name on any of the lists, Jason was surprised to see the name of Bettina Whitney on top of the stack. Surely he would have remembered that socially prominent name. He checked the date of her appointment. February 20th. He had been skiing in Aspen for two weeks at that time. Claude Franco's office had covered his patients, and he had to admit he'd paid no attention to the files of new patients who didn't return to his own office for a follow-up appointment. Notes on Bettina's file said she had transferred to Franco's office. He was even more surprised to find Marvin Stokes named as the only man, other than her husband, that she had slept with.

Marvin Stokes and Bettina Whitney! He threw the file on his desk and paced the floor, unsure of what to do next. There was no way he could reveal to Paul or his attorney that Marvin Stokes had sex, not with fifteen-year-old Brooke Whitney, but with her mother, Bettina. Her medical file was protected by the doctor/patient privilege, which could only be broken by a court order. That was a task for attorneys, not doctors. By leaking a patient's file, he would be violating the federal Hippa law that protects healthcare information, and he could lose his medical license. By refusing to release the file, he was withholding information that would be of benefit to Paul's defense. There was no question which choice he would make, even with the knowledge that he was risking his doctor's license.

He placed Bettina's file conspicuously on the printer and left the office. He drove past Cowboys, searching for Harry's ancient Karmann Ghia. Inside, he sidled up to Harry at the bar and dropped his office keys into Harry's pocket. He told the bartender he only had time for a quick one, because his dippy nurse had called and said she failed to lock the office door, thinking he was still in the lab. She lived thirty miles outside of town, so he'd have to go back to lock the door himself.

Harry was puzzled by the poke in his ribs and the feel of keys dropping inside his pocket. Dr. Barkley otherwise ignored him, while he tapped idly on the bar waiting for his drink. Harry fingered the keys, wondering why the doctor needed him to lock or unlock that office door. A message was hidden there somewhere. He dropped a five-dollar bill beside his half-empty glass and left the bar.

In the doctor's office, he put on rubber gloves, surveyed the office, and moved to the printer, where he briefly reviewed Bettina's report. He made a quick copy and laid the original back on the doctor's desk.

When he returned to the bar twenty minutes later, the space beside Jason was still vacant, and the doctor was moving his empty glass in a circle of wetness on the bar. Harry held the key beneath the counter, wiped it clean of finger prints, rolled it in a napkin, and pushed it near Jason's glass.

"Give me a long one," he said to the bartender. "I've finished my work for the day."

Jason deposited the napkin in his pocket and left the bar. Harry could hardly wait to deliver the information he'd gathered to Carmela.

Chapter Thirty-Two

Harry sat chatting with Rosemary when Carmela arrived at the office the next morning. They heard her coming in the back door, and Rosemary hurried to fix her boss the usual cup of coffee with cream.

"Harry's here," she said, splashing coffee into the saucer as she set it in front of Carmela. They both yelled in dismay.

Harry followed Rosemary to the office and leaned against the door-jamb. "What's going on in here?"

"Just cleaning up Rosemary's mess. It's a good thing she's a secretary. She'd never make it in the restaurant business."

"Be careful, or I'll let you get your own next time." Rosemary flipped out of the office, closing the door behind her.

"What's the latest?" Carmela asked.

Harry handed her the report from Dr. Barkley.

"My God. Where did you get this?"

"I have friends in high places."

"It's hard to believe Marvin was sleeping with Ms. Whitney. He wouldn't be sleeping with both of them, would he? He could have infected Brooke. The rape test should show that. We still don't have it."

"Maybe we're back to asking what started the fight between the Whitneys. I suspected it had something to do with their daughter. Would never have dreamed the wife was involved with Stokes."

Carmela grimaced. "It changes the whole complexion of our case. If it turns out Marvin didn't rape Brooke, it will be harder to prove he abused Cody. I've been banking on finding the person who abused him, and Marvin was the best bet. It looks more doubtful now."

"He still could have done it. A sex addict is potentially a sex offender, and many of them don't discriminate among their victims. I think Cody's mother is ready to cooperate. I was at her house yesterday when Travis and his partner came to arrest her. When I got there, she was packing to leave town, and I told her she ought to talk to her lawyer before she ran. I was going to take her, but I decided I should stay and delay the police as much as possible. She headed over to Ross Barney's office just before Travis arrived to pick her up. I thought she'd gotten away, but old 'eagle-eyes Hawk' caught on to what we were planning and followed me to Barney's office."

"He told me about that."

"You've got a smart man there, Carmela. I'm not convinced he'll make the greatest husband, but knowing you, I suspect you can tame him."

"Harry, you should stick to investigating. You're not so good at match-making. Travis and I are not seeing each other anymore."

Harry frowned. "That's too bad. His wife's death was a big blow. He needs all the support he can get."

Carmela stared at Harry, a little surprised at his concern for Travis. "He's a big boy. He can take care of himself."

"Yeah, he's tough. What people don't understand is that behind that shield of toughness is a weakness—policemen need support when they're hit with emotional problems. It's one thing to be a bruiser on the football field, something else when you're hit with the death of someone you loved. All the air gets knocked out of you. Some guys never get up when it happens."

The scene of her first meeting with Travis flashed across Carmela's mind. She'd knocked him flat and seen him recover many times when he was knocked flat. But Harry might be right. This one she didn't understand, maybe because in the past she and Travis had supported each other when one was knocked down. She had to admit, while he was gone, she found herself depressed more often than usual, turning down invitations from friends with whom she used to socialize.

"So did Travis arrest her?"

"No. The attorney had talked her into returning the kid to the foster home and he went with her to the police department for questioning. They told her Marvin had been found and was being returned to San Carlos that evening, and they no longer needed her."

"So the police told her when Marvin was being returned?"

"Yes. That's the way I heard it."

"Is there anything else we need to discuss?" she asked Harry.

"I went out to the Scarboroughs, and the parents let me talk to Cody's little friend. He denied having talked to Cody about anything, but I had a feeling he was leaving something out."

"Too bad."

"Not too bad for the kid. He shouldn't be mixed up in this mess. I'm still trying to get verification of the real reason for Marvin Stokes's marine corps dismissal. I'll let you know when I find it."

"Thanks, Harry. And thanks for being nice to the Scarborough kid."

"I also talked to Glorietta. She was pretty closed mouthed. Ms. Whitney stayed within hearing distance, which may have influenced her some, but I got the feeling she felt the girl needed some protection. I couldn't find out who from. I need to talk to her when her boss isn't around."

He left, walking past Rosemary's desk without his usual affectionate goodbye. She looked up. "I hope you're taking that gloom with you. We don't need any more around here."

He waved and left without speaking.

As the sun set, San Carlos County sheriff's deputies, weary from their six-hour drive from Denver, parked near the back entrance of the jail. Both—anxious to unload their passenger and get home to a hot meal and their families—noticed with some irritation that the local TV station had sent a cameraman to record the event. As they pulled Marvin Stokes from the rear seat of the van, they paid no attention to the woman who walked over from a car parked nearby.

"Lucille!" Marvin's hoarse voice shocked them. They froze as a shot rang out and Marvin Stokes fell at their feet, bleeding from a hole in his forehead.

Chapter Thirty-Three

Images of a bloody corpse lying at the feet of shocked policemen greeted Carmela from the local news channel as she sat down for breakfast the following morning. She reached to turn to another station, when the name Marvin Stokes stopped her. She sat at attention, searching the screen in hopes the information was wrong. The last Carmela knew, Marvin Stokes was in a Denver jail awaiting extradition. His wife had an attorney to protect her interests, yet the news report stated that she had shot her husband. Why would she have wanted him dead? Because she'd learned that he had raped a fifteen-year-old girl? Or could it be she'd learned that he abused her son?

Carmela dropped her cup of coffee into a saucer. She had spent weeks gathering evidence and preparing for a cross-examination of Marvin Stokes concerning the tape-recorded description of what he saw—or didn't see—on the mountainside, his military record, and his contacts with the Whitney family. That work would be useless now, but she saw a greater benefit from his death—*if* it was true that Lucille had proof that he was the abuser. The court would surely dismiss the case against Paul, and even if it were not dismissed, she felt confident that, with his wife's testimony, a reasonable jury would come to the conclusion that Marvin Stokes, not Paul Morrison, had sexually abused Cody Vernon.

From another angle, she could renew her motion to the court that Stokes's tape recording of the scene on the side of the mountain should be barred from use by the state because the person who recorded it was not available to testify at trial. And since his deposition hadn't been taken, Carmela had had no opportunity to cross-examine him.

However, if Lucille didn't have proof regarding her husband's abuse, the case just got tougher. Without Stokes alive, how could she convince a jury that he was the culprit?

The newspaper article said his wife shot him between the eyes. The question was: why did Lucille Stokes want her husband dead? Carmela refilled her coffee cup as she mentally sorted through the files in her brain, much like the process of searching the documents in her computer read-out of the case. The clicking stopped when it came to the Whitney health report obtained from Dr. Barkley. Bettina's list of sexual contacts included Marvin Stokes, which meant that Marvin's contact included his wife and Brooke's mother, Bettina Whitney. Would Brooke's rape kit reveal another of his contacts? And would another victim be Cody Vernon? If so, that news would make any mother want to kill her husband.

But where would Lucille have gotten that information? Had Harry been talking out of school? It wasn't like him, but the investigation must start with him.

The TV news switched to the weather report, so Carmela turned it off and pushed cold toast between her teeth, chewing viciously. Every time she got a break in this case, someone kicked the props out from under her. Given all the twists and turns, she had to prepare for a scenario where Lucille had no proof of his guilt. This latest event, the murder of Marvin Stokes, was more likely to be a burial rite than a resurrection for her trial.

The question of why Lucille Stokes chose to kill her husband had to be answered. Would the answer reveal that he had abused his stepson? Would Carmela be able to get that evidence in front of the jury? If she pursued that avenue, would her case fall apart if the jury sided with the victim of the gunshot wound instead of the wife who pulled the trigger?

She went to the whiteboard in her workroom to map a pattern of links among prominent characters who had played a part in the action. She put Lucille's name in the middle of the chart. Who were her contacts? Carmela drew a line to Harry's name. He had revealed to Carmela more than one conversation with the wife.

She drew another line to the name of Reverend Paul Morrison, Lucille's primary counselor, with documented contacts even though he had been warned not to have contact with her.

She drew two more lines to the names of Travis Hawk and Bettina Whitney. She began listing the information that each person had, which might have precipitated Lucille's fury. She added a red line on the path that led from Harry to Lucille. Had Harry revealed to Lucille that her husband would be in a van arriving at the San Carlos county jail Saturday evening, not knowing her anger might lead to murder? If so, where had he gotten that information? From Travis? From PT? And why hadn't he reported his findings directly to her? Carmela felt cold sweat dripping between her breasts; her hands were moist. Surely Travis would not have set in motion an action intended for the sole purpose of doing away with the one witness who might allow her to win Paul's case. She wiped her hands and placed his name beside Harry's, in the middle of the web.

What about Bettina Whitney? Any reasonable juror should be able to connect the adulterous relationship between her and Lucille's husband to his murder. She drew another red line between Lucille, Harry, and the Whitneys.

A less obvious connection led to Paul and Dr. Barkley, who initially had revealed to Harry the adulterous relationship of Bettina's husband. Paul reported consultations with Lucille concerning her marital problems, meetings which the church secretary said led to gossip among the parishioners. If Lucille had a crush on Paul, was that enough reason to want Marvin dead? To Carmela's knowledge, Paul would have no access to the police department's plan to transfer Marvin back to San Carlos. Nor would Jason. And, for heaven's sake, neither of them would pass information to Lucille that might hurt her or lead to a confrontation between the couple. Nevertheless, Carmela drew blue lines from Paul's and Jason's names toward Lucille's.

As she laid aside her colored markers, Carmela sighed. Her work had shown only one thing. Practically everyone involved in this case had the information and a possible reason for wanting Marvin Stokes dead, and an angry wife was the logical person to carry out the act. Travis Hawk was the connection to the police department where the information about his return was documented.

She returned to her desk and closed her files. She must talk to Harry. If necessary, she would also talk to Travis. She shrugged, admitting to herself that they had been acting like two immature kids. She could not let their personal affairs interfere with winning her case.

That evening she sat with Harry at the local lawyers' watering hole, drinking Hornitos. "Harry, this is critical. Did you have any idea Lucille was going to kill her husband?

"Lord, I didn't know she had killing in her. I guess it's the quiet ones you have to watch out for."

"I'm interested in knowing how she found out the exact time that he was being brought back to San Carlos on Saturday."

Harry shook his head. "Your guess is as good as mine. The press were there too."

Carmela suspected that what they both knew was more than a guess. "Have you talked to Travis this week?"

"Travis?"

She sat looking at him, waiting for an answer.

Harry took a long swig of his drink, his eyes shifting around the room. He cradled his glass in both hands.

"You remember Captain Hawk, don't you?"

Harry didn't bother answering her sarcasm, wondering where this conversation was going. "I ran into the captain yesterday while he was looking for Lucille."

"Did you discuss the fact that Marvin Stokes was being delivered to the San Carlos jail that night?"

"No. I wasn't aware of it at the time."

"Did he mention it to you?"

"Nope. Had no reason to."

Carmela relaxed. "Don't worry about it."

Harry leaned forward, resting his arms on the table, and looked straight into Carmela's eyes. "What's going on with you and Travis?"

"What do you mean?"

"Don't play coy with me, Carmela. You'd have to be blind to pretend things are alright between the two of you."

Carmela sat looking at Harry, her cheeks sucked in between her teeth. Moments passed and she relaxed, knowing he deserved an answer. "I'm not sure," she said, "but I suspect his wife's death set into motion some vile disturbance, and the same poison is killing our relationship. On the one hand, he is loving, thoughtful, caring. On the other hand, he's uncommunicative and controlling. He's tried to accept my defending homosexuality, but it turns out to be more than he can stomach."

"I'm sorry as hell, but the man should understand that your job is to defend your client, no matter who he is. How is the minister holding up?"

"He's doing okay. Just wants this to be over."

"How will Stokes's death affect your trial?"

Carmela smiled and shook her head. "Maybe I can turn it to our advantage. I'm hoping the jury will prefer to believe a dead man was guilty—someone they don't have to throw in prison—than a nice preacher who has a clean record."

She returned to the office, satisfied that neither Harry nor Travis had passed on the information that Marvin Stokes was being returned to San Carlos at five o'clock on Saturday.

Chapter Thirty-Four

On Friday, Carmela met Aviva for lunch to compare notes on family cases they shared through Child Protection Services. Her friend arrived, laid a laptop on the chair between them, and gave Carmela a weak smile.

"What's the matter?" Carmela asked.

"I'm worried. What's going on between you and Travis?"

"Not much. Why do people keep asking me that?"

"Carmela, you and I have been friends for years. We can be open with each other. What's going on?"

"Travis and I are at an impasse . . . or it may be over."

"That's what I figured. Tony and I were at the Corral last night, celebrating his birthday, when Travis came in with PT on his arm. They weren't on police business, for sure. Neither was in uniform, and she was wearing a very revealing dress. Both were drinking heavily. They were dancing like—well, you know what I mean. All I can say is, Travis wasn't acting like a man engaged to be married to some other woman."

"Travis is no longer engaged—at least as far as I know."

"Oh, Carmela! I'm so sorry. But why would he rebound to PT? She's married, isn't she?"

Carmela nodded. "Yes—but it's not what you think, Aviva. PT's husband is in Afghanistan. He's okay with having Travis take her out on special occasions while he's gone. And no matter what else I may say about Travis, he's honorable. He wouldn't take advantage of the situation."

"There you go! Making excuses for him again. I wanted to scream at them, but Tony wouldn't let me."

"Good for Tony. This is probably a case that a man understands better than a woman."

Aviva sat back in her chair and stared at Carmela. "Well, what's come over you? You just said you were breaking up with the bum. Now you're defending him."

"No. I'm not on his side. I just understand where he's coming from. He says he married Carolyn after I left, partly to hurt me. That still hurts, and I wonder if his gross behavior with PT in front of you was done for the same reason. He knew you'd tell me."

"I'm sorry."

"Don't be. Our talking is helping me put into words what I've been struggling with since he returned from vacation. I've known there was a serious problem between us, but I haven't been able to admit it."

"You seem so crazy about him, Carmela. Are you sure you aren't making up excuses for why you should split?"

Carmela smiled again. "Could be. Travis and I have developed a physical attraction for each other, which is the best I've ever had. That's hard to give up."

"That will eventually bring you back together."

"No. He obviously doesn't care for me the way I care for him. His love for me didn't keep him from marrying Carolyn. It didn't keep him from turning away after Carolyn died. He doesn't want me on his team anymore." She smiled. "I've been benched."

"I've never thought of you as a bench warmer."

"There. You've defined one of my biggest faults. I'm not satisfied being second on anybody's list. I guess that's why I refuse to fall for his efforts to reconcile."

"You know, Tony's going to be very upset when I tell him what's going on. He'll accuse me of causing the break-up."

"Why? How could you have caused it?"

"Telling tales out of school."

"You won't be the only one. Half a dozen people will tell me they saw Travis and PT together, so don't worry about it."

"I thought you were keeping your relationship a secret."

"Well, maybe only one or two. Harry and Rosemary probably saw them. They'll let me know."

"You should go out and have some fun, too. Chuck is single. Why don't we arrange something with him?"

"Your ranch manager? Maybe someday when I've retired. I can't imagine any sane person wanting to put up with my current professional and personal craziness."

"Think about it. I can't imagine any male *not* wanting to put up with you."

"We've been talking about Travis's emotional problems. I have mine, too, Aviva. I think it began when my parents left me with Grandma and Grandpa. I thought they should love me too much to leave. Obviously they didn't, but I keep looking for someone who does. At the time, I thought school was what I wanted, but deep down, I needed my parents. This whole problem with Travis makes me see that I used his friendship to replace my parent's love. Now, when he rejects me, I just withdraw into a little cocoon. That's where I've been for a while. I'm in the dark, unable to make decisions about where I'm going. On the other hand, I feel independent, happy taking care of myself. Maybe I'll leave San Carlos when this trial is over."

Aviva reached across the table and squeezed Carmela's hand. "It isn't all bad. Remember, beautiful butterflies develop inside a chrysalis and then come out and fly free. You will, too."

"You're such an optimist, Aviva."

"Don't worry, kid. I'm already creating a list of potential replacements for Travis. There must be someone who does body searches as well as he does."

Carmela threw her napkin at Aviva and left.

At home that night, Carmela went through the house collecting all of Travis's remaining paraphernalia, packing it in boxes from the garage. Underwear, tee shirts, and socks he'd left in the laundry room. She left a message on his home phone asking him to come by and pick them up. "Please also leave my house key on the kitchen table." She hoped this was her signal that "over" meant over.

It was midnight when she awoke to find Travis standing beside her bed. "What are you doing here?"

"You told me to come get my things."

"They're downstairs."

"I saw the boxes, but there are some things you've taken from me that I didn't find." He sat on the edge of her bed.

Carmela scooted away and pulled the covers over her shoulders. "What's missing?"

"The rest of my life. You can't deny that we've been like one person from the day you moved here. Losing you is like losing a family member. And it doesn't seem to bother you at all."

"You aren't looking deeply enough, Travis. Don't blame me for what's happened to us since I went to law school. I was devastated when you married Carolyn, and you acted like I didn't exist—a lot like my parents did when they left me here. Lately, you've made it even clearer that I'm not someone you want. And you didn't give me your heart, Travis. If you had, you wouldn't have married Carolyn just because I went off to college. And," her eyes narrowed, "I know about you and PT." She sat up in bed. "I, on the other hand, have not been chasing around since you left."

"No? How about the night you spent with Troy out at the ranch?"

Carmela shook her head. "I didn't spend the night with Troy. Nothing happened while I was there. I was drunk, but he's a gentleman. Which is more than I can say for some people."

Travis stood and threw her house key on the dresser, where it slid to the edge in slow motion and fell to the floor. He left the room, and she heard boxes banging into doorframes as he carried them to his car. She crept downstairs to make sure he'd locked the door after he left. He had.

While the last of autumn leaves fell from the trees, Carmela's house sat like a tomb, a resting place for the dead. Carmela abandoned it for long hours of work, even declining Aviva's invitation to a Thanksgiving dinner. Prissy continued to sit on the fence, spitting at her when she returned after dark, as if she blamed Carmela for her loss. Carmela finally spat back. "Why don't you go live with him, you hussy? You're two of a kind. I hear you at night, flirting with every tomcat who comes around." Prissy ignored her.

Inside, she poured a drink and shook her head. I'm becoming a bitter old maid that even a cat can't love. The drink burned her throat. But this is not the end of my life, she decided. Bella still loves me. She called Aviva and left a message that she would be out to ride tomorrow.

Bella lifted her spirits as no human could. Feeling slightly better on the way home from her ride, Carmela stopped by the office to see what emergencies had arisen while she relaxed at the ranch. A notice from the court announced that jury selection in the Morrison case would begin January 12, 2015.

Chapter Thirty-Five

The month of December was historically a time when little was accomplished at the courthouse. The staff crowded onto the docket all the minor cases that had stumbled through the year, with the intent of starting the new year with the big, serious cases aimed at settling or going to trial immediately. Carmela spent the month preparing witnesses.

January entered as if it were angry at the whole world. A nasty wind whirled snowdrifts across the main highway and county roads, bringing travel on the streets of San Carlos to a standstill during the weekend before the start of *The State of New Mexico vs. Paul Robert Morrison*. Deer, cattle on the BLM grazing range, and wild horses struggled to survive on the mountainside. Old-timers opined that it was the worst storm in the history of the state. Many rural citizens listed in the jury pool were unable to travel to San Carlos. Judge Salazar ordered that jury selection would be delayed until Wednesday, January 14. Rosemary complained that she'd have no fingernails left to chew by then.

The snowstorm was giving Carmela two more days to make sure all her bases were covered. She was delighted when a friend from law school, Mark Gordon, now practicing in Albuquerque, called to encourage her and offered to help with jury selection, which had become one of his specialties. He just happened to have some free time because one of his cases had settled, and he admitted he'd been following her case with jealous interest. They worked late into the night, analyzing the jury questionnaires and discussing the makeup of the potential pool and the types of jurors who should be dismissed or kept.

Another coup came when the national Gay and Lesbian Alliance unexpectedly offered to cover the expenses of Dr. Margery Carter, an expert witness from Columbia University, who came prepared to convince the jury that *gay* was not another word for *pedophile*. Dr. Carter's expertise in the areas of pedophilia, child molestation, and male-male sexual molestation was expected to educate the jury about the research debunking any preconceived opinions that homosexuality and pedophilia were connected.

Carmela enjoyed working with witnesses she had culled from Harry's contacts. He had found church members, coaches, the church secretary, parents, and community leaders who would testify to Paul's reputation for honesty and good works. If the reputation of Marvin Stokes became an issue in the trial—which it could only if the prosecutor made the mistake of introducing information about the tape recording of Paul's and Jason's meeting on the mountain—she had a slew of witnesses who could counter that item with negative testimony about Stokes's character, including his less-than-honorable discharge from the marine corps. Carmela didn't expect the DA to be that stupid.

Finally, Carmela worried about the psychological effect the snow delay might have on the jury pool. Would it create anxiety in some, or exultation in others eager to play an extra two days in a seldom-seen snowstorm of this size in San Carlos? What remnants of these emotional disruptions would enter the jury room and render it more difficult to get a reasoned verdict? Her mind wandered to the scene of the Garden of Eden, high in the Sangre de Christo Mountains, and she wondered how the animals there were faring. No doubt the snake was doing fine, curled in his nest deep in the ground.

The postponement created a bad case of nerves for Carmela. To kill time, she called her hairdresser and asked to have her long, sun-flecked tresses braided and circled around her head, similar to her neighbor who belonged to the Southern Pentecostal Holiness Church. She felt only a little guilt for playing to the jury. She struggled to stop wondering how Travis would like it.

On the morning of jury selection, Rosemary took one look at Carmela's new hairdo and giggled.

"What's so funny?"

"Do you really think the jury won't know you're playing the religious card?"

"How will they know I don't wear my hair this way all the time?"

"Everybody in this town knows how you wear your hair, Carmela."

"What many don't know, however, is that I was sprinkled with wet chard in Whole Foods. Maybe my baptism is just now taking effect."

Harry sat in the waiting room listening to their silly argument. "I'm with Carmela on this issue. The hairdo will sit well with the men on that jury because it will remind them of their mothers or grandmothers, and they won't dare question the truth of what such a woman says. For some, it will remind them of their wise wives, knowing of course, that when night comes, she'll loosen the braids and that hair will come down in all its glory, just for him. "

Carmela smiled. "I didn't realize a mere hairdo might have such an impact on the jury. I think you're both over-reacting."

The door opened and Paul entered to find Rosemary throwing her arms around Carmela. "I'm sorry. You do look fabulous, and if the jury doesn't think so—what do they know?"

Carmela laughed. "Too late to worry about it now." She looked at Paul. "I trust the jury won't punish you for my impulsive choice of a hairdo. Rosemary doesn't like it. If we lose, she says you'll have a legitimate complaint to file against me."

"Do they allow prisoners to file complaints from their prison cell?" His words killed the levity in the room.

Carmela hurried over to Paul and reached for his hand. "You aren't going to prison, my friend. Don't forget, when we walk into that courtroom, you will be surrounded by people just like those who came to hear your Sunday sermons. They are looking for the truth. They believe what you say, because they trust you. I hope they trust me enough that they won't hold my hairdo against you. Together, we have to lead them to the river. Can you help me do that?"

Paul nodded, blinking tears from his eyes. "Yours is a good analogy. Converts trusted me with their lives when I baptized them in the river. Today, I'm trusting you with mine, and the hairdo just might help."

"Remember that the jurors can feel our vibes. They want to be with winners. If we appear confident, they're more apt to be on our side."

Paul straightened his shoulders and nodded, trying to smile. "I'm with you."

"Let's go."

Chapter Thirty-Six

Along line of spectators, masked in knitted scarves and caps, bundled in winter coats against the icy blasts of wind sliding down the Sangre de Christo Mountains, stood outside the courtroom, waiting for the doors to open at 9:00 a.m. Two security officers were caught off guard when the crowd, including international newsmen plus others from around the state, filled the hallway and begged to be admitted. With tight lips, the officers closed the heavy doors and stood together, hands behind their backs, daring the disgruntled crowd to push them aside. Inside the courtroom, selected police officers were assigned the tiresome job of standing guard by the doors, but they agreed that this assignment was better than walking the streets in two feet of snow. The officer in charge reached for his cell phone and called for a backup. If the crowd began to push and someone had to be arrested, they would need help.

"First time we've had to turn people away since the Maesta's murder trial," one of the officers muttered through the side of his mouth. "Who'd have thought the whole town would want to sit in on this one?"

The other officer laughed a deep gargle and coughed to clear his throat. "Well, you know, sex sells, no matter what kind it is. Shoulda' held this trial in the school gymnasium and sold tickets. We'd a made a fortune."

"Makes me wish I'd asked to be assigned inside. How come Juan and Manny got those jobs?"

"They're smarter than we are."

"Hard to argue with that."

"What I don't understand is why people would want to sit all day just to watch 'em pick the jury. They'll hear the same questions over and over, and Lord knows, those that want to stay on the jury will lie where it's necessary, and the others will be honest and they'll get kicked off. That's the way it goes."

"My question is, who in his right mind would want to be on this jury?"

"Anyone that has a strong opinion one way or the other."

"Don't you figure everybody does?"

"From what I hear, the preacher doesn't have a chance of gettin' off. People are mad because so many priests have been getting away with abusing kids in this state, and everybody wants to make an example of this guy."

From inside the courtroom they heard a gavel pound for silence, and the court clerk shouted for everyone to stand. They relaxed, certain that when the Honorable Adam Salazar took his place at the dais, high above the plaintiffs, the defendant, and curiosity seekers, the crowd would calm down. Judge Salazar didn't put up with disruptions and was famous for putting the unruly in the slammer.

The DA and his entourage of assistants filled the chairs at the long table nearest the jury box. Only Carmela, Paul, and Mark Gordon, who would assist in the jury selection, were seated at the defense table.

A low buzz of whispers circled the room. Carmela surveyed the table of the three prosecuting attorneys, and wondered whether her decision to go it alone had been sound, or whether the jury would be swayed by the idea that three lawyers can't be wrong if only one can be found to challenge them.

"You may be seated," the judge said as he settled into his leather chair.

In his opening remarks, the judge explained that seventy people had been called as potential jurors and that only fifteen would be chosen. Three of those would be available, in case one or more of the twelve jurors became ill or could not serve. He explained that the panelist would have the opportunity to claim how serving would be a hardship or that they had a conflict of interest, in which case they would be dismissed. All others would be questioned by counsel and the judge to determine whether they would be accepted or dismissed from the panel. He explained that the procedure to be followed would allow the DA three peremptory challenges, which meant that he could dismiss three potential jurors without stating a reason. Carmela could dismiss five potential jurors without stating a reason. Each side could dismiss any potential juror for a legal cause.

If twelve were not seated from this panel, another round of citizens waiting in the wings would be called.

Carmela watched the body language of each person as the jury boxes filled. As all attorneys knew, the case could be decided by one negative juror who could influence the whole panel. She wanted to find that person and dismiss him or her, without stating a reason. She hoped to find jurors with open, inquiring eyes, not afraid to look at the defendant—jurors interested in seeking the truth, not those with minds made up. Mark was busy making notes on a large chart as each person's name was called. Paul was following her advice to show interest in each person without seeming either afraid or too confident.

The attorneys had been given a roster of the persons called for jury duty, and the DA stood at the podium and began questioning various members to determine their eligibility to serve and whether they held prejudices or prior knowledge of the case; whether they knew the parties or their attorneys, and whether they could be fair in determining a verdict in this case.

Carmela and Mark listened carefully and made notes on their registry—a plus, minus, maybe, or what questions to ask when it came their turn. In the afternoon, the DA closed his voir dire, and Carmela greeted the tired panel with an energetic smile, which helped to wake them. She was more interested in creating a pleasant relationship with them—hoping they would like and trust her—rather than digging into their personal histories.

She and Mark had already ruled out several of the panel while listening to their answers to the DA's questions. They wanted no teachers who might be so sympathetic to children they could not be open minded in their judgment. They wanted no one from the legal community who would have already decided the verdict, or young mothers who feared for their own children's safety. They looked for young adults who were a part of the current social society, who might have friends who were gay, church members who trusted their ministers, business owners and politically active people who were knowledgeable about various social trends within the community.

At five o'clock, the DA closed his voir dire, and the judge excused the jurists, repeating his orders not to discuss the trial with each other, family, friends, or enemies, nor to read newspapers or watch TV news.

The judge spoke to Carmela. "Let's finish with the jury selection tomorrow."

Carmela heaved a sigh of relief. She and Mark would have time tonight to review their notes and target the panelists they felt would make the best jury. Tomorrow would be exciting—if their final decisions proved to bring together a perfect jury. She, Paul, and Mark slipped past news reporters and settled in at the office, where Rosemary had spread a supper takeout from Momma Maria's Truck Stop.

"How's it going?" she asked.

Carmela looked at Paul. "We're doing alright. I think we have the potential for seating a jury that will listen to us." She looked at Mark. "However, I don't think we can relax. How did you feel?"

"You're right. I felt better about the selections than I had expected to." He looked at Paul. "The jury decision in this type of case depends so much on the social and political background of the community as a whole. As I've mentioned before, studies of San Carlos residents show it is about forty-five percent liberal and fifty-five percent conservative. Liberals are more apt to come with an open mind and can go either way on this kind of issue. Conservatives are more apt to hear the evidence and weigh it against their family and church standards. It's harder to move them to accept new ideas. The fact that they are church-going people rests in your favor, unless the gay issue pushes them beyond their comfort level." He looked back at Carmela and then to Rosemary. "We're doing as well as could be expected."

Chapter Thirty-Seven

Jury selection resumed first thing the following morning. Carmela already knew exactly which persons on the panel she suspected had a prejudice and those whom she believed were open-minded and willing to weigh the evidence carefully. She'd relied upon Mark's expertise. After only two hours, she sat down and the clerk began calling the names of panel members, giving each attorney the option of accepting or excusing that person. Carmela used a number of peremptory challenges to dismiss panelists who refused to look at her or Paul. She worried that she would be left without a challenge when an obviously prejudiced person appeared. The prosecutor was accepting every panelist without a challenge, which worried Carmela. He obviously wanted to send the message that any jury they selected would be leaning in the direction of finding the defendant guilty.

By late afternoon all twelve seats were filled, plus three other members were chosen to serve. Judge Salazar thanked the other panelists for coming and excused them from the courtroom. To the chosen jurors, he explained the preliminary details of the proceeding.

"The case before you is *The State of New Mexico versus Paul Robert Morrison*. The defendant is accused of knowingly and intentionally looking upon, touching, or feeling the body or private parts of a child under eight years of age." He emphasized that the defendant was innocent until proven guilty beyond a reasonable doubt, and cautioned them not to discuss the court proceedings with any person, including spouses and family members. They were not to read newspapers or watch TV. He denied Carmela's motion to sequester the jury and announced that the court would be in recess until 9:00 a.m. on Tuesday morning, skipping Monday in honor of the Martin Luther King holiday.

Carmela reviewed the list of chosen jurors and counted a rancher's wife, a casino worker, two government employees, a CPA, two older house-wives, a college professor, two college students, an artist, and employees from Walmart, a hardware store, and Sears. In general, she was pleased that the jury box was filled with diverse men and women with whom she was comfortable or that she felt would remain neutral and open minded. She had doubts about one government employee, though, knowing it took only one juror to cause a mistrial.

Another question in her mind was the testimony from some jurists who said they had not read stories about Catholic priests who had been accused of sexually abusing young boys in their churches. How could they have missed those stories, unless they didn't read newspapers at all? Mark assured her that the uninformed were more apt to be people who had not made up their minds on the subject and, therefore, might be more open to persuasion.

Carmela sighed, pleased that she'd have the weekend plus the holiday to focus on her opening statement, due on Tuesday.

She continued to worry about the fact that Cody would be a wit-ness for the prosecution. His testimony could end any hope she had of winning this case. However, there was no way she could avoid the legal right of the victim to testify. She had argued against using the child as a witness and had asked the video interview taken by the Children's Protection Services should be used instead. She had presented a report from a victim's advocate that argued children who had been abused were too traumatized to be competent witnesses, and that the experience itself would cause further traumatization. However, Judge Salazar had inter-viewed Cody and determined that, under New Mexico law, the child could be a witness because he understood the difference between lying and his duty to tell the truth.

On Tuesday morning, with preliminaries completed, Judge Salazar directed Roman Sedbury to present his opening statement. Carmela relaxed as he spoke.

"Good morning, ladies and gentlemen. Thank you for accepting your duty as American citizens to serve on this jury. You are faced with the important task of protecting the children of this community from a sex-ual predator. The state has charged the Reverend Paul Robert Morrison with "knowingly and intentionally looking upon, touching, or feeling the body or private parts of six-year-old Cody Vernon in the basement of the Southern Pentecostal Holiness Church of San Carlos, following a Cub Scout meeting.

"On September 6, 2014, Cody Jordon appeared at his church for a Cub Scout meeting. The purpose that day was to convert the church basement into a workroom for the Scouts, a place where they could build their cars and hold their annual races.

"Cody is an innocent six-year-old boy who trusted his pastor. He had gone to him for counseling when he lost his hero father in the Afghanistan war, and again two years later, he sought help to accept the fact that his mother had remarried. Testimony from the child's mother will show that the minister became a substitute father in the child's mind."

"Objection," Carmela said. "The mother could not know what was in the child's mind."

"Sustained."

Sedbury frowned but continued. "Cody went to the meeting that day excited about helping with the Cub Scout project. He left the meeting a victim of sexual assault."

Carmela objected. "Prosecution has no proof of when or where the unproven assault occurred."

"Sustained," the judge said.

"Who was in the basement alone with the child at the time?" the DA asked his audience. "We will present evidence that the man Cody loved and trusted, the minister of his church, the man on trial here today"—he pointed to Paul—"was the only person who remained in the room with the victim after the Scout meeting. He is the man the police interrogated about the assault and eventually arrested.

"The defense will tell you that the child had been crying before he arrived at the Cub Scout meeting and suggest that he had been abused before he came, but the mother will testify that the reason he was upset when he left home was because the family was late in leaving for the meeting. It seems obvious that the minister later used the child's tears as an excuse to pick him up, place him on his lap, and sexually abuse him."

"Objection! The state has no proof that the child was abused at that place or time."

"Counsel, approach the bench."

"Your Honor, Mr. Sedbury knows his statement cannot be supported by hard evidence, but he's introducing it to prejudice the minds of the jury."

"Reverend Morrison has admitted that he put the child in his lap to console him," Sedbury countered.

"That hardly rises to the point of admitting he abused the child. I'll strike that statement," the judge said.

Carmela returned to her seat, pleased with the strike, angry that the DA had gotten away with putting the idea into the minds of the jury.

"What happened next?" the DA asked, and answered his own question: "The minister called the parents and told them the child had complained of being abused and that he had reported the incident to the police. The defense will argue that no guilty person would have called the police to report his own sexual assault, but let's consider the advantage the minister had by calling the police himself and how much more damaging it would have been to him if the child had gone home crying and the parents had made that call."

Sedbury then emphasized the fact that Cody attended church regularly and that Sunday-school teachers would describe the child's joyous involvement in religious training and his pride in having memorized the ten commandments. The teachers will testify that Cody often quoted the commandment, "Thou shalt not lie." After a dramatic pause, the DA continued. "Finally, the state will present evidence that this highly respected minister has been leading a double life."

Carmela jumped to her feet. "Objection. May we approach?"

The judge nodded and frowned at the DA. "Mr. Sedbury, we determined some time ago that your taped interview with Mr. Stokes was inadmissible as hearsay. What other evidence do you have?"

"We will submit copies of email correspondence from Reverend Morrison's computer addressed to other homosexuals over a long period of time."

"Those emails do not prove that Paul Morrison is a homosexual, and even if they did—which we do not concede—it would not be evidence that he is a pedophile, and that is the question the state has raised."

The judge waited for Sedbury's reply.

"I have an expert witness who will testify that most sexual abuse to children is performed by homosexuals, and we will present evidence to prove that the minister himself is gay."

"Your Honor, Mr. Morrison's sexual orientation is irrelevant, and the evidence should be excluded under Rule 11-402 and Rule 11-403. The expert the state intends to offer will have no foundation or reliable scientific facts to support his opinion. If he is allowed to testify, his opinion will be challenged by an expert who has competent and reliable research showing that most sexual abuse of children is done by family members or close friends who are not homosexual," Carmela said. "And there is no proof in those emails that Reverend Morrison is gay. They only show that he was counseling gays who sought his spiritual advice."

"Well," the judge said. "I'll let it stand, but be prepared to back up your statements, Mr. Sedbury."

Carmela returned to her seat, hoping she was concealing her disappointment. It was now clear that this would be a battle to clarify the status of modern research on pedophilia.

Carmela had hoped this case would not be decided on the issue of homosexuality. Sedbury was making sure it would be. She had expected him to drop a hint further into the trial that Paul was gay and to let the jury's imaginations do the dirty work. He obviously hoped the emails would overcome the court's hearsay ruling that disallowed the playing of Marvin's sighting on the mountainside. Despite her surprise, Carmela concluded it was just as well that the gay issue had come out early. Her expert was prepared to do battle with the state on the subject of gays as pedophiles. Her major concern remained the possibility Cody would point to Paul as his abuser. If that happened, she would have to convince the jury beyond a reasonable doubt that Cody was confused and traumatized by his circumstances.

Sedbury continued with what he considered the arrow that would pierce the heart of her case. "We will present evidence to show that Reverend Morrison spent a great deal of time corresponding with homosexuals via emails, " he told the jury.

Next, Sedbury reached the topic he suspected she would use in an effort to cement the jury's doubts about Paul's guilt. "Defense will suggest to you that the defendant is not the real perpetrator of this crime. When that happens, ask yourselves one simple question: who was the man in the church basement with the child when the abuse was reported?"

As the DA continued, he returned to his list of witnesses and what the jury should expect their testimony to prove. As the list lengthened, Paul sank lower in his chair, and Carmela straightened, to remind him that while the jury was busy listening to the arguments, they were also watching Paul's reaction. He must not act like a loser, and Carmela was pleased that he responded by adjusting his posture. After all, he was a public speaker. Part of his job as pastor of a church was to connect with the congregation on a one-to-one basis. He looked at the judge and then allowed his eyes to slide to each person in the jury box, making each believe he or she was the most important person in the room, moving his attention to the next juror before one felt uncomfortably targeted.

Frowns dissolved as the beneficiaries of his attention shifted their focus to Carmela. She relaxed, believing the pastor was making reassuring contact with the jury. Whether it would resonate when they returned to the jury room was another question.

Summing up his arguments, Sedbury walked in front of the jury. "Your finding that Paul Robert Morrison"—he pointed at Paul—"is guilty will allow the court to send this man to prison, where he will not have access to helpless children. Do what is best for our community. Return a guilty verdict." He sat, struggling to hide a smirk as he closed his folder, quite pleased with himself.

Chapter Thirty-Eight

Carmela stood, looked each juror in the eye, and quietly affirmed: "I am happy to inform you that your task as a juror will be much simpler than the state has suggested." There was an audible sigh and relaxation of bodies in the jury box. They were listening, their questioning eyes saying, "tell us how."

"First, you don't have to decide whether Cody Vernon is telling the truth or whether he is lying about what happened in the church basement. You see, Cody Vernon never said he was abused *in the church basement.* Believe me when I say that placing the scene of the crime in the church basement is a figment of the district attorney's imagination. If he can convince you, beyond a reasonable doubt, that the abuse took place in the church, he believes it will be easy for you to come to the conclusion that someone in the church did it, and that person would be the Reverend Paul Morrison.

"On September 6, 2014, there indeed was a Cub Scout meeting at the Southern Pentecostal Church in our city. It was an exciting day for the Scouts, who had been carving their wooden cars, preparing for the annual race, each one hoping to be the winner. That day, they would clean out the basement, giving them room to work on their projects at the site of the race. Pastor Morrison and nine Scouts were present when Cody Jordan arrived. Pastor Morrison will testify that he was busy when Cody arrived, wiping tears from his eyes, and that he assumed Cody would stay and talk to him about his problem after the other Scouts left.

"I urge you to listen carefully to Cody and the other witnesses. Not one witness will point to the church basement as a site where the abuse took place. In fact, Cody has not said what happened to him or where it happened, and it is not your task to determine where it took place, but it makes your job easier to know up front that nothing criminal happened in the church, as the DA would have you believe. Nor did anything happen *after* the Cub Scout meeting. Testimony from the child will show that whatever happened to Cody occurred *before* he went to the Cub Scout meeting. How do we know? We can safely say it happened before Cody came to the meeting, because Cody was crying when he arrived. Evidence will prove that after the meeting, Reverend Morrison asked Cody why he was sad, and at that time Cody confessed that *he* had sinned. The questions then become: When had he sinned? Where had it happened? At school? On the playground?" Carmela paused while the jury considered these options. "Or could it have happened at home?"

Eyebrows rose. Frowns multiplied. Some heads nodded.

"Think about it," Carmela said and moved back to the table, giving them time to consider that possibility.

"Second, don't let the state distract you from your sole duty as jurors. The district attorney is asking you to find Paul Morrison guilty of the court's finding of probable cause. Remember, that finding was based upon argument made in front of a municipal court judge with a minimum amount of evidence—just enough to say 'maybe' something happened to the child. Let's take it to trial and let a jury decide if there is proof beyond a reasonable doubt that this man abused the child. Notice that it is just as likely that nothing happened, but a jury must listen to all the evidence and make a final decision on the pastor's guilt or innocence. You are that jury.

"Let's look at the evidence that will be placed before you—evidence that you must weigh in reaching a decision in this case.

"The district attorney has tried to plant in your minds the idea that Reverend Morrison is guilty as charged. However, the judge will give you very clear instructions before you go into that jury room that you must assume the defendant is innocent until the evidence, not the DA, has convinced you beyond a reasonable doubt that he is guilty. He must first be given the benefit of the doubt. You must find him not guilty, unless you are firmly convinced by all the evidence presented that he touched Cody Vernon inappropriately that day *in the basement of the church*. If you have a reasonable doubt about *what* happened that day, or *where* it happened, then you must find Paul Morrison not guilty.

"Indeed, there is a big difference in what the district attorney and I—" she pointed to the DA and to herself, "are required to do, and it is important for you to understand that difference as you listen and watch the proceedings this week. The district attorney has laid down his charges." Carmela picked up a magnifying glass from her table, continuing, "But you hold the magnifying glass. You are Sherlock Holmes. My job is to show you the cracks in the district attorney's case, the false statements, the facts that will make you realize that there is a reasonable doubt about what the district attorney is telling you.

"That's right. It may surprise you to learn that my job does not include proving to you that Paul is innocent. As he sits before you right now, *he is innocent.* The burden is on the state to come up with real evidence that proves to you beyond a reasonable doubt that Paul is guilty of improperly touching Cody Vernon.

"The fact is there is no proof beyond a reasonable doubt that Paul is guilty as charged, if you agree that some other person is just as likely, or more likely, to have done it. Was there a different person who had a suspicious history of collecting child pornography, who might be described as a pedophile, and who had access to this child? If so, without having to decide the guilt of some other person, all you need to do is determine that the evidence places a reasonable doubt in your mind about whether Paul Morrison is guilty of the crime.

"There also should be a reasonable doubt in your mind as to the pastor's guilt if there is no evidence to show that he has a history of child abuse or, for example, a history of viewing child pornography. The district attorney has told you that Reverend Morrison communicated on the Internet with men guilty of selling child pornography. What he did not tell you is that Reverend Morrison's response to everyone involved in these communications was limited to his pastoral duties to listen to the caller's problems, to suggest that writer seek counseling for what bothered him, and to urge him to be saved in the blood of Jesus Christ—which is a teaching of the Southern Pentecostal Holiness Church, where he is pastor. We will show that Reverend Morrison notified the FBI of one of these contacts, because of his concern that the writer was involved in a ring of nationwide pornographers. An FBI agent will testify to the defendant's cooperation in their efforts to find and prosecute offenders.

"Finally, on this subject, we will present evidence that the child's step-father, Marvin Stokes, did indeed indulge in—"

Roman Sedbury jumped to his feet, shouting, "Objection."

Judge Salazar banged the gavel on the walnut base on his desk. "Counsel will approach the bench."

The jury grew tense as the attorneys walked to the dais.

"What's this all about, Roman?"

"Your Honor, Miss Jared knows that she cannot include facts in her opening statement that cannot be supported by legal evidence during trial. Mr. Stokes is dead! Furthermore, Mrs. Stokes cannot testify because spousal privilege survives her husband's death." Sedbury's face flushed the color of his tie.

Judge Salazar looked at Carmela.

"Your Honor, this is a different issue. The wife has indicated a willing-ness to waive the spousal privilege and testify that her husband, Marvin Stokes, collected child pornography via the Internet, and the law allows the wife to testify against her dead husband if there has been a crime. Furthermore, a police witness will testify to Mr. Stokes's criminal pos-session of child pornography. More importantly, there will be testimony that it was Mr. Stokes, not the child, who told the police that the child had accused Paul Morrison of abusing him. Finally, the child's statement to the stepfather about the defendant's abuse—if there was such a state-ment—is hearsay and inadmissible."

The judge looked at Sedbury. "I'd say your objection died along with the husband—and with the wife's change of heart, Mr. Sedbury. His death makes my prior ruling void. Ms. Stokes may testify. Let's get on with it."

Carmela relaxed, seeing this win comparable to a perfect landing past the first hurdle in a steeplechase competition. The attorneys left the dais, and Carmela continued her opening statement. "As I was saying, we will present evidence that the child's stepfather did indeed indulge in the ille-gal gathering and distribution of child pornography. A military expert will testify that this practice was the basis for Marvin Stokes's dismissal from the marine corps."

A general sigh emanated from the jury box.

"One other important conclusion you *don't* have to reach is whether Marvin Stokes, the victim's stepfather, now dead, was the actual perpe-trator. This is not a trial to find out 'who done it.' Your only task is to decide whether Paul Morrison abused Cody Vernon. Even though it isn't our duty to prove the truth of anything in this case—because the burden of proof is on the state—evidence will show that Cody was not abused in the church basement, and Paul Morrison is innocent of the false charges made against him. You should, therefore, find him innocent of all charges.

"It is understandable that you may say, 'We read the papers and are angry about the Catholic priests who vow to be celibate but often prove to be pedophiles.' Those facts anger us, also, but we cannot assume that all priests or pastors break their vows or that those who do are all pedophiles. We will present scientific surveys, which show that those Catholic priests who break their vows. What I'm asking you to do, as good jurists, is to look at this man, judge him on the basis of his character and his public acts, weigh the good that he has done for this community, and not judge him on the bad acts of other clerics."

Carmela smiled at the jury, pleased that some of them seemed to have gotten her message. "After you hear all the evidence, I will have another opportunity to speak to you, and I will again ask you to find Paul Morrison not guilty of the charges against him and to send him back to the family church where he was doing great service in this community. Thank you, and may God bless you."

Paul sucked in a deep breath as she sat beside him. He leaned over and whispered, "Will I be breaking my pledge if I say 'I love you'? You were wonderful."

She shook her head, biting her cheek to keep from laughing. She was relieved when the judge glanced at the clock and informed the jury that they were dismissed for the day, reminding them that they were not to discuss the case with anyone, even spouses. They were not to read newspapers, nor watch the news on television.

"When they return," Carmela whispered, "they'll be chomping at the bit to get this trial completed. Let's hope that bodes well for us."

"The jury is dismissed for the day. I will see counsel in chambers."

Curious and wondering who was in trouble, Carmela followed the DA. She waited while the judge removed his robe and made himself comfortable behind his desk. His demeanor was solemn.

"Roman, I've listened closely to both these opening statements and have come to the same conclusion that I suspect both of you have. This case rests on the testimony of one witness: the child. I have to agree with the defense. There probably was not sufficient cause presented in the initial hearing to order this matter to trial, and I can't see that you've offered anything solid to leave it here. Wouldn't you agree that the state's last hope is to have the child point to his accuser? If he doesn't, you are dead in the water. While I cannot order you to, I strongly suggest you put him on as your first witness, and let's get this thing over with."

Sedbury turned a pale ash color, and while he struggled to control his anger, his face flushed red. "Your Honor, I spent hours in my opening statement outlining to the jury all the reasons they should find this man guilty. It's not just the child's testimony they should consider."

"I'm not so sure. The law says the abused person must name the abuser. So far, we have no proof that the child was even physically abused. You have no witness to the act; the child has not specifically named a guilty person; and if the child cannot find him in the courtroom, then the defendant cannot be found guilty as charged. We can hear your arguments for days and come up with the same result. There is a motion for a directed verdict before the court, and I'm inclined to grant it. I'd like to hear the child's testimony before I decide."

Sedbury slumped in his chair. "The jury has the right to hear all our witnesses, Your Honor."

The judge raised his eyebrows and looked toward Carmela.

"I move that the court find in favor of my motion for a directed verdict at this—"

"Okay. Okay," Sedbury interrupted. "I'll put the child on first."

"Thank you. That's all."

Carmela could hardly breathe as she returned to the courtroom. "Let's go," she said to Paul and Mark Gordon, and she led them out of the courtroom through a back door.

"What's going on?" Mark asked.

"You won't believe this. The judge just laid down the law to the DA. He has to put Cody on as his first witness, and if he doesn't point to Paul as the abuser, the judge will announce a directed verdict dismissing the case. We'll win!" She turned to Paul. "You'll be a free man."

Paul opened his arms and hugged her tightly. "I can't believe it."

"All my work for nothing," Mark said with a mock frown.

"Well, it ain't over till it's over. It all rests with Cody," Carmela said. "We won't get any sleep tonight."

Chapter Thirty-Nine

At home, Carmela found a note from the local flower shop, saying that a bouquet addressed to her had been left at the door of her neighbor, Ms. Peña. Before Carmela had time to go inside, Ms. Peña popped out on her porch and hurried down the steps, carrying a large bouquet of roses.

"These are for you, dear. I'll bet they're from that sweet Detective Hawk who rescued Prissy, don't you? He's so thoughtful."

Carmela smiled, took the roses, and thanked Ms. Peña. "Yes, he's very thoughtful," she said and wondered if this was his next step in mending fences. It seemed improbable, considering Aviva's report that his dancing with PT seemed far beyond friendship. She placed the flowers on the coffee table and set about removing her coat, her snow boots, and wool scarf before moving to the bedroom, where she leisurely undressed and took a shower. It was dark when she returned to the kitchen and popped a frozen dinner into the microwave oven. Cautiously, she moved to the front room, where she circled the coffee table before sitting down in the half-lit room and reached over to pluck the gift card between her index and middle fingers.

The bell chimed on her microwave, and she laid aside the note, stood somewhat disgruntled with herself for hoping the flowers were from a man who had the power to hurt her so deeply. How long would her heart say yes and her head say no when he made new overtures?

"Ouch!" She burned her hand on the blasted microwave container, and ready-made tears rolled down her cheeks. She went back to the roses and stared at the familiar "T" he used for signing his notes to her. No name, just the initial he had used to communicate with her since grade school. Hungry, she wound her fork through the pasta and her wine glass emptied quickly. She supposed she'd have to call him.

He answered, "Travis here."

"You shouldn't have sent me roses. However, they're beautiful, and I thank you. Are we celebrating something?"

"Yes. I thought you did a great job in court today."

"You were there?"

"I talked the chief into thinking we needed someone to get a hands-on report of how the case was going."

"And he sent you to put a hex on it."

"You know I wouldn't have done that even if I could."

She didn't respond.

"I told you I have been going to therapy. "

"Yes. You said you were told to mend fences. So that's what this is all about?"

"I didn't think of it that way, but I guess you could say that. I sent them because I love you."

Carmela had no response to that, and Travis broke the silence. "John thinks my problem is all tied up with what happened between Billy Joe and the college guy. We're working through that."

"I'm glad to hear it."

"Is there any chance I can see you? Maybe go out to dinner?"

Carmela blinked fresh tears from her eyes. "Travis, are you having an affair with PT?" The words came softly, but pierced her heart like needles. She had to know.

"You know me better than that, Carmela. How could you even think it?"

"People talk."

"Aviva. She saw us at Cowboys. I ought to apologize for that, but the truth is, it was a bad night for PT, and I was trying to help. She had just gotten word this week that her husband lost a leg when a road bomb hit his jeep. She'd been off work and was exhausted, trying not to cry in front of the kids. Her husband called me and asked if I'd help out. He said she needed to feel human again."

The silence between them was painful.

"I'm sorry, Travis. I sometimes forget what it is to be human myself. Forgive me. I'm glad you helped her. You should have sent her the roses."

"No." The silence was palpable. "You're the only woman I've ever sent roses to, Carmela. You're the one I love." It sounded like a confession.

Carmela relaxed and wiped away her tears. Was she a fool for believing him? It didn't matter. He was the one who touched her soul. Her ranting to Aviva that she did not plan to be only one in a crowd of women in a man's life now seemed childish. She knew her weakness. She needed Travis and he said he needed her. "What are your plans for tonight?"she asked.

"Nothing I can't change."

"I've already eaten supper, but I might rustle up some dessert."

"I'd like to come over for dessert."

She hung up the phone and bent forward to breathe in the essence of the heavily scented roses. Winning her case would be a major victory. Was it possible that she and Travis could also settle their differences, put them aside, and simply love each other? Earlier she had come to the conclusion that they could not, but what she really wanted right now was to be in his arms, to tell him what he wanted to hear, and to share with him the possibility that she would win her case.

Chapter Forty

The district attorney entered the courtroom smiling, ignoring Carmela. Why was he so cheerful? Could he possibly have talked to Cody and knew what he was going to say? There was a strange tension in the air as the judge entered and the bailiff called the court to order. The judge ordered the district attorney to call his first witness.

"We call Cody Jordon. Your honor, we request that a worker from the Child Protection Services be allowed to accompany the child."

"Any objections?"

"No, sir."

The bailiff hurried to a side door and led Aviva Romero and Cody to the clerk's desk, where the child was sworn in. She directed him to the witness stand, where he climbed into the chair, and Aviva stood outside the stand. Cody looked at the judge who smiled and explained to him that the lawyer would ask him some questions and he should answer them with yes or no and not just shake his head. Did he understand? He said yes, and the judge smiled again.

"Cody, my name is Roman Sedbury. I'm the district attorney and I will ask you some questions, like your teacher does at school." Pointing to the jury, he said, "These men and women want to hear your answers, so speak directly to them. Do you understand?"

He nodded.

"Is that a yes? Please say it out loud."

"Yes." Cody's eyes slipped from the DA to Carmela and the defendant seated beside her. His eyes opened wide, surprised to see his pastor there. He looked at the jury suspiciously.

"My first question is: what is your full name?"

"Cody Lee Vernon," he whispered.

"Just a little louder, please."

"Cody Lee Vernon."

"Do you know your address?"

"Seven two eight Buffalo Lane, San Carlos, New Mexico."

"Great. Do you know your mother's name?"

"Lucille. Her last name isn't like mine because she got married again after my father died. His name was John Vernon. He was a war hero."

"You're a very smart little boy, Cody. Thank you for helping me. You're very proud of your father aren't you?"

"Yes, sir."

"Do you remember your stepfather's name?"

"You mean Marvin?"

"Yes, Marvin. Do you know his full name?"

"Marvin Stokes." Cody's voice had gotten softer, and his lips quivered. He looked again at Paul and tears threatened to fall from his eyes.

"We've almost finished, Cody. We're going to talk now about the Cub Scouts. "You like the Cub Scouts, don't you?"

"Yes, sir."

"And did you build a race car in Cub Scouts this year?"

"Yes."

"Do you remember the day you finished your race car for the big contest at church?"

He nodded.

"Is that a yes?

He nodded again and whispered, "Yes."

"Were you happy that morning when you went to Cub Scouts with your new car?"

His eyes settled on Paul. "I don't remember."

Carmela's heart sank. He must have wiped the incident from his memory.

"Do you remember who took you to the Scout meeting?"

Cody looked around the room and back to Paul. "Marvin always took me."

"Were you and Marvin the only ones in the car that morning?"

"No. We had to take Rusty to work."

The DA looked surprised. Who was Rusty? Had his staff overlooked a possible witness?

"When you got to the church, who was the first person you saw?"

He thought for a long time. "I don't remember."

"Was the Reverend Morrison there?"

"Yes. He was helping put up the racetrack."

"What did you do?"

"I watched."

"Were you happy?"

"Not much." He looked at Paul again.

"Why weren't you happy?"

"I don't remember."

"Did you have a headache?"

"Can I go now?"

"We're almost through, Cody. Let's remember that morning back at the church basement. Did you leave when all the other Scouts left?"

"I don't remember."

Frustrated, the DA asked, "Do you recall sitting on the preacher's lap and talking to him after everybody else left?"

Cody looked at the DA without answering.

"Did you tell him why you were sad?"

Cody turned to look at Paul and blinked rapidly. "I told him it was a sin to lie. But he knowed that already."

"Had he lied to you?"

"No."

"Had you lied to him?"

"I'm going now." He slipped off the chair.

Sedbury frowned at Aviva, and she lifted Cody to her lap. He continued. "What was the secret you and the preacher had together?"

"I told him I'd sinned, but he told me it wasn't my fault, and I only had to tell God when I sinned. But then he told the police!"

"Were you angry because he told the police?"

"Yes. They won't let me go home."

"Is this just one of the secrets you had with the pastor?"

Cody began crying. The DA was ecstatic. There were secrets between the two of them! This was enough evidence to overcome a ruling of directed verdict.

"I rest my case, your Honor."

Carmela stood. "I wish to cross examine, Your Honor."

The judge frowned. He had no right to deny her request, but she was taking a tremendous risk. She very well might reveal evidence that would hurt her case. It was a gutsy call.

"Continue," he said.

Aviva had been wiping tears from the child's face.

"Hello, Cody. My name is Carmela, and I have a very few questions to ask you. First let's talk about Rusty."

Cody shook his head. "I don't want to talk about Rusty." He looked at Aviva. "Can I go home?"

"Please, Cody. Just one more minute. Was Rusty in the car when Marvin delivered you to the Cub Scout meeting?"

"No. He got out at McDonald's."

"How long has your uncle lived with you?"

Cody looked at the jury as if he were searching for someone he knew, and then he looked at Carmela with squinted eyes. "He's only visiting. He's got a job now, and he's going to find another place to live so I can have my room back."

"So he's been sharing your room while he visits?"

"Yes, but it's too little. I don't have room for my train set any more."

"When did he start working at McDonald's?"

"I don't know." Cody's face brightened. "But he brings me a free hamburger if I do what he tells me to."

"What sort of things does he tell you to do, Cody?"

"Keep my toys off his bed."

"What else?"

"Not wake him up in the morning."

"Anything else?"

Cody squirmed in his chair and finally whispered, "Sometimes he wants me to touch him."

The room became so quiet Carmela could hear the breathing of the jury.

"Can you show us where you touch him, Cody?"

He pointed to his genital area, and tears slipped down his cheeks.

"Did you think that was a sin?" The child didn't answer, and she asked, "Is that the sin you confessed to Reverend Morrison?"

Cody became angry and stared at Paul.

Carmela paused. She had maneuvered herself into another corral, gate closed. She should sit down and let his testimony free her client, but the possibility remained that the pastor could have asked Cody to touch him, also. She needed that question answered.

"Is there anything else you want to tell us about what happened that day at the church?"

"I'm still mad because when I told God about my sin, it was suppose to be a secret."

Carmela was relieved. Paul's mistake in the child's mind was calling the police, not touching him.

"Cody, did you believe that touching Rusty was a sin?"

"Yes, when he hurt me."

"Thank you, Cody." She looked at the Judge. "I have no other questions."

"Mr. Sedbury?"

The DA stood. "Cody has anyone other than Rusty ever asked you to touch them?"

"No."

"Have you ever touched anyone besides Rusty?"

Everyone waited for his answer. Finally, Cody shook his head. "No. It's a sin to tell a lie." He began sobbing and buried his face on Aviva's shoulder.

Paul jumped to his feet. "Cody!" He turned to the judge. "Please stop this!"

The judge slammed his gavel for order and the police guards in the room came to attention. Cody slid from Aviva's lap and ran down the steps into Paul's arms. The judge shook his head and wearily asked, "Mr. Sedbury, have you finished with this witness?"

Under the judge's angry glare the DA answered, "Yes, sir."

"Ms. Jared, do you have other questions?"

"No, Your Honor. The defense rests."

"The court hereby enters a directed verdict of not guilty. I thank the jury for your service. You are now dismissed. Counsel will come to my chambers."

Paul pulled the child's arms from around his neck. "You have been a brave young man, Cody—a hero like your father. I'm so sorry you were hurt and I'll do everything I can to make it right. Remember, this was not your fault, son. Please forgive me."

Cody nodded. "Can I go home now?"

"I'm afraid not, but I will come to see you every day. We'll play with your car. Okay? We will be best friends. Be a brave boy, and remember God loves you."

Aviva took Cody's hand and led him from the room.

A confused jury followed the bailiff out of the courtroom. The district attorney walked to her table and shook hands. "I'm sorry for this mistake, Carmela. The world is not a perfect place."

Carmela closed her eyes and the image of Eden crossed her mind. "No," she said. "But we have to keep trying." She turned to Paul and her associates and accepted their hugs and congratulations, blinking tears and thoughts of snakes from her mind.

"I have to go to the judge's chambers for a minute," she said to Paul, "and we have to meet the press when I come back. Stay here."

"I will. Like I've said before, you're an angel, and I'm convinced that if I'm with you, I'm in heaven!"

"Hang on to that!" she said and pushed her notes and other documents on the table toward Paul and Mark. "Would you two drop these off at my office? We'll be there shortly." She hurried to meet with the judge, afraid everyone would disappear before she returned.

Chapter Forty-One

A rash of reporters and TV cameras met the attorneys when they exited the courthouse following the meeting with Judge Salazar. At her side, Paul searched the crowd and waved to Jason and Travis, standing at the back of the crowd, slapping hands as if they were the best of friends sharing a victory.

"Ms. Jared," one reporter called, "How does it feel to win this case?"

"Justice won this case," Carmela said. "An innocent man was falsely accused of a horrible crime, and the court correctly cleared his name. Today should be a new beginning of a war on the cancer of child abuse in our neighborhoods, our churches, our Scout troops, and our homes. Reverend Morrison is a fine citizen who has contributed much to this community, and we should be proud of our country's legal system and our own court, which has brought justice to this matter. Thank you for spreading that word to our fellow Americans. Paul?"

"I cannot tell you how happy it makes me to stand here today to acknowledge that I am gay and to have the American justice system find that I am innocent of the false charges made against me because of my God-given sexual preference."

Carmela smiled. She had not known he would use this victory to announce that he was gay, but it didn't surprise her. She had heard him tell Cody he was a hero for standing up for truth; how could he do less?

"I encourage everyone to continue fighting the battle against sex abusers by questioning the actions of all members of the public who have contact with your children, including teachers, Scout leaders, sports participants, and family members. Thank you. And I must thank my attorney, Carmela Jared, who has bravely led this fight for justice. I actually can't thank her enough." He turned to embrace her as the crowd cheered.

Carmela turned to Travis, who had pushed through the crowd to her side.

"Congratulations," he said. "Where to?"

"The office. I have to share this with Rosemary and Harry."

"Did everything go the way you wanted it to?"

"Yes, but I'm a basket case. I worried constantly that something would go terribly wrong." She pointed to the sky. "Somebody up there likes me, as Paul would say."

"I've never doubted that. Let's go. By the way, we arrested Rusty at McDonald's within thirty minutes of Cody's testimony. I understand he confessed, with a little help from our investigators."

"Thank goodness. I hope this is his only offense and that he can get some help with his problem before he's out on the street again."

Within minutes they were at her office. "What are all these cars doing here?" Carmela asked as they pulled into the parking lot. She soon found out when Travis opened the door, and a crowd of friends, and friends of friends, sang out: "For she's a jolly good fellow, for she's a jolly good fellow. For she's a jolly good fellow, that nobody can deny!"

Carmela blushed and hugged Rosemary, who had been on the telephone spreading the good news of the victory. Attorneys who had snickered when the judge embarrassed her at court hearings were now lifting their glasses to her success. Carmela wondered if some of them had a personal interest in this win for gay rights.

Confetti began flying and champagne corks popped. Paul and Jason were the happiest celebrants, but Rosemary and Harry vied for the honor. Carmela wondered if she would be sweeping confetti from the office forever. Travis returned to work but said he'd check back later to see how the party was going.

By one o'clock, the crowd headed to Cowboys for lunch and further celebration. There, she found herself lifted to sit on the bar while the crowd continued to make speeches, sing songs, and relish the victory for hours. Exhausted, she called Travis and begged him to take her home.

"I can only drop you off," he said. "I've pulled a double shift. But I promise to make it up to you."

Carmela's disappointment was replaced by curiosity when she found a UPS envelope by the door with Troy's return address. On the back of the envelope, he'd drawn an Indian chief shooting an arrow at a birth certificate. What did it mean? What had he found? She tore into the envelope, and pictures of the commune where her parents had lived fell out. Tears filled her eyes as she recognized Savanna in front of a tent, stirring a large iron pot of—food, laundry, soap? Other pictures showed her father working on their old van, a small boy playing nearby with a scraggly dog. That must be Troy. The image showed rolling hills, no trees, no water in sight. A garden plot with few plants.

This was what her parents had saved her from by leaving her with her grandparents, who loved her and made their cozy home *her* home. This was the life Troy had inherited instead of the public school where she excelled, which paved the way for law school, which prepared her to win an "unwinnable" case before the courts.

She checked the handwritten agreement confirming that Rosita Herrera was married to Buck Jared, and next was Troy Leader's birth certificate. A third paper documented the name changes of Savanna and Buck Jared to Angel and Marcus Leader. That must have happened before Troy's birth. Had they known when they created these names that Carmela would never be able to find them? She quietly returned the documents to the envelope and placed it on her desk.

Carmela went upstairs, undressed, and stepped into the shower. Slowly she tested the sharp, hot streams of water that massaged her exhausted muscles and then slathered lavender bubbles over her body. Her brain refused to rest and kept hopping back to the trigger points that she'd dealt with over the past few months. First, the treasure-filled envelope from Troy. There was no proof, however, that the two of them were blood brother and sister. She had a lot to discuss with Troy.

And Brooke came to mind. While she had not been directly involved in the girl's case, she worried that someone might be dropping the ball by not following up on what was in the teenager's best interest. She'd ask some questions the next time she saw Aviva.

And Lucille. Would her attorney be able to get her released from jail while awaiting trial for Marvin's murder? How soon could Cody go home? She must see that he and Paul were re-united.

She smiled as she recalled the peaceful look on Paul's countenance. Would he really give up his career as a minister? What direction would his life take? She hoped he would stay in touch.

The hot water began to cool just as her thoughts turned to Travis. He had been a part of her life from the day she came to live with Grandma and Grandpa. For better or worse, she knew they would always be connected.

Chapter Forty-Two

Travis brought breakfast to Carmela in bed and apologized for having to report for work. "I've already used my vacation days, you'll remember."

"It's okay. I'm going back to the gym to make up for all the time I've missed. Spinning class starts at noon. Come by if you have time."

However, it wasn't Travis who set up his bicycle next to hers. "Good morning, Counselor. I didn't expect to see you here. I thought you'd be off to some exotic paradise to celebrate your victory."

"*Our* victory, Paul. And why aren't you at church preparing for tomorrow's sermon?"

Their conversation was interrupted by noisy directions coming from the instructor. Only minutes into the class, Carmela found herself perspiring, her muscles insisting that she slow down. Paul, instead, seemed to be enjoying the challenge of beginning the exercise anew. Carmela was embarrassed that she had confronted him with a question about his career. He had said he might not resume his job as a religious minister, and while she was curious, it was really not her business.

"Do you have time for a snack?" he asked as the class finished. She was surprised but pleased.

"Yes. I was planning to stop by Whole Foods. Why don't I meet you there?"

Paul hesitated then nodded. "Just stay away from the vegetable bins. We got into trouble there last time."

Carmela laughed. "Not me. As I recall, that sprinkling made a big difference in my life." She walked away and half an hour later sat down at one of the booths, where Paul was devouring a seafood salad.

"You left me curious," he said between bites. "How did that accidental sprinkling affect your life?"

"It seems to me that my life has always followed an undirected and surprising course. My mother told me I was born in the family van beside the road, because they didn't have time to get to the hospital. When I turned six, they left me here in San Carlos with her parents so that I could enroll in public school. It was my choice to go to school here, but I thought they would stay with me. I was devastated when they left. It was by accident that I was introduced to Travis Hawk, who later became the most important person in my life. All these things seemed to be unplanned."

"But you also went to law school. That had to have been your choice, an important direction for your life."

"Yes, but until yesterday, when I won your case, I've never been sure that it was a smart decision. Going away caused me to lose Travis to another woman, and both my grandparents died while I was away. I came back here alone, with nothing but a sterile career to look forward to." She smiled. "Things didn't look up until you accidentally baptized me."

Paul shook his head. "I don't think I can take credit for that. God moves in mysterious ways."

"You're too modest, Paul. You touch many lives, every day. You make a difference. I'm not sure I do."

"Do you honestly believe you haven't been a positive force in my life—and Jason's? How about Cody's and Lucille's? And Travis's. By the way, I've had an opportunity to talk with him since his wife died, and it's obvious to me that you are his polestar. You shouldn't underestimate your influence on people's lives." He stood. "We should continue this discussion, but now I have to run. I'll see you in class on Monday."

Carmela pushed her salad aside. "Thank you, Paul. This conversation may have been more invigorating than a second baptizing would have been. I do hope you'll stay in touch."

"Of course I will. In fact, I'm moving in with Jason this weekend, and he asked last night if it would be appropriate to invite you over for dinner soon. He thought Travis might like to come, also. The two had a chance to talk outside the courthouse, Jason says, and he thinks they may have gotten past the experience on the mountain."

"God does move in mysterious ways! I'm sure we'll come if you invite us."

"And to answer the question you asked earlier: I've decided not to return to my calling at the church. This victory has given me a greater opportunity to reach the public with the message that child abuse must be stopped. I've already had contacts with two national organizations that want my help. I'm excited about it. Also, I have a duty to stay in Cody's life. I want to make sure he recovers from this trauma. I feel responsible for what happened to him on my watch."

"Then you won't be leaving San Carlos?"

"Not in the foreseeable future. Let that be a warning when you walk past the vegetable bins while the sprinklers are on!"

On the way home, Carmela received a call from Aviva and pulled over near the river walk to answer. Snow still lingered on the trees and bushes bordering the trickle of water hurrying south. Carmela left the heater on to avoid cold toes.

"Hey, I see you survived the party yesterday. You were still going strong when Tony and I left. Congratulations, again. We're so pleased for you."

"Thanks, Aviva. I couldn't believe the response from other attorneys. You'd think I won a Supreme Court case."

"You might as well have. This is important. What are you doing today?"

"I just had lunch with Paul. He's decided to give up his local ministry and to get involved with national organizations fighting child sexual abuse. Which reminds me—what's going on with Brooke's case?"

"Not much. We have a hearing coming up to determine whether she would be safe if we sent her home. We still don't know whom she had sex with. If it was Connor, it would fall under the Romeo and Juliet exception to sexual assault, and she could go home, but she refuses to admit that he was the one. If it was an assault by Marvin Stokes, she could go home safely because he's no longer a threat. Who does that leave? Her father? He's the most likely culprit, but she refuses to name him, and his lawyer knows all the tricks for protecting him. He seems amenable to staying out of the home and submitting to supervised visitation if the court will allow her to go home, so that may be the best we can do without her cooperation."

"I suppose she will be ordered into therapy, to make sure someone is continuing to monitor her condition."

"Yes, that will be the maximum supervision we'll get."

"And how about Cody Jordon? Is there a family member somewhere who will care for him until his mother is released?"

"Yes. Lucille's parents live in this county, and they've asked to take him. We've just completed an investigation of their home, and he'll be going there next week."

"I heard Paul tell him he would be seeing him daily. Is that possible?"

"Oh yes. He came out this morning and has made arrangements to get Cody to Sunday school tomorrow."

"Well, everything seems to be in good hands. I'll stop worrying."

"And get back out here to ride your horse. She's been in mourning."

"I'm sorry. I'll be out tomorrow. Maybe I can talk Travis into coming."

"I'll expect you. Tell Travis I'll fix some lunch. Oh, and Troy will be back at work."

Carmela turned off the engine of her car and stared at the beautiful river scene. Life was like that, she thought. Today it was flowing peacefully. Tomorrow it might be tumbling over the rocks. Why had she thought only weeks ago that she might leave San Carlos after the trial ended? Now she understood that no matter where she lived, life would still flow at will. For the present, dark times had passed. She had made peace with Judge Salazar. She and Travis were back on track. She had won her case. What more could she ask for?

She drove by the office and found Rosemary directing the cleanup and answering nonstop telephone calls.

"No emergencies?" she asked. Rosemary shook her head vigorously and pushed her toward the door, while she assured a caller that Carmela would be out of the office the rest of the week.

"That suits me fine. I'll go home and surprise Travis with a special dinner. Fried chicken I can do, and if I burn it, I'll dig out the last of the frozen chocolate cake and he'll forgive me."

As usual, cooking a full sit-down meal took longer than she'd planned for, and she was still in her exercise clothes when she checked the clock. She left everything on "warm" and hurried to the shower, hoping he would be late. As the hot water began to cool, she reluctantly reached over to turn it off.

"Need some help?" Travis asked, standing outside the shower.

"What did you have in mind?" she asked. "I know how to turn off water."

"I'm running a special for a certain female attorney who won an impossible case." Blocking her way from the shower, he reached in and turned off the hot water and turned on the cold. "This is the shower they give the coach at the end of the game when his team wins the World Series."

Carmela screamed and he dodged the bar of soap she threw at him. The towel he wrapped around her was warm, and he carried her to the bed, where he kissed every pulse he could find on her body. She allowed his massaging until she stopped shivering.

"Travis, you know you're crazy, don't you? I keep telling you I hate you, and you give me a cold shower as if that will fix things. Don't you understand what hate means?"

She watched as he undressed. "Umm huh. It means we have to make up. That's the part I like best."

"I give up," she said, and pulled the covers over her head.

"That's what I've been waiting to hear," he whispered as he pulled aside the blanket and eased his body over hers. "If I'd had any brains, I'd never have spoken to you after you hit me with that soccer ball the first time we met. That's the first thing I forgave you for—which proved I was crazy."

"But look where it's gotten you. Is that why you continue to push your luck?"

"I suppose so. I can't complain about where I am." He sighed and nuzzled her warm neck. "Though maybe you could spend a little more time on top."

Carmela laughed. "Travis you just refuse to be serious, don't you?"

"On the contrary, I'm very serious. I'll admit it's hard for me to always respond to you as if we were two professionals meeting in a boardroom. To me, you're still the snotty-nosed kid who tried to beat me at everything we did. And too often you won. I admired that about you, but I wasn't about to tell you so. I still find it hard to tell you how impressed I am with what you do as a grownup. It just seems to me you ought to know. It's like we read each other's minds. That's why I've always thought you knew, even after I married Carolyn, that you were the one I loved."

"I did know that, at some level, but knowing only made it worse. I wanted you next to me, the way you are now. I wanted you to be mine, and I wanted to be yours."

"Can we agree that, beginning right now, I am yours, and you are mine?"

"I think it's time."

Travis moved over her body again. "As of this moment, I declare that I, Travis Hawk, am yours, and you, Carmela Jared, are mine. We are married. Death to anyone who challenges it."

"And mud in the eye to anyone who dares suggest that, as a married couple, we exchange trade secrets when our cases overlap."

Travis chuckled. "Leave it to you to legalize pillow talk."

Acknowledgments

As I mentioned in the acknowledgments in my last book, *Rebel on Horseback*, books are never published full-blown from the author's imagination. They hatch there, develop wings, and fly from the nest to visit talented friends and editors who read, critique, encourage, and share the excitement of publication. I am indebted to the following—and many more—for having shared their time and talents in the making of *Love Is a Legal Affair*.

Critique club members and independent readers of this novel are Valerie Stasik, author of *Incidental Daughter* and editor of the New Mexico Book Association's newsletter, *Libro*; Bethany Baxter, whose latest book is *What the Horse Knew*; John Meeks, author of *Bogey's Final Gift*; Reverie Escobedo, who has a story to tell; Kate Curry, author of *The Man in the Fedora*; and Donah Grassman from Colorado; plus many, many more, including family members Mitch, Nicole, and Marian Davenport. I am grateful, too, to my friends who are regulars at the Homegrown Authors table at Santa Fe's Farmers Market, who kept asking, *How is your book coming* and *Is it finished yet*: Sandi Wright, author of the popular children's book, *Santa Fe Sam*; Nancy King, author of *The Stones Speak* and other novels; Elaine Pinkerton, author of *The Goodbye Baby* and other novels; Belinda Perry, author of *An Old Woman's Lies*, who also writes historical Westerns under the pen name William Luckey; and Pat Goehe, author of *Annemarie and Boomer Wait for Grandma.*" Please visit the Farmers Market on Tuesdays, May through November, to meet these and other local authors.

My great thanks goes to Louren Oliveros, Esq., of the law firm of Gorence & Oliveros, PC, in Albuquerque, NM, who graciously gave of her time to read and critique the legal issues in this book. I had the privilege of attending one of her jury selection sessions and was not surprised at her professional skills. Having practiced law myself, I understand the value of her gift of time and expertise and shall always remain in her debt.

Love Is a Legal Affair is a book that could not have been published, as is, without the excellent editorial skills of Mary Neighbour, of MediaNeighbours.com and Susan M. Waterman, PhD, of Custom Editing & Word Crafting.

Beyond her editing skills, Mary is the president of the Santa Fe chapter of APSS (Association of Publishers for Special Sales) as well as the author of the beautifully written fictional slave novel *Speak Right On*, which is in its second printing.

She and her husband, Andrew, are responsible for the excellent design, cover, and photography exhibited in *Love Is a Legal Affair* and for my website, www.davenportstories.com. I thank them and look forward to their continued participation in the marketing of my books.

In addition to her editing career, Susan is manager of the New Mexico Book Association office in Santa Fe; she can be reached at susan@susan-waterman.com.

About the Author

Maxine Neely Davenport's love of writing was born and flourished in Oklahoma's farming and ranching country, Colorado's mountains, and Santa Fe's creative environment. Her world has always been full of stories, first as a journalist and later as a short-story writer and novelist.

From Latta, a small country school outside of Ada, Oklahoma, she attended East Central University. After marriage, she moved to Colorado and completed a masters degree in American literature at Colorado State University, where she was particularly influenced by Ernest Hemingway's writings. She later attended Oklahoma University Law School and attended one summer session at Oxford University. She then practiced law in Colorado Springs until 2002.

Since that time, she has lived in Santa Fe and has published a book of short stories, *Saturday Matinee*; a murder mystery, *Murder Times Two*; a modern Western, *Rebel on Horseback*; and now, *Love Is a Legal Affair*.

She is the mother of three children, seven grandchildren, and three great-grandchildren.

Visit www.davenportstories.com to learn more about the author and her books.

Questions and Topics for Book Club Discussion

1. As a judge, would you have granted Carmela Jared's claim of "conflict of interest" sufficient to grant her request to withdraw from the appointment as a defense attorney for the minister? Why or why not?

2. In small towns, attorneys often find it impossible to limit their practice to a specialized area. Should the judge have assigned this case to an Albuquerque attorney who did specialize in criminal defense? Had Carmela lost the case, would a higher court likely have found grounds to overturn the ruling based on inadequate representation?

3. Was the story of Carmela's being left with her grandparents by her hippy parents believable?

4. Was the relationship between Carmela and Travis believable as children? As teenagers? As adults following his marriage? Was it difficult to approve of their intimate relationship after his separation from Carolyn?

5. Did you find Reverend Paul Morrison a sympathetic character before he revealed he was gay? Why? Why not? Did you find yourself more sympathetic or less sympathetic to him after that revelation?

6. Was Carmela's sudden determination to take on the case, and win it, after she discovered his secret, believable?

7. Was Lucille, wife of Marvin Stokes, a sympathetic, believable character? Did you understand the motivation that drove her to murder?

8. Were you surprised, pleased, or dissatisfied with the revelation that Troy might be Carmela's half sibling? Was it distracting? Did Troy and

Carmela come across as possible children of the same father? Why or why not?

9. Did you enjoy Rosemary's and Harry's repartee throughout? Did they seem fresh and funny or too much like ordinary secretaries and private investigators in novels?

10. Would you recommend this book to other readers' clubs?

To My Readers,

Thank you for reading Love is a Legal Affair. *If you wish to write a review of this book, or of* Saturday Matinee, Murder Times Two, *or* Rebel on Horseback, *please go to* Amazon.

You may also visit my website, www.davenportstories.com, *and leave your comment there. I would love to hear from you.*

Maxine

Made in the USA
San Bernardino, CA
24 August 2017